Harper, did you ...
Vicki suggested t...
sell books, yes? Draft something to let
her know I can't make that change
because it screws up the entire
second act. Love you!

Everywhere I go,
there Connor is.
Why?!

NO ONE
WAS SUPPOSED
TO DIE
AT THIS WEDDING

NO ONE WAS SUPPOSED TO DIE AT THIS WEDDING

A NOVEL

CATHERINE MACK

MINOTAUR
BOOKS
NEW YORK

First published in the United States by Minotaur Books, an imprint of St. Martin's Publishing Group

NO ONE WAS SUPPOSED TO DIE AT THIS WEDDING. Copyright © 2025 by Catherine McKenzie. All rights reserved. Printed in the United States of America. For information, address St. Martin's Publishing Group, 120 Broadway, New York, NY 10271.

www.minotaurbooks.com

Designed by Omar Chapa

Endpaper design by David Baldeosingh Rotstein

Endpaper art: confetti © Karlygash/Shutterstock; tickets and napkin © Mega Pixel/Shutterstock; crumbs © sergio34/Shutterstock

The Library of Congress Cataloging-in-Publication Data is available upon request.

ISBN 978-1-250-32613-3 (hardcover)
ISBN 978-1-250-40886-0 (Canadian edition)
ISBN 978-1-250-32614-0 (ebook)

Our books may be purchased in bulk for promotional, educational, or business use. Please contact your local bookseller or the Macmillan Corporate and Premium Sales Department at 1-800-221-7945, extension 5442, or by email at MacmillanSpecialMarkets@macmillan.com.

First U.S. Edition: 2025
First International Edition: 2025

10 9 8 7 6 5 4 3 2 1

For Catherine Richards

Murder, like life, is about choices. It's never an accident. It's right there in the definition—an *intentional* act. Because you have to want it, for it to happen. You have to be ambitious. And sometimes, stopping yourself from doing it takes more effort. But it's not inevitable. It never is.

—ELEANOR DASH, *WHEN IN ROME*
(THE VACATION MYSTERIES #1)

Every murderer is probably somebody's old friend.

—AGATHA CHRISTIE, *THE MYSTERIOUS AFFAIR AT STYLES*

NO ONE
WAS SUPPOSED
TO DIE
AT THIS WEDDING

PROLOGUE

If a Body Drops in a Broom Closet, Does It Make a Sound?

My name is Eleanor Dash, and I'm the bestselling author of the Vacation Mysteries series.

That's not *immediately* relevant to my current situation, but it feels like something you should know about me from the jump.

I write murder mysteries for a living. I think up ways to kill people and then I do it. On the page, that is. I haven't *actually* killed anyone.

Not yet.

Oh, wait, that's not true. Not *technically*.

But that was a story for another book. So.

Moving on.

Despite the fact that I wing most things, you should also know that I always figure out the who, what, when, where, and why of the murder(s) before I start writing. I *enjoy* doing this. It's a fun puzzle to me. To figure people out—their motivations, hurts, and resentments. Why are they striking out? What was the last straw? How are they going to do it?

It's fascinating.

I mean, have *you* ever thought about it? What might push you to the brink so you'd see the most terrible act as a solution to your problems?

You don't have to answer that, but it's not a rhetorical question.

Not entirely, anyway.

So, why am I telling you all of this before we even get to the first chapter?

There's a method to my confession, I assure you.

Let me, as they say, set the scene.

I'm at Emma Wood's wedding to Fred Winter, her co-star in a movie called *When in Rome*. Emma's been my best friend since childhood, and this movie is based on a book I wrote ten years ago that's been (finally, and oh my God, I can hardly believe it!) adapted into a film. They wrapped filming two days ago in Santa Monica, and then the entire cast and crew came to Catalina Island for the wedding.

Because Hollywood.

It's been a balmy October day on this lush island one nautical hour off the coast of Los Angeles in the Channel Islands. But though you can't tell from the lingering sunset bathing the Descanso Beach Club in a warm orange glow, there's a hurricane heading our way, because of course there is.

You didn't think we were going to be at a wedding on an island *without* a storm, did you?

Okay, good. Because this is that kind of book.

Everything that can go wrong will.

Don't say I didn't warn you.

Anyway, a lot of shit has happened since we got here yesterday, but the most important thing is that, just now, when I was trying to find the bathroom during the wedding reception, I ended up finding a dead body in the broom closet instead.

I know, right?

No one's supposed to *die* at a wedding.

But the person lying next to a stack of boxed toilet paper with a cake-cutting knife sticking out of their back is dead.

I've had some drinks, but not so many that this fact escapes me.

The large pool of very red blood forming a halo around their body is one clue.

Their open-eyed gaze into the middle distance is another.

There's no doubt about it: I'm staring at a freshly dead person in an eight-by-ten room. And the smell of their death—the iron tang of their blood, the fluids the body releases at that pivotal moment, the *anger* that drove the knife that deep into their back, right up to the hilt—is almost overwhelming.

I put a hand out to steady myself, then stop before it touches the wooden doorframe.

Fingerprints. I don't want to leave any, my murder-writer brain tells me even in this moment of panic.

I take a couple of shallow breaths and try to clear my thoughts. I need to tell someone about this, someone in authority, so they can call the cops and start up all of the things that come with a body.

Police. Suspicion. Fear. Questions.

So, first of all, *fuck*.

And second of all, *again*?

And most of all, though it's not strictly my job, I'm probably going to have to solve this thing.

I mean, I'm right here on the spot. I told you I like puzzles and planning murders. Untangling the knot isn't the same as tying it, but they're related activities. And, as the *"again"* above suggests, this isn't my first non-literary homicide. Three months ago, I was involved in a whole thing in Italy when I was on a tenth-anniversary book tour for *When in Rome*. I almost died and three people actually did.

I figured out who the murderer was just in time.

To save my skin, that is. Too late for the other victims, unfortunately. Bygones.

I have some expertise in this department, is all I'm saying.

Some of the other guests do, too.

Plus, on closer inspection, I *know* the victim, so . . . I've got to do it. I have to at least try to figure out the who, what, where, when, and why.

I get that you might have some questions, potentially about my choice to rhyme in a situation like this.

I do, too.

But I promise that everything important will be explained in due course.

And hey, we can solve this together, right? You'll help me out?

Great.

Let's begin.[1]

---

[1] Hello again. Eleanor here. Welcome to the footnotes. Yep, this book has them. Why? Because they're awesome. But they're also optional. If you want to skip them, do. I promise not to drop too many clues in here.

TWO DAYS EARLIER...
Thursday

CALL SHEET FOR WHEN IN ROME—DAY 50

PERSONALIZED FOR **ELEANOR DASH**

YOUR CALL TIME: 7:30 A.M.

This is our last day of filming!
Base camp will be in the alley behind Shutters.

Reach Shawna directly for any additional questions.

OCTOBER 23

83 DEGREES

SUNRISE 7:05 A.M./SUNSET 6:09 P.M.

LOCATION: SHUTTERS ON THE BEACH

1 PICO BLVD., SANTA MONICA, CA 90405

Producer	Director	Assistant to the Director
Tyler Houston	**Simone Banerjee**	**Shawna Kassel**
555-610-8220	555-789-0643	555-834-1212

SHOOT CALL—8:00 A.M.

SCHEDULE:
Scene 102—Cecilia and Connor EXT Shutters
Scene 103—Cecilia and Connor INT Shutters

CAST
1. Fred West (Connor Smith), scenes 102 & 103
2. Emma Wood (Cecilia Crane), scenes 102 & 103
3. John Parsons (Waiter #1), scene 103
4. Ken Simon (Connor Smith stand-in)
5. Naomi Smith (Allison Smith), scene 103
6. Eleanor Dash (Extra), scene 103
7. Harper Dash (Extra), scene 103

CHAPTER 1

Can You Forget That You're Wearing a Mic?

"What should we toast to?" Emma says to Fred as she leans across an intimate table at Shutters on the Beach that's nestled into the tall palm fronds that surround the greenhouse section of its restaurant, Coast.

It's midday, brunch things on the crisp white tablecloth, a bottle of Dom Pérignon sweating in a silver bucket, the sun dappled through the cream sailcloth providing some shade above.

"To you," Fred says, raising his fluted Champagne glass, the bubbles sliding up the inside of it, and clinking it against Emma's as his periwinkle eyes twinkle with mischief. "To us."

"To Rome," Emma says. Her chestnut mane tumbles in beachy waves to her bare, thin shoulders. She looks young, innocent, and *happy*. "To the Giuseppes for bringing us together."

"In death?"

"In life."

Fred raises his glass and starts to take a drink—

"That's not what happens in the book," I say to my younger sister, Harper, under my breath. "And this dialogue is cringe."

"And CUT!" Simone Banerjee pulls her headphones from her ears and glares at me across Video Village. She's wearing a pair of dark blue coveralls with her name embroidered over her left breast where her heart *should* be. "Did someone explain to The Writer that there's no talking while we're rolling?"

Shawna Kassel, Simone's early-twenty-something assistant, shuffles nervously from foot to foot. She's wearing an expression I associate with new mothers trying to keep their toddlers from having a tantrum in public. "I *did* tell her, Simone. I'll tell her again."

"Excuse me," I say, putting up my hand. "Are you talking about me?"

"Is The Writer talking *again*?"

"No, Simone. I'm taking care of it. Reset, everyone! We go in five."

There's a collective sigh from the cast and crew as Shawna beetles her way toward the table where Harper and I are sitting.

It's the last day of filming on *When in Rome*, the movie, and when they asked us if we wanted to be extras, I jumped at the chance. Who wouldn't want to be an extra in a movie based on a novel you wrote? The whole experience has been exciting and surreal, terrible dialogue notwithstanding, and the first day I walked on set and saw the world I'd created in my imagination made real, I *cried*.

I know, right? That's not like me.

But anyway, I watched as many of the shoots as I could over the last forty-nine days, and now here Harper and I are, dressed as ladies-who-lunch in enough makeup that it feels like a Halloween mask.

"You're in *trou-ble*," Harper says. They've swept her dark hair back into a low chignon and given her features more definition. She looks older than thirty-three, and more severe than usual.

"I don't *ca-re*," I sing back, but that's probably not true. No one likes being called out on a film set. Especially not one where Simone is in charge.

I shift my focus to her as she picks up her clipboard and writes something down. Probably a demerit point for me that I'll hear about later.

She's hated me since high school—LA is a *very* small town—and I knew there'd be problems between us when I learned she was going to direct *When in Rome*.

"Um, Eleanor?"

I look up into Shawna's scared face. She's got unruly strawberry blond hair and pale green eyes. I met her on day one of filming, and I swear she's aged ten years in that time. Working for Simone will do that to you.

"What's up, Shawna?"

"Sorry, but it's about the talking. You can't talk during a scene."

"I muttered under my breath."

"But you're mic'd up? Remember, before you came on set, they put a microphone on you?"

"I remember." The mic pack is resting against the small of my back, and the wire to it that's hidden in my bra is itching under my costume in the worst way. But I'd agreed to speak a line in this scene and so it had to be done.

Besides, maybe I didn't care if everyone heard what I thought of the dialogue in this scene. Because it's dreadful.

People always tell me that my books would "make a great movie." And I always answer, "Or a terrible one." It was my stupid joke and now I'm paying for it.

Don't put things into the universe that you don't want coming back.

Anyway, filming's almost over, and I don't have script approval,[2] so it's too late to do anything about it. But for the record, the *original* dialogue was much better than the lines Emma and Fred were delivering at the beginning of this chapter.[3]

"Well," Shawna says, "anything you say on mic goes into our headsets. So we can hear everything."

"We could *all* hear it, headsets or no," Emma says with a laugh. She's holding an empty Champagne glass in her left hand. Normally, the

---

[2] My film agent assures me that no book writer gets script approval, but I should've asked for it anyway. Don't ask, don't get.

[3] The mystery was better, too, though I knew it would be changed to fit into a movie format.

Champagne in a scene is colored water, but knowing Emma, she's figured out a way to sneak real Champagne on set.

It's the sort of thing we would've planned together until recently. Now she goes to Fred first, which is as it should be, but I already miss the intimacy we had.

Emma is *that* Emma, by the way. Emma Wood, who commands $5 million a picture.

We grew up next to each other in Venice Beach, and Emma's the reason I got a publishing deal. And, more relevant to this particular story, she's playing *me* in the movie. I mean, not actually me, but Cecilia Crane, my alter ego.[4]

"I spoke the truth," I say to Emma as I pull a face she's more than familiar with. "Sue me."

"I like to avoid litigation wherever possible," Emma says sweetly as she rises and walks to my table with grace. "But I'm sure David will be very happy to hear your thoughts about the script."

She means David Liu, the screenwriter of this shit show.

I mean the movie I'm very happy is being made.

"Surprisingly, he's proven unreceptive to my notes."[5,6]

"You don't say?" She smiles at me again as she reaches down and grabs my hand, pressing a folded piece of paper into it like we used to do in school, passing notes in the hallway with our special handshake.

She taps my palm three times in rapid succession, our code for *keep*

---

[4] Quick primer: Cecilia Crane is the protagonist of *When in Rome*. She meets a private investigator named Connor Smith on vacation in Italy and ends up working with him to solve a series of robberies and, eventually, a murder while they conduct a whirlwind romance. The book was loosely based on my own trip to Rome ten years ago where I met the real Connor Smith and we solved some major crimes.

[5] "Notes" is the Hollywood term for, well, notes on screenplays. In Hollywood, everyone has an opinion on your writing, and the screenwriter is expected to incorporate all of them.

[6] Not my notes, though. David didn't even acknowledge the multiple emails I sent him.

this to yourself, and I slip the paper under my place setting. I give Emma a questioning look, but she's already turned away and gone back to her seat.

"Anyway, the thing is," Shawna says, doing that thing again where she hops from foot to foot, "we need to wrap in time for the party? And Simone would like to bring this in on time and on budget?"

That's been Simone's refrain since day one of filming: "We're bringing this plane in on time and on budget." And while it's annoying to hear over and over, I don't blame her for this.

She's a female director. She only gets one shot.

So maybe I should cut her some slack? The sisterhood and all that.

Ha ha. No.

And okay, before you judge me, I *was* prepared to flip the page and start over, but Simone started calling me "The Writer" on day one and that was that.

"She won't do it again," Harper says to Shawna. "I promise."

"I can speak for myself."

"I know. That's the problem."

"Aren't you supposed to be on my side?"

"You'd think a girl whose book is being made into a major Hollywood film would be *happy.*"

She's right. Because Harper's the one who always calls me on my shit.

And I *was* happy. I *am.*

When my film agent, Rich, called a few days after we'd returned from Italy to tell me the *When in Rome* film was finally happening, I'd been over the moon. After the book was optioned[7] ten years ago, it had lingered in development[8] for years, and I'd given up hope of it ever seeing the screen.

---

[7] Hollywood doesn't buy the rights to your book until they're making the project. Instead, they "option" it, paying the writer a fraction of the eventual purchase price to hold on to the possibility of making it.

[8] Hollywood speak for "Don't call us, we'll call you."

But all of the publicity surrounding my almost-murder in Italy had revived interest in the project. They already had a script and they wanted to rush it into production.

I'd whooped in delight and spun Harper around the kitchen, and then Emma had called, brimming with excitement. They'd offered *her* the part of Cecilia Crane! We were going to have *so much fun!*[9]

It seemed like a dream, especially when it was confirmed that Connor was going to be played by Fred Winter.

The Fred Winter! One-time Oscar-winner, big-time movie star.

Emma's had a crush on Fred since high school, when he burst onto the scene in a schlocky surf movie that showed off his, well, *assets*. Ever since she disclosed that in an interview at the beginning of her career, people have been fan-casting them in movies.

And then there was the location. I'd been worried we were going back to Italy, which seemed like a bad idea with one of the people who tried to kill me still on the loose. But they'd decided to film in California. I could visit the set as often as I wanted, and Instagram about it to Harper's content.

It all seemed too good to be true.[10]

"I'll keep quiet," I say to Harper, and I feel bad for embarrassing her. This was supposed to be an amusing day for us, being extras in one of the last scenes, which calls for Emma and me to share a moment of eye contact, like she is looking at her future self—and, of course, she is![11] "I didn't mean to ruin the day."

"One minute to slate!"

---

[9] For the record, Emma speaks in exclamation marks, not me.

[10] Which, of course, it was! Okay, yes, I do use exclamation marks sometimes. Sparingly.

[11] Did you notice how my best friend who's my <u>exact</u> same age is playing me <u>ten years</u> younger?

"It's fine," Harper says. "They always do several takes. Simone will get over it."

"Right," I say, but somehow I doubt it.[12]

I try to make eye contact with Simone to calm the waters, but she's deep in her clipboard. Plus, trying to speak to her would involve everyone hearing what I had to say, which I'm sure neither of us would appreciate.

She's probably heard this entire conversation, anyway. Of course she has. I never turned my mic off. Amateur mistake.

Oh, well. Maybe I'll find time to talk to her at the wrap party. Though, I don't know what the wrap party's going to change. But I can always hope for the best.

Hope for the best and expect the worst, my mother used to say. And then she got hit by a drunk driver and died way too young, so I guess she knew what she was talking about.

Sorry about that. That got dark for a minute.

We *are* at the beginning of a murder mystery, though.

You should know it's going to get dark.

"Places!"

I snap away from my memories and glance over at Emma's table. A makeup artist is touching her up while the continuity girl refills her glass to the level it was at the beginning of the scene.

Emma seems so serene and calm, and then Fred[13] reaches across the table and touches her hand briefly. An intimate gesture that makes her beam.

They began dating right after they met in pre-production. They kept their relationship under wraps for the first month, but then it burst out

---

[12] News flash: Simone does not get over it.

[13] Imagine Captain America with a smirk. Dark blond hair, steely blue eyes, a strong jaw, and a hint of something underneath.

of them after they filmed a particularly dramatic scene, and the cat, as they say, was out of the bag.[14]

And I'm happy for her. I am.

I mean—Fred Winter!

Everyone says they're perfect for each other, and I think so, too. I've even been taking credit for their match because, hello, if I never wrote the book, they never would've met.

So that's all of us.

Am I forgetting anything?

Oh! Emma's note.

I slip it out from under the place setting and unfold it in my lap.

"Quiet on set!"

I glance down at the note. Instead of Emma's handwriting, it's written in letters cut out of some publication like a newspaper or a book.

SomEonE Is GoiNg To Die At The WedDinG.

Ah, *hell*.

"And . . . action!"

_____

[14] This is an unfortunate expression to use for reasons that will become clear later.

SYNOPSIS OF *WHEN IN ROME*—THE MOVIE

Written by David Liu

We open on CECILIA CRANE (25) arriving in Rome for a month-long holiday. Cecilia's parents died suddenly when she was eighteen, leaving her in charge of her younger sister and forcing her to put her dreams on hold. But her sister is launched now, and it's Cecilia's time to explore.

Enter CONNOR SMITH (35), the handsome, devil-may-care private investigator she meets on her first day. He's been hired by an insurance company to investigate a series of bank robberies. Cecilia loves mysteries—and finds Connor irresistible—so she ends up tagging along in his investigation. It's thrilling and fun, and soon Connor and Cecilia tumble into bed together.

Connor also introduces her to the glitterati of Rome, including NAOMI ROGERS (35), a model/actress who's filming a B movie in town. Cecilia feels uneasy around her, but that's probably her insecurities showing. Connor assures her that there's nothing between them and shows her how invested he is in her in the bedroom. This is the life!

But then another robbery occurs, and this time the police find a dead body in the tunnel that was dug to gain access to the bank. The dead? GIANNI GIUSEPPE (30), the son of a local Mafia capo. The police quickly establish that this was cold-blooded murder, and the stakes have officially been raised.

Cecilia's scared, but she's also fairly certain she's figured out a pattern to the robberies. They've all taken place on important Roman holidays and within a four-block radius of the epicenter of the celebrations. The next event is happening in a few days, and she and Connor need to make sure that the thieves/murderers are caught.

She convinces Connor to go to one of his police contacts—INSPECTOR TUCCI (60). They bring him their evidence, but Inspector Tucci is dismissive. He doesn't have time for amateurs looking to cash in on the finder's fee offered by the banks.

Crestfallen, Cecilia persuades Connor that they can find the thieves themselves. The lure of the finder's fee is real, and Connor agrees. They stake out the most likely bank on the night of the festival of San Marco and catch the culprits in the act! The police establish that the capo killed his son because he was about to betray him, and he's going to jail for life.

Connor collects his finder's fee, and it's time for Cecilia to return home. They share a tearful goodbye at the airport and Connor leaves. He'll join her in LA in a few weeks.

But then Cecilia makes an impulsive decision: She returns to the hotel to find Connor and Naomi together! Naomi Rogers is *actually* Naomi Smith! This was all a long con—they identified Cecilia as an heiress and had a plan to defraud her of her inheritance.

More than that—they were behind the robberies in the first place! But now Eleanor is an accessory to their crimes, whether she knew it or not, and she can't go to the police. She can, however, pay blackmail to Connor and Naomi for the foreseeable future.

The moral of the story: Don't fall for con men when you're on vacation.

CHAPTER 2

Does Being #1 on the Call Sheet Mean You're Famous?

They do seven more takes of the scene I interrupted before Simone's satisfied, and I keep my mouth shut through each of them except for when I'm required to deliver my line.

I can't help it if my thoughts are visible on my *face*.

I'm not an actress, just a writer.

Besides, I'm fixating on the note Emma slipped me, a sick feeling in my stomach. Is it serious or just a joke? People in the public domain get crazy messages all the time, even writers. Emma's had plenty of stalkers over the years, and I have one, too. Crazy Cathy is more silly than scary, but that doesn't mean I don't take her threats seriously.

But this note is from someone who knows there's about to be a wedding.

And that's been a closely kept secret.

I try to find a way to speak to Emma about it, but every time I get close to her between takes, Shawna beetles me away with an apology. Harper tells me to behave, so I tuck the note into my pocket and resolve to talk to Emma when we wrap for the day.

But that's not how it works out.

Instead, when the scene is done, they shoot another scene Harper and

I aren't in, and then the crew breaks the set down while everyone's taken to their trailers to get changed for the wrap party.

Since we don't rate trailers, I resign myself to catching up with Emma later, and Harper and I walk down the boardwalk to our house in Venice Beach. Then I go for a quick swim in the brisk, choppy ocean.

I spend a minute treading water, looking into the horizon. The sky is that perfect, clear blue washed in sunlight I associate with coastal California. It always calms me, making my brain more logical and less prone to overreacting.

The note is probably nothing. Despite what I do for a living, danger doesn't lurk around every corner. And the threat wasn't specific to Emma—it said *someone* was going to die at the wedding. If she was a target, they'd name her.

I release a long, slow breath and tell myself to relax. The film is done, and all there's left to do is celebrate.

I think the official term for this moment is "the calm before the storm."

I swim back to shore, dry off, and change into a sage-green silk dress with Harper hurrying me along like she always does, though no one will notice if we're late or even if we don't make it to the party.

But Harper hurrying me is kind of our thing, even though I've been her surrogate parent since our parents died when I was eighteen. I had to grow up overnight and become *in loco parentis*, but you can't stand in for your parents.

I'm not sure exactly when we switched roles. It was probably not long after I crushed her dreams by publishing a novel she didn't know I was writing, making it patently obvious I was no longer putting her first.

Harper was supposed to be the writer in the family. And while me publishing a book didn't make it impossible for her to do so, it didn't *not* make it impossible either. Then she took a job as my assistant, which I offered her because I thought it would give her enough time to write *and* make money, but it didn't work out that way. Instead, she took five years to write a book no one wanted to buy and she's given up writing. She says she's over it, and I hope, rather than believe, that's true.

All this to say, she finally gets me out the door, and when we're half-way there, we run into Oliver Forrest, my on-again boyfriend. We had four good years until I fucked it up, but we reconciled this summer in Italy. Which I've just realized probably wouldn't have happened but for the fact that someone organized an entire book tour to kill me.

I should thank them, I guess?

Oliver is standing under a tall palm tree that's perfectly framed by the setting sun with the Santa Monica pier behind him, the Ferris wheel's blinking colored lights visible against the fading sky. He's wearing a light beige suit and a white shirt with the collar open, and with his curly brown hair and tanned face, he looks like Jonathan Bailey with a literary bent.

"Why does Oliver always look like the hero in a romance novel?" I say to Harper.

She shrugs but smiles. She likes Oliver almost as much as I do.

"I heard that," Oliver says, taking my hand in his. I'm still at the stage when I feel giddy around him, and his touch feels like an invitation to do something we can't in front of Harper.

"You were meant to," I say, and give him a wink.

He winks back. "Ladies, you both look lovely."

"This old thing?" I say, nodding to my very new dress. It has a high neck and a low back. Harper's wearing something similar in ballet pink, and we've both got our hair in a high ponytail.

We look like, well, *sisters*.

"Thanks, Oliver," Harper says. "You look nice, too."

Oliver's phone beeps in his pocket.

"Do you need to check that?" I ask. "It might be a publishing emergency."

Oliver smiles. He's an author, too, and it's a joke between us that there are no emergencies in publishing, only predictable disappointments.

"It's just a weather alert."

"How do you know?"

"Because I set a special chime for those."

I start to laugh. "That's . . . adorable. And a bit odd."

"Why odd?"

"Because the weather's always the same. Warm and sunny. It's why people live here."

"Tell that to the hurricane."

"Hurricane?"

Oliver gives me a rueful smile. "Hurricane Isabella. Scheduled to make landfall in Southern California in the next forty-eight to seventy-two hours."

"Hurricane *Isabella?*"

Isabella is one of the people who tried to kill me. She's in jail pending her trial, but you don't just stop being afraid of someone because of a little thing like prison bars.

"It'll probably be a tropical storm by the time it makes landfall," Harper says. "It's been all over the news."

"You know I don't read or watch the news when I'm writing."

"*Have* you been writing?"

I look away. There's a surfer in a black wetsuit trying to mount a wave. He almost makes it up, then tumbles off his board.

I wrote Book Ten of the Vacation Mysteries series[15] in a fever dream after we got back from Italy. But I've got another book to write, and so far, I haven't been able to produce anything. My agent, Stephanie, checks in weekly, and I'm hoping that I'll be able to focus now that filming is over.

"I will be next week. But in the meantime, is there really a hurricane named after my attempted murderer heading toward us?"

"It's not named after her," Harper says. "It was just the next name in line from a preassigned list."

---

[15] In case you're interested, the title is *Amalfi Made Me Do It.*

"Uh-huh."

"First sign of a narcissist . . . thinking everything's about you . . ."

"That's a bit harsh, isn't it?" Oliver says.

"Wait until you hear what she did on set today."

"What? Again?"

"Hush, you two, we're going to be late."

I link arms with both of them, and we walk to Shutters. It's a white-and-gray shingled building with shutter-clad windows located next to the boardwalk. There are restaurants on the first two floors and a five-star hotel above. A clutch of palm trees with white lights strung around their trunks light the path to the main entrance. There's a red carpet, and a small line of people dressed in finery waiting to get in.

We give our names to the large man in a tight black T-shirt who's manning the list.[16] We're on it, though I have a moment of panic that we won't be because imposter syndrome, and then we're whisked into the party.

It's on the second floor in the formal dining room. Two sets of French doors give out onto a balcony, which is a great place for a cocktail and a view of the sunset. Easy jazz is playing—why is it *always* Kenny G at events like these?—and there are soft pink tablecloths with gorgeous flower arrangements made up of slightly darker peonies. There's a copy of *When in Rome* on every table and strings of fairy lights hanging from the ceiling.

The air smells great, too, pungent with the hors d'oeuvres being passed around by young, hot waiters in blue aprons—things wrapped in phyllo, glistening olives, avocado, and salmon roe. The drink of the evening is an Aperol spritz.[17]

---

[16] Not to be confused with the *New York Times* bestseller list, which is probably even harder to get onto.

[17] It's the signature drink of the book.

It looks like the whole cast and crew are here—over two hundred people—and there's a hierarchy to the party just like there is on set.

#1 and #2 on the call sheet[18]—Fred and Emma—are at the apex on the balcony. A group of people is swirling around them, coming in for air-kisses and declarations of fabulousness. Emma's wearing a white off-the-shoulder number that shows her fantastic collarbones—you'd, well, *die* for them—and Fred's in a blue chambray linen shirt with black slacks. He's got just enough buttons open to show off his toned chest and . . . no. I'm not going there.

Anyway, they're at the center of it all, and they deserve to be because they're the stars of the show, but also, it's their engagement party.

You got that from the Prologue, right? That the wedding where someone is going to die is Emma and Fred's?

Yep, that's right. Soon after their relationship went public, Fred popped the question.

I thought it was fast.

Emma said it was romantic.

I pointed out that he had a reputation as a player.

She told me he'd sown his wild oats and was ready to settle down.

I showed her a calendar and said that getting engaged that fast was how half of Hollywood ended up with second and third marriages.

Then she said I couldn't take credit for their relationship if I didn't want them to get married, and also, did I want to be her maid of honor or what?

I shut my mouth after that because she was right. I mean, *I* was right, it *was* too fast, but I've noticed that people don't listen to that kind of advice. And, okay, I *did* want the credit. And to be her maid of honor. We'd planned that out since we were little girls. There was no way I was letting that job go to whoever her second choice was.

---

[18] The daily shooting schedule. First position on the call sheet goes to the most important actor on set.

So, I arranged a quick bachelorette for her in Napa and even invited Simone—though she barely talked to me all weekend—and thanked my lucky stars that my maid of honor dress was from Vera Wang rather than the hideous monstrosity she threatened me with as punishment for not being 100 percent pro her getting engaged in less time than it takes to make a movie.

"Earth to Eleanor," Oliver says, waving a hand in front of my face. "You in there?"

"Present."

"You going to tell me who everyone is?"

I lean on him gently. "Who don't you know? Emma you've met. And Fred."

"I have," he says.

He likes Emma, and we all spent time together when he and I dated the first time.

He was a little starstruck when he met Fred. Or maybe his reaction was because Fred looks an *awful lot* like Connor Smith. More than once on set I'd gotten the two of them confused, especially from behind. They have the same broad shoulders, blue eyes, and a smirk that's made scores of women tumble into bed even though they knew it was a bad idea.

"Who else do you want to know?"

"Who's that?" Oliver points to Simone. She's wearing something other than her coveralls, for once, though it *is* in the jumpsuit family. The burnt orange color was made for her, and her dark brown hair is down and curled. She's wearing a delicate gold necklace that pops against her clavicle, and her skin is a couple of shades darker than when we started filming from being out in the sun all day. As much as I hate to admit it, she's stunning.

"That's the director."

"Does she have a name?"

"She can't seem to remember mine."

"So, that's Simone. Hmmm. You probably intimidate her."

I touch his arm, pushing him away playfully. "Please."

"You can be very intimidating."

"She's hated me since high school."

"Did you steal her boyfriend or something?"

I look down at my shoes. Was that it? Was all this animosity because of some dude whose name I don't even remember?

Okay, okay, I do remember who he was.

Whatever. Bygones.

"I haven't done anything to her this year. Or even this decade."

"Why don't you try to talk to her about it?"

"Honestly? She scares me."

He tips his head back and laughs, catching Simone's attention. She turns toward us and scowls.

An actual scowl! Like a cartoon villain.

"Did you see that?"

"Maybe that's just her face."

"Uh-uh."

Oliver taps my arm. "Bygones, remember."

"How did you know I'd said that in my head?"

His eyes dance. "I almost always know what you're thinking."

"That's scary."

"Or kismet. Who's Harper talking to?"

My eyes swivel through the crowd. Harper's standing next to a man about her height who's wearing a seersucker suit and a woman in a variation of Simone's pantsuit.

"The woman is Shawna, Simone's assistant. And he's David Liu."

"Ah! The Writer."

"The *Screenwriter*."

Oliver taps me gently on the nose. "We hate him, too?"

"He massacred my book."

"Massacred?"

"He changed all of the dialogue," I say. "And the ending is stupid."

"It's a screenplay, not a book. There were bound to be differences."

"He could've left some of it. You know dialogue is my thing."

Oliver smiles down at me. "Is there anything he could've done that would've pleased you other than transcribe your book word for word into Final Draft?"[19]

"I'm being a brat."

"Little bit."

"Fine. But we'll see who's right when the reviews come out."

He shakes his head, then nods into the crowd. "Here's someone you *do* like."

Allison Smith is walking toward us, Connor's ex-wife.[20] She's wearing a yoke-collared red dress that accentuates her slim frame. Her natural hair borders her face, and her brown eyes are surrounded by the perfect smoky eye.

She's gorgeous, and everyone in the room watches her as she walks to David and plants a kiss on his lips.

"Whoa," Oliver says. "I did not see that coming."

"Don't you remember that he was at the funeral?"[21]

"That was him?"

"I thought you were good at details?"

"I had my mind on other things."

"Such as?"

"The dead." He raises an eyebrow at me.

"Oh, right. I was thinking about him, too, of course."

And I was. I just wasn't so distracted that I didn't notice Allison had brought a date to a funeral.

---

[19] Final Draft is a screenwriting software.

[20] I found out he was still married to her <u>after</u> we'd been together for a year. It was <u>awesome</u>.

[21] The funeral was for one of the people who was murdered in Italy.

I didn't know who he was then, or how Allison met him. It wasn't the time to ask. But then, at the table read,[22] there he was. There they *both* were. Because Allison had been hired to play the character based on her in the movie. He'd even suggested her, she'd told me at the craft services table one day with a giggle.

"Well, they're dating."

Oliver cocks his head to the side. "We want Allison to be happy."

"Of course we do."

"And she seems it. She looks marvelous."

"She does."

"What, then?" Oliver asks.

"Don't you think it's suspicious that he suggested they cast her and now they're dating?"

"You think he's taking advantage?"

"I think he has an agenda."

"What?"

I watch as David wraps his arms around Allison to the jealous eyes of half the men in the room. "I haven't figured it out yet."

"Let me know when you do."

"Fine. Let's go say hi to the happy couple."

We push our way through the crowd until we get to Emma and Fred. Emma's face lights up when she sees me.

"Finally!"

"I wasn't late."

We give each other a hard hug, even though we just saw each other this afternoon.

"Are you okay?" I whisper into her ear.

"That stupid *note*," she says, her voice trembling slightly.

I pull back and Fred must catch something in my expression. "What's going on?"

---

[22] Where all of the actors sit around a long table and read the script together.

Emma shakes her head. "I was just saying I can't believe there's a storm coming to ruin our day!"

"Perhaps you should consider moving the wedding to the mainland?" I suggest.

"Absolutely not," Fred says. "As I told Shawna *and* the wedding planner, the location is nonnegotiable."

Oliver's mouth twists like it does when he's suppressing a laugh. "We make plans, and God laughs."

"What's that? Oh, yes. It will all work out, though. It always does," Fred says with the certainty of someone who hasn't had anyone say no to him in twenty years.

"Fred used to go to Catalina as a kid," Emma says, smiling at him indulgently. "He's always wanted to get married there."

Fred's cheeks tinge pink. Oh my God. Fred Winter is *blushing*.

"It's only that the wedding is all planned," Fred says. "And it's too late to change it."

Emma smiles at him again because he's fucking adorable, but then her eyes cloud with impending trouble.

Before I can ask her what's wrong, Tyler Houston, the film's producer, joins us on the balcony. He looks like his job—sandy hair in an expensive haircut, a well-cut dark blue suit with a chambray shirt and a conservative tie, broad shoulders, an air of authority. Straight out of central casting.

He's been a shadowy presence on set, more felt than seen. But I picked up enough scuttlebutt to know something's brewing between him and Fred. And by the look on his face, it appears that it's about to boil over.

How fortunate for us.

Not that I'm looking for drama. Only that's what *you've* come here for, right? I mean, a body is going to drop in forty-eight hours. Maybe sooner. And you know me well enough by now—even if you're *just* getting to know me—to know I'm bringing you to this party for a reason.

Something important is about to happen.

"You must be joking!" Tyler says to Fred in a voice that carries over the din of the party and stops it in its tracks like a record scratch.

"What is it, Tyler?"

"I've just discovered this little trip to Catalina this weekend isn't in the script!"

Fred shrugs. "And?"

"I am *not* paying for your wedding. Bad enough that . . . I've already paid for *enough*."

· "I don't know what you're implying. But I agreed to do this film as a personal favor and—"

"A favor to me? Ha! That's a joke."

"What did I ever do to you?"

"Please. You want me to tell everyone here, plus *People* magazine?"

"I'm sure everyone would be *very* interested to know whatever it is you think I've done. Do tell us. In fact, David, come here. Maybe you could whip up a suitable scene for us on the spot?"

David walks toward the group slowly. He glances at Emma, who looks like she wants to sink through the floor and disappear, then shakes his head. "I'm mixing out."

"That figures." Fred looks around and catches Emma's eye. She's on the verge of tears. "I'm sorry, honey."

"Let's just go."

"Yes, Fred," Tyler says, disdain dripping from his tongue, *"run along."*

Fred mouths a second apology to Emma, then does a roundhouse maneuver that ends with his fist square in Tyler's face.

He falls to the ground without a sound.

SANTA MONICA GOSSIP

@SMGossip

#BREAKING: A fistfight broke out at a party at #shuttersonthebeach tonight. Rumored to have been in attendance are the cast of "When in Rome," which just wrapped production in LA. Starring Emma Wood & Fred Winter, who've been heating up the set since filming began, sources tell me this was their engagement party & they're set to marry this weekend on Catalina Island. More to come.

10:34 PM · October 23 · Twitter for iPhone
624 Retweets 59 Quote Tweets 1,295 Likes

FRIDAY

CHAPTER 3

Do You Go Right to Hell If You Like Gossip?

I regret to inform you that no one died in this fistfight.

In fact, in the end, it wasn't much of a fight. Despite the impressive punch, Tyler was out for only a couple of seconds, and then he sprang up like a jack-in-the-box and assumed some kind of karate pose that was, frankly, a bit embarrassing.

For him.

But before he could get off whatever Karate Kid move he learned from Mr. Miyagi, two security guards grabbed him under the armpits and removed him from the restaurant with a swiftness I had to admire.

The party broke up quickly after that.

Emma and Fred left in their car, wanting to split before the paps started circling like vultures. When it became obvious there wasn't going to be any more free food or drinks, Harper, Oliver, and I tripped back down the beach and got dinner at the Waterfront, where we tried to talk about other things than what we'd just witnessed.

We had a pleasant dinner, and then went home to bed.

Not all three of us. Harper has her own room.

We share a lot but not *that*.

Just in case you were worried.

"What do you think all of that was about?" Harper asks the next day in the car. We're on the 405 headed to Long Beach, where we're going to catch the ferry to Catalina Island.

Oliver's driving and I'm in the passenger seat. Harper's in the back, sitting in the middle so it's easier for us to talk. She and I would rather sit in the back with Oliver driving, but he draws the line at that. "I'm your boyfriend, not your chauffeur," etc.

Fine.

"Fred and Tyler?" I ask. Because sometimes I can read minds, too.

Okay, it was probably obvious who she was talking about.

"That was *extra*, as the kids say."

I laugh. "How do *you* know what the kids say?"

"I'm on TikTok enough."

"Ugh." I shudder.

TikTok is the worst.

And no, I'm not saying that because none of my books have blown up on there.

Not *exclusively*.

"What do you think, Oli?"

He curses under his breath as a driver in an oversized Escalade cuts him off. "I think I shouldn't be driving in this traffic."

Oliver wanted to leave at "the crack of awful," as Harper called it, under the false impression that getting up before the sun would allow us to avoid the fate we're in right now. But LA traffic is eternal. The only way to avoid it is to stay at home.

"I did offer to get us a car," I say.

"You did."

I let that lie there. I've learned a thing or two in this second go-around.

Things like saying *I told you so* aren't conducive to happiness.

"So, what about Fred and Tyler?" I ask him. "Any theories?"

"I just write books for a living."

"Brilliant books."

"Books no one reads," he says matter-of-factly.

I pick up his hand and kiss it because what can I say? His last book sold, as he likes to put it, twelve copies, even though it was his best book by far. But the book business isn't a meritocracy.

It does make it a bit awkward, though, between us, when he gets the amazing reviews[23] and I get the book sales. I keep trying to convince him to write a book with me, but I think that feels like failure to him.

Or he just can't see us writing together.

I don't like thinking about that.

It feeds right into my insecurities.

"They were friends," Harper says into our awkward silence.

"Who?"

"Fred and Tyler. They went to film school together at UCLA."

"How do you know this?"

"TMZ."

"You read TMZ?"

"You do, too. You didn't see the video from last night?"

"There's a video?"

"Eleanor, everyone has a phone. Of course there's a video."

"They should've had the party at the San Vicente Bungalows," I say. "They take your phone away there."

"Aren't you always complaining that's pretentious?"

"Well, yes, but since this affects me, I have a different opinion."

"This is why we love you," Oliver says.

I savor the word "love." Sometimes I still can't believe it.

I smile at him, but he's concentrating on the road. "I think this is our exit."

"Right. Shit." Oliver starts maneuvering over four lanes of traffic.

---

[23] *The New York Times* called his last book "dazzling." They didn't even review my book, just did a profile about me, which sounds nice, right? But is also kind of telling.

"Does TMZ know why they were fighting?" I ask Harper.

"Something about bad blood over their last film together," Harper says.

"*Julius Caesar?*"

"Yep. It was a box office disaster."

"Why is that Fred's fault?" I ask.

"It was his idea, I guess. Plus, his performance was . . ."

I start to laugh, remembering it. "Terrible. And that curly white-blond wig was certainly a choice."

"I think it made less money than *Gigli.*"

"Right. But then, why work together again?"

"Hollywood?" Harper says.

"Hmmm." I think back to the note Emma slipped me yesterday. Could Tyler have sent it? But no. Tyler didn't know about the wedding until last night, though that could've been an act.

This is the problem with hanging out with film types.

You're always questioning their authenticity.[24]

"El's right, though," Oliver says. "Why would Tyler hire Fred to be in *When in Rome?*"

"Tyler and Fred optioned the book together," Harper says.

"Did I know this?" I say.

"Honestly, it's like you just got into the business sometimes."

"I know I have you looking out."

"Didn't you promise you'd start reading your contracts before you signed them?"

"That was for the future."

"Did you?"

I watch the road. I signed a big new deal when I'd gotten back from Italy, and I'd *tried* to read the contract. I really had. But that shit is *boring.*

---

[24] You should be doing that, too, because I already told you that it's <u>that kind of book</u>.

"I did my best. But I made sure my agent and lawyer read everything twice."

Harper sighs.

"I heard that."

"You were meant to."

"So they had a fistfight over bad box office?" Oliver says. "That's a bit extreme."

"I don't think it was just that," Harper says.

"What then?" I ask.

"Apparently, Tyler and Emma were an item."

My stomach falls like this is a rumor about me. "That's not true."

"Are you sure?"

I slump down in my seat. The sad thing is, I'm not. Emma and I haven't been as close the last few years. Not because anything happened, but life goes like that sometimes. Friendships slip away or fall into disuse. You have to work at them like any relationship.

But even so, Tyler doesn't seem like her type. Plus, she has this rule about not sleeping up. She doesn't want to be seen as one of *those* girls. The ones who sleep their way to the roles of a lifetime because whether that still goes on or not (it does), everyone thinks it does. She chose a public life for work, but she doesn't want a public private life.

I didn't point out to her that marrying Fred Winter went against that in the worst way possible.

I only thought it.

But we're all a bunch of contradictions. It's what makes life interesting.

"It could explain the level of anger," Harper says. "If he's jealous."

"Is he coming to the wedding?" Oliver asks.

"Tyler?" I say. "I think so. The whole cast and crew are. It was the only way to keep it quiet. They'd pretend it was a shoot for the movie—"

"Wait, wait, wait . . . Are you telling me everyone thinks they're coming to watch you and *Connor* get married?"

"Not actual me and Connor, just the fictional ones."

"Why is this the first I'm hearing about this?"

"I'm pretty sure you've told me that the less you hear about Connor, the better."

"You're right. If I never had to hear another word about that guy, it would be too soon."

I pat him on the hand while Oliver turns down the road to the ferry.

Part shipyard, part boat dock for the rich and famous, sailboats line a series of piers while the ocean glistens under that same bright blue sky from yesterday.

My spirits lift like they always do when I'm near the water.

Today's going to be a good day.

I can feel it.

"Oh Christ," Oliver says as he parks the car. "What's *he* doing here?"

Or maybe not.

WHEN IN ROME

ACT 1, SCENE 1

INT. HOTEL BAR – NIGHT

TITLE. ROME

CECILIA CRANE (25, bright, attractive, but <u>tired</u>) is pulling a large suitcase behind her. She looks lost and just wants somewhere to <u>rest</u>.

Her eyes light on the bar—mahogany, low lights, glass bottles glowing—it beckons to her like a lover.

She sits down on a bar stool with a slump, then takes out a TOURIST GUIDE to Rome. She thumbs it nervously, then checks her phone for the time. It's **10:00 A.M.**

A BARTENDER approaches.

                    BARTENDER
      Benvenuta, signorina.

                    CECILIA
      Non parlo Italiano.

The Bartender smiles and switches to accented English.

                    BARTENDER
      Would you like something to drink?

                    CECILIA
      Can I have an . . . Aperol spritz?

                    BARTENDER
      Si, naturalmente.

                    MAN (O.S.)
      Put that on my tab, Eduardo.

Eduardo nods and walks away to make the drink.

Cecilia looks over to a dapper MAN (35, Captain America with a smirk) sitting two stools over. He's wearing a suit, and there's a fedora on the bar in front of him.

                          CECILIA
            I can buy my own drink, thank you.

                          MAN
            But why would you want to?

He moves one stool closer. Cecilia is wary, but he's <u>very attractive</u>.

                          MAN
            Connor Smith. And you must be Cecilia Crane.

                          CECILIA
            How did you know that?

He points to her luggage tag on the suitcase by her feet. Her name is written on it in all caps: **CECILIA CRANE. VENICE BEACH, CALIFORNIA.**

                          CECILIA
            You're observant.

                          CONNOR
            Comes with the territory.

                          CECILIA
            What's that?

                          CONNOR
            My profession.

                          CECILIA
            Are you some kind of Sherlock Holmes?

                          CONNOR
            Something like that.

                         CECILIA
     Hmmm. Connor . . . Smith, did you say? Sounds
     like an alias.

Connor hesitates for a beat, then laughs it off.

                         CONNOR
     I may be a man of mystery, but that's not one of
     my secrets.

                         CECILIA
     I wonder.

                         CONNOR
     What?

                         CECILIA
     About your secrets.

                         CONNOR
     I'm good at keeping them.

                         CECILIA
     Is that supposed to recommend you?

                         CONNOR
     Hmmm?

                         CECILIA
     That's what we're doing, right? Flirting?

Connor gives her a slow smile. Her knees weaken.

                         CONNOR
     You're American, aren't you?

                         CECILIA
     The luggage tags again?

                         CONNOR
     More your manner.

                              CECILIA
          Really? Everyone usually thinks I'm Canadian.

                              CONNOR
          One of those faces. Honest.

                              CECILIA
          People are always handing me their phones and
          asking me to take their pictures. I could make a
          killing if I was a thief.

                              CONNOR
          I like the way you think.

                              CECILIA
          Oh?

He raises his eyebrows suggestively. Then there's the
POP of a Champagne cork.

                              CECILIA
          I've always liked that sound.

                              CONNOR
          Like a party beginning. You never know what
          might happen.

                              CECILIA
          Exactly.

They smile at each other, leaning in closer as the CAM-
ERA pulls back to reveal the back of a WOMAN watching
them . . .

CHAPTER 4

Does Anything Good Ever Happen on a Ferry?[25]

I scan the parking lot full of Teslas and town cars, looking for whoever it is that's set Oliver off.

I should know without looking because there's only one person who makes Oliver react this way.

Connor Smith.

You didn't think we were doing this book without him, did you?

I wish.

If you weren't around for the Italian tour, or haven't picked up the vibe from context, Connor and I used to have a thing. Before me and Oliver, but also, ahem, briefly *during*.

Anyway, Connor's getting out of his James Bond–mobile, some fancy, baby-blue sports car. He's wearing one of his signature linen suits, and his dark blond hair is cut and feathered short, and even I can admit the look suits him.

Ha! Is *that* where that expression comes from?

Quick primer for those who skipped the footnote: Connor is one of the protagonists of my book series. He's also often the antagonist. In my head, anyway. TL;DR: We solved some crimes together in Italy ten years

---

[25] These chapter titles are <u>all</u> rhetorical questions, by the way.

ago, had great sex, and I wrote a book about him, which he wasn't happy about and kind of blackmailed me over. Then I found out he was married to Allison and we broke up, but I had to keep writing about him because that's what the public—and my publisher—wanted.

Since we both got book-famous ten years ago, he's been kicking around Hollywood taking odd jobs as a script consultant, hanging with the semi-famous, dating inappropriately young women, and living off the proceeds of my books.

I'm sure he does other things as well, but that's what I know for sure.

"Did you not know he was coming?" I ask Oliver as Harper climbs discreetly out of the car to give us a moment.

Oliver runs his hands through his hair, his dark brown curls springing back. "Did you?"

"Not specifically, but, like I said, the whole cast and crew were invited."

"Is he one of those?"

"He has a consultant credit." I look him in the eyes. They're dark brown and usually I get lost in them, but right now they have a serious cast I need to make disappear. "I definitely told you that, Oli."

He gives me a crooked smile. "I must've blocked it out."

"I *do* talk a lot. You can't listen to everything I say."

He touches my hand, and I know we're going to be okay. "Probably not."

I have to ask, though. "Are we okay?"

"Yes," he says, then kisses my hand for emphasis.

"Good." I kiss him. Not with passion but with assurance. *This is it*, I want to tell him. I'm not going anywhere. I'm here. Forever.

It's a lot to convey with a kiss.

I do my best.

I think he gets it.

Eventually, we break apart and lean our foreheads against each other. "It's only two days," I say.

"What could go wrong?"

We should both know better than to say something like that out loud by now.

Connor would keep his distance if he knew what was good for him. But instead, he joins us in the line for the eight a.m. ferry that fifty others are waiting to board, waving at us like we're old friends who haven't seen one another in a while.

Situational awareness has never been Connor's strong suit.[26]

"I hear I missed quite the show last night," Connor says with a laugh as he pulls up to us.

"Good morning, Connor," I say.

I've found that sometimes an air of formality is the only thing that gets to him.

"What? Oh, yes, good morning, Eleanor. Harper. You're both looking well."

"And me? Am I not looking well?" Oliver says, putting his hands on his hips and jutting out his left leg like he's posing in a fashion show.

"I, uh . . ."

Harper snorts. "This is *awkward*."

Connor assesses the three of us. The last time we were all together was at a funeral, but that didn't *quite* count as a reunion. We didn't speak, just nodded across the grave at one another.

"Things are bound to get awkward," I say, "when the only two people who haven't slept together are you and Oliver."

Oops.

Am I ever going to learn to shut my stupid mouth?

No, right? The answer is no.

Fine. FINE.

Also, it's not even accurate. Harper hasn't slept with Oliver. Or me, obviously.

---

[26] Another "suit"-based expression. English is fascinating.

I pointed that out earlier with my joke about the three of us *not* going to bed together.

"Sorry, everyone. I can't always control what comes out of my brain."

"If it wasn't awkward before, it is now!" Harper says, and we laugh.

"So, last night?" Connor says, eager for the gossip.

Oliver sighs. "It was a dramatic evening."

"Bound to happen," Connor says, "given the players."

"Do you know something?" I ask.

"Tyler and Fred have been spoiling for a fight for months."

"How do you know that?"

He fidgets with his hair, a sure sign that he's hiding something. "I'm observant."

"Uh-huh."

"Where were *you* last night, Connor?" Harper asks. "Not like you to miss a party."

"I was . . . working."

"Doing what?" I ask.

"Something confidential."

"That can't be good."

"Ha ha." Connor fixates on something over my shoulder. "What's *she* doing here?"

"A popular question today," Oliver says dryly as we all turn to look.

Allison and David are stepping out of a Land Rover. Allison's wearing a white pantsuit, and David has a beachy vibe going with linen shorts and a dark blue Lacoste polo. His classic Wayfarers cover his eyes, and even though I have a dislike of him that's probably unwarranted, I can see his appeal. Allison looks happy, anyway, which should be the only thing that matters.

I make a shushing gesture with my hand to stop whatever Connor's about to say. "Quiet. They're coming over here."

Allison and David walk up, arm in arm. David tips his glasses up onto the top of his head and smiles at us in an open and friendly manner.

And it's then that I remember. David is *nice*. Allison is nice, too, and she wouldn't be with a man who wasn't. Except Connor, but she was young when she met him, and we're all entitled to one mistake. Me included.

"What a beautiful day for a wedding." Allison points to the ocean, which is a deep blue and glittering in the sun.

"The wedding's tomorrow," Connor says.

Oliver clears his throat. "Always *so* precise."

"I just like facts."

I'm about to let out a sarcastic response, something about how he wouldn't know a fact if he saw one.

I know, not my best work.

But I stop myself and take a deep breath instead.

Maybe more oxygen will help me make better decisions?

"Will we get blown into the sea with this storm, do you think?" David asks.

"We'll be fine," Allison says. "Remember all that fuss about Hurricane Hilary? And then nothing."

"Mudslides, road closures, Palm Springs underwater . . ." I say.

"Yes, well, that won't happen to Emma and Fred."

"Why not?"

"Disrupt #1 on the call sheet's perfect day?" Allison says. "The weather wouldn't dare."

"Besides," Oliver adds, "they wouldn't let us over there if there was any real danger."

Allison tips her head back and laughs. "The regular tourists? I agree with you. But the Hollywood demand set? That's a different story. Actors who command ten million a picture don't take no for an answer."

"Especially when it's their wedding day," David says.

Wait. They know about the wedding. Could *David* be the one who sent that note to Emma? Using cut-out words *would* be something a (bad) scriptwriter would do.

But why?

"How did you know we're going over for a real wedding?"

David shrugs his shoulders. "Doesn't everyone know?"

"No, it's a secret."

"Not after last night," Allison says.

"Is that when you learned about it?"

Allison raises her hand to her heart. "I swear to tell the truth, the whole truth, and nothing but the truth."

"Sorry."

"To answer your question, I've been hearing rumors about them getting married for weeks, so we weren't surprised that it was their wedding, were we, David?"

He shrugs. "Plus, there isn't a wedding in the script, so . . ."

"How many people know that, though?" I say. "Outside of production."

"There's hundreds of copies of the script out there once you start filming something," David says. "It was a dumb plan. Emma's probably."

Allison swats his arm playfully. "Now, David. Emma's one of El's best friends."

"I think the line's moving," Harper says, tugging on my arm. "What's wrong with you?" she mutters to me under her breath.

"I'll tell you later."

We don't say anything more as we get on the boat, a white ferry that can hold a couple hundred people. As far as I can tell, all of the other passengers are the movie's cast and crew, a nice tight-knit group of people whose names I've been struggling to remember since shooting started.

Before you judge, you should know, I'm terrible with names, and there are so many people on a set, often dressed similarly in jeans and black T-shirts, that it's almost impossible for someone like me to keep track.[27, 28]

But like with so many things, I should do better. So I spend the

---

[27] If there isn't an actual medical syndrome named for this phenomenon, there should be.

[28] Oh, great, I just googled it, and it turns out it might be a mild form of aphasia. AWESOME.

first half of the ride mixing among them, listening to them rehash what happened at the party, and adding in details where I can. They weren't out on the balcony, so I tell them what I saw, without spilling the beans about the wedding, and wait for them to repeat the rumors Harper told me in the car.

They know Emma and I are friends, though, so they don't say anything when I wonder aloud why Tyler hates Fred so much.

But I can feel their thoughts, like a weighted blanket.

And that's what makes me think it's true. Because the crew always knows what's happening. Like the house staff in a British mansion. They disappear into the background and see *everything*.

Which means Emma and Tyler had a thing. How serious and for how long, I don't know. But it couldn't have been something positive in her life. If it was, she would've told me about it. And now it's surfacing like a bad penny, right before her wedding.

That can't be good.

I mean, it isn't. Foreshadowing and all that. You know the drill.

"Are you investigating something?" Connor asks me when I wander back toward the front of the boat looking for Oliver and Harper.

"Why do you ask?"

He stares down at me in the same way that he did when we met ten years ago. Seductive *AF*. "Because I know you."

"You were watching me, you mean?"

He raises a shoulder. I think about avoiding the question, but maybe he's heard something. Connor's a magnet for scuttlebutt.

"They're saying there's something else behind that fight last night. Between Fred and Tyler."

"That set was full of exes."

"Like who?"

"Fred and Simone had something years ago when they did their first film together."

"Gross."

He smirks. "And you've heard about Tyler and Emma?"

Ugh. That means it's true.

"I don't want to believe it." I bite the edge of my thumb. "What about David, the screenwriter? Does he have something against Emma?"

"I heard she got him fired off a picture a few years ago."

"That can't be right."

Connor raises his eyebrows at me. "Actresses."

"You *were* married to one." The wind picks up and blows my hair around. I tuck it into the back of my shirt. "So, Tyler picked a fight with Fred because of jealousy?"

"It's not just that."

"What, then?"

He cocks an eyebrow. "Why do you want to know?"

"Because she's my best friend and Fred is her fiancé."

"And you like gossip." He smirks. "I know you, remember?"

I feel a blush creep up the back of my neck. Connor's always had way too much impact on me, despite everything he's done. "Didn't we agree in Italy to let the past be the past?"

"If I recall, our agreement was more of a financial nature."

"Right," I say. "You stopped blackmailing me, and I made sure you didn't go to jail."

"I kept *you* out of jail."

"The point is—there weren't going to be any games between us any-more. Right?"

He tilts his head like he's considering it. "You really want to know?"

"Tell me."

"The case I'm on . . . It's *Fred.*"

CHAPTER 5

Is the First Sequence in a Movie Always the Setup?

"*Fred* is the case you're working on?" I repeat what Connor just told me as our ferry chops through the waves toward Catalina. "What?"

Connor makes a shushing motion with his hand, even though we're away from the rest of the passengers. "I can't tell you too much. It's confidential."

"Maybe I can help you with whatever it is you're investigating? I know these people."

His mouth twists. "Because you're so Hollywood and I'm an outsider?"

"That's not necessarily a bad thing. But yes, you are. That's probably why Tyler hired you."

"And here I was thinking it was my world-famous investigative skills."

I try not to roll my eyes. I might not entirely succeed. "Those are invented."

"Excuse me, I was making my living at this before I met you."

"Barely."

"And yet you want to work with me."

I take in and exhale a long, slow breath. "I do." I pause. "Please?"

Like I suspected it would, this word affects him. I'm not sure if it's something I've ever said to him before.[29] But I know him. I've been writ-ing about him for ten years, my fingers flying over the keyboard like I'm playing a ballad on a piano. I don't know which parts I made up anymore, and which parts were there to begin with. He's bent to the pages, too, becoming more like the fictional Connor than he was in the beginning.

"If I tell you, it will stay between us?" Connor says.

"Of course."

I may be crossing my fingers behind my back.

I mean, obviously.

He nods slowly, sealing the pact. "Fred owes Tyler a lot of money."

"For what?"

"*Julius Caesar*. It lost millions. Tyler financed the film, but Fred was the guarantor."

"What does that mean?"

"If the film didn't make Tyler's investment back at the box office, Fred guaranteed he'd repay up to a certain amount."

"Why would he do that?"

"It was the only way to get the movie made. He's been obsessed with it for years."

"How much?"

"Twenty million."

"Yikes," I say. "I assume Tyler's asked for payment?"

"Of course. But Fred hasn't paid."

I cock my head to the side. "Where do you come in? Does he want you to threaten him?"

"That's not my style."

"You're right, you used Guy for that."

I mean Guy Charles, Connor's former business partner. They had a falling-out at some point over the last ten years that I never got an

---

[29] Okay, maybe I said "please" once or twice in the bedroom, but I don't like to think about that.

explanation for. Not that this is unusual. Connor generally operates on a need-to-know basis.

"Where is Guy, anyway?" I ask. "I haven't seen him since the funeral."

"I have no idea," Connor says. "And good riddance."

"You ever going to tell me what happened between you?"

The corner of his mouth lifts. "Unlikely."

"That tracks." I tap the side of my face, thinking. "So, if it's not violence, what are you supposed to do exactly?"

"Tyler wants me to track down Fred's assets so he can seize them."

"Like in a lawsuit?"

"Yes."

"And?" I say.

"And what?"

Why is everything always so hard with this guy? Sigh. "Any luck with your investigation?"

"I only started looking into it last week."

The ferry hits a large wave, rocking us up, then down. My stomach turns with the beginning of seasickness. Or it might just be proximity to Connor.

"How long has he owed the money for? *Julius Caesar* came out last year, right?"

"That's right. But it takes a while to know what the total tallies are going to be. That happened when the accountants closed last year's books in March."

"So long before we started filming."

"Yes."

"Have you spoken to Fred?"

"Not yet. I thought I'd gather as much information as I could before I confronted him."

I nod my head slowly. "That's smart."

He gives me that half smile again. "I learned it from you."

"How?"

"The Vacation Mysteries? Our literary adventures?"

"You read the books?"

"Of course I read them."

Okay, interesting.

I'm not sure why, but I always assumed he didn't read the books. Not since he read a galley of *When in Rome* and discovered he could blackmail me for using his name without his permission.

But that's all behind us, I guess. He isn't in my newest book contract. It was part of what we'd agreed to in Italy.

It doesn't make us friends.

"I thought that film cost one hundred and fifty to make?" I say.

It was all anyone talked about in the press surrounding its failure.

"It sold well overseas—I don't quite understand the accounting. But twenty million is a hefty sum."

"For you and me, yeah. But Fred should be good for it. Hasn't he been paid millions per picture for years? Or did he buy some island in the South Pacific I didn't know about?"[30]

"As I said, I haven't been investigating long. Perhaps he's simply withholding payment for some other reason."

"Such as?"

"Emma." He takes a step closer. "A jealous man can make irrational decisions."

Our eyes lock and I wonder what exactly he means. That's one of the (many) problems with Connor. He speaks in riddles and ellipses, and it's exhausting trying to puzzle it all out.

Also, we've been looking at each other for way too long.

I pull my eyes away and watch the waves beat against the boat.

We're approaching the port in Avalon, a half-moon bay with a steeply rising mountain behind it covered in lush greenery. Candy-

---

[30] There's at least one celebrity who should be canceled but somehow isn't who lost a lot of money this way.

colored buildings climb the mountainside in a way that reminds me of the Amalfi Coast. But because of the name, I can't help but think of the mists of Avalon, that made-up place in Camelot.

But wait . . . King Arthur and Guinevere—an epic marriage that ended badly because the bride was in love with another man.

Oh dear.

I think about the note Emma received yesterday.

Is life imitating art?

"Would Tyler make threats?" I ask. "Is he that angry about the money?"

"Do you know something?"

"I'm just speculating." The boat bumps up and down again. I'm glad this ride is almost over. "We're here. We should get ready to disembark."

"Don't say anything to Emma," Connor says.

"I won't."

"Eleanor . . ."

"What? I said I won't."

I catch sight of Oliver approaching and take a step away from Connor. Which is a mistake.

You don't allay fears by stepping away suddenly.

"Ready to go?" Oliver asks as he arrives next to me, but what he wants to know is—what's going on?

"Connor's been hired by Tyler to investigate Fred," I blurt, my voice high-pitched and rapid, like it always is when I'm nervous.

"Eleanor! I *just* said not to tell anyone."

"You didn't mean Oliver."

"I meant everyone."

"I don't have any secrets from Oli."

Oliver shakes his head as the boat slides into the dock. "Are we done here?"

I link my arm through Oliver's. "Definitely."

* * *

After the ferry docks, we're met by a flotilla of golf carts, there to take us to our accommodations. Not everyone fits into the wedding venue at the Descanso Beach Club, and I made sure Harper, Oliver, and I got one of the private villas nearby.

Part of me wanted to have a romantic weekend with Oliver, but I didn't want Harper to feel left out. She grumbled about being our third wheel, but I knew she didn't mean it.

That doesn't mean I don't have plans for her this weekend.

There are a couple of wedding guests I have my eye on for Harper.

Not that she can't find her own dates. It's just that she doesn't. Or she did, but the last person she was involved with was Connor, and that was a terrible idea.

So that's what *was* on my agenda.

Only now it looks like I also have to figure out who sent that note to Emma.

Could it be Tyler?

But why send the note to Emma if he was mad at Fred?

"Someone is going to die at the wedding"—it's so vague it feels hard to take it too seriously under this perfect sky.

But you can't trust the weather these days.

Storms come whether they're forecast or not.

And there's a tempest on the way.

"Eleanor," Oliver says, "what were you talking to Connor about?"

"I told you—he's investigating Fred."

"But why were you talking to him in the first place?"

"This is our golf cart," Harper says, pointing to a white cart with the number 10 on its side. There's a young man in a blue-and-white uniform sitting behind the wheel. He gets out to help us with our luggage, and then we settle in—Harper and I in the back, Oliver up front—while the driver, Tommy, gives us a tour.

"Santa Catalina Island is twenty-two miles long and eight miles wide, making it seventy-six square miles covering almost forty-eight thousand acres with a coastal perimeter of fifty-four miles. For a point of comparison, Manhattan is thirteen miles long and two miles across at its widest point. Of course, Manhattan's population is 1.6 million people, where the permanent population of Catalina is only four thousand, mostly here in Avalon, with a smaller concentration in Two Harbors, which is located on the other side of the island."

Tommy speaks in a bored drone. He's clearly delivered this spiel many times before.

"The highest peak on the island is Mount Orizaba, at over two thousand feet in elevation. The island is also known for its wildlife and dive sites. It was first settled over seven thousand years ago and was originally inhabited by various Southern California tribes, including the Tongva. The Spanish were the first Europeans to claim it. It was then turned over to Mexico, and eventually the United States."[31]

We're driving at maximum golf cart speed along the two-lane main road. To the left are small shops painted in bright yellow and stark white. To the right, dozens of boats are moored inside the breakwater. Up ahead of us is a massive round structure that's painted white with a terra-cotta roof—the Casino, which sits on a point overlooking the Pacific. It's ten times bigger than any other building.

Whatever Tommy says, gambling is clearly the island's most important commodity.

"Where is everyone?" I ask, pointing to the nearly empty high street.

"Most people left because of the storm." His tone says that we shouldn't be here either.

"Sorry you had to stay," Harper says.

"That's fine, miss. Catalina Island has long been a stop for smugglers, gold diggers, and pirates. There have also been hunters and missionaries, and it became a resort a hundred twenty-five years ago."

"Do you think he's talking about us?" I whisper to Harper.

---

[31] Tommy's preset spiel can be found, in part, on the Catalina Island website.

"Smugglers, gold diggers, and pirates, oh my!"

We laugh as our cart moves through a small roundabout onto St. Catherine Way, which will take us to a second, more secluded bay where the Descanso Beach Club is located.

"In 1915, a fire burned down half the buildings in town, which led to the island being sold to William Wrigley Jr. of chewing gum fame. In 1921, Wrigley even had the Chicago Cubs do their spring training here. They trained here until 1951. And Wrigley invested a lot of money into the island, building the Casino." Tommy points to it as we pass.

Oliver looks back at me. "I assume that's where Connor will be spending the rest of his time?"

I smile at him. "No doubt."

We drive past the Casino, and the golf cart takes a left and starts going up the hill. The engine sounds like it's working overtime, but that doesn't detract from the beauty. We're surrounded by palm trees and flowering bushes, and the air smells floral and sweet.

"Catalina Island has always been a popular destination for Hollywood, especially during the 1930s, '40s, and '50s. More than five hundred films, documentaries, and commercials have been shot here over the years."

We crest a turn and arrive at a complex of forty white villas with red-tile roofs and balconies overlooking the bay. We're in a two-bedroom. Emma's staying in one of the villas near us. She and Fred came over on a private boat early this morning because arriving by ferry didn't quite fit with her ideas for her wedding.

We'd laughed about that when she told me, because our lives have ended up so differently from what we'd imagined when we made Barbie and Ken get married on a floating barge in the canal near our houses in Venice Beach. Back then, she wanted to be an astronaut and *I* wanted to be an actress.

You never know where life is going to take you.

That's not a clue, just an observation.

The golf cart lurches to a stop.

"The Beach Club is down that path," Tommy says, pointing to a paved path that winds through the terra-cotta-tiled villas. "The tennis court is up there. There's a map of the property inside, and here are your keys."

He hands us three sets of keys, and Oliver tips him as we grab our bags.

"Say," Tommy says, suddenly shy. "Can I have your autograph?"

"Oh, you've read my books?"

"I . . . You're not Emma Wood?"

Harper starts to laugh. "No, she's not."

"Sorry, miss."

"It's fine."

"I'll be getting back to the marina to meet the next ferry." He blushes as he ducks into the golf cart and puts it in reverse. It starts to beep like a truck backing up.

"You okay, El?" Harper asks.

"Of course, why do you ask?"

"Not every day that you get confused for Emma."

I give her a look. "It happened more than once on set. I mean, she *is* playing me."

"Fictional you."

"Yes, yes. Let's go in, shall we?"

Inside, the villa is a little outdated with lots of red tiles and reddish-brown wood, but it has an incredible view of the water and Descanso Beach below.

"You never answered my question," Oliver says.

"Which question?"

He gives me a look because he knows that I remember, well, kind of everything.

Which is a curse, if you're wondering.

I mean, would *you* want to remember all of your worst moments like a highlight reel every night before you fall asleep?

Oh, that happens to you, too?

So you know.

"El . . ."

"He approached me," I say.

"Why?"

"He's working his case."

"Why would he think that you'd know anything about Fred?"

I loop my arms around his neck. "Emma's my best friend. It makes sense to talk to me. Plus, it's Connor. Who knows how his mind works?"

Oliver grimaces. "Oh, I know how his mind works."

"He's not that bad," Harper says.

We both turn. "What?"

"I'm not saying he's perfect or anything. I mean, he's still *Connor*. But he's been trying to do better. You know, reform his ways or whatever."

"Since when?"

"Italy," Harper says. "He took the blame, right? And you don't have to pay him anymore."

I get that sick feeling in my stomach that I had on the boat. "Why are you defending him?"

"No reason." Harper busies herself at the table. There's a welcome basket on it, full of wine and fruit. "So, what's on the agenda for today?"

Oliver and I exchange a look because Harper is acting weird.

Not that I'm not grateful to her for distracting us from my conversation with Oliver.

Connor is a sore subject that I'd rather bury than exhume.

"Emma said there'd be a schedule." I spot a piece of paper on the kitchen counter. I pick it up.

It's written in letterpressed lettering on thick paper.

Welcome to
Emma and Fred's Wedding!

SURPRISE!

That's right! We're not filming any scenes from the movie. Instead, we're on a journey to start our lives together! We're so excited you could be with us for our big day!

We've got lots of fun activities planned for you over the next several days.

But first, we'd love to keep this wedding in the family—so please, no posting of pictures or videos while you're here.

We also ask that you leave your phones in your rooms/ villas, as per the conditions of our contract with *People,* who'll be providing an exclusive look at the wedding for their readers!

In the meantime, here is the schedule for the weekend!

FRIDAY

12:30 p.m.—Lunch—Descanso Beach Club
2:00–5:00 p.m.—Afternoon activities
- Glass-bottomed boat tour
- Snorkeling

Let Shawna know which activity you'd like to do and when.
6:30 p.m.—Rehearsal Dinner—Descanso Beach Club

SATURDAY

9:00 a.m.—Exhibition tennis match—Fred & Emma vs. Eleanor & Oliver
11:00 a.m.—Ropes course
12:30 p.m.—Lunch—Descanso Beach Club
6:00 p.m.—Wedding, followed by dinner & dancing until dawn!—Descanso Beach Club

A MIDNIGHT MURDER WILL BE SERVED.

Wait, *what?*

STORM WATCH From Friday 8 PM PDT until Sunday 1 PM PDT

Issued By Los Angeles, CA, US National Weather Service

Affected Area The Channel Islands, including Santa Catalina and San Clemente

Description STORM WATCH REMAINS IN EFFECT FROM 8 PM PDT THROUGH SUNDAY AFTERNOON . . . Flash flooding caused by excessive rainfall and high surf around the Channel Islands is expected.

Action Recommended AVOID affected areas. An evacuation order may be issued. Be prepared to evacuate on short notice.

CHAPTER 6

Is It Okay to Be a Bridezilla If Someone Is Trying to Kill You?

When I find Emma in her room twenty minutes later, she's inconsolable.

"A midnight *murder*? Did you see, Eleanor? Someone is planning on killing me at my wedding at midnight!"

She's sitting in a green rattan chair in front of a bank of windows. The sun is filtering through in a way that makes her seem lit from within, a visual that's accentuated by the white linen dress she's wearing.

Fred is standing behind her in white pants and a blue chambray shirt. As I meet his gaze over Emma's head, it strikes me again how very much he looks like Connor.

"It's a typo," I say as I sit down next to her and gather her in my arms like a child. "No one is going to kill you."

She wipes at her cornflower-blue eyes. "A typo! It was supposed to say 'buffet.' How does that get changed into 'murder'? There aren't even any letters in common in those two words."

"There's the *u* and the *e*. You know how autocorrect is."

She shoots me a look. "But I checked it. Shawna checked it. The wedding planner checked it. You did, too, right, Fred?"

Fred and I exchange another look, and I'm 100 percent certain that Fred did not check the wedding schedule to make sure it didn't refer to an upcoming murder.

Not that I blame him for that.

I'm not good at reading the fine print either.

"Of course I did, love." He pats her gently on the shoulder.

"Then how did it happen?"

"Maybe someone thought it was a theme wedding?" I say. "Because of *When in Rome*? That's what you can say if anyone notices."

"No one chooses *murder* as their wedding theme!"

"Which makes it original."

"I guess." She sniffs. "Did *you* notice?"

"Well, yes, but you know I'm a stickler for detail."

I hold my breath because this is not true. Like I just said, I'm terrible at details. This is what I have Harper for. Emma knows this, but she's distracted right now, so maybe she'll forget.

"You think people will believe the theme wedding thing?"

"I do."

"And when there isn't any murder mystery to solve, what then?"

"They'll be too drunk to notice," I say. "There's an open bar, right, Fred?"

This is an item I'm certain he took care of. If I know one thing about Fred, it's that he loves an open bar.

"I certainly ordered one. If the studio wasn't being such a bunch of ass—" He stops himself, his face turning red. "Maybe there *will* be a murder," Fred says through his teeth. "The more I think about it . . . I bet Tyler had something to do with this."

"Oh, Fred," Emma says. "Not this again."

"I'm telling you, Em. He wants to ruin me."

I squeeze Emma and stand up. "Ruin you? That's a bit dramatic isn't it?"

He gives me a hard stare. "You don't know Tyler."

"You're right, I don't. But still. You're starring in his movie. He needs that to succeed. Bad publicity won't help."

"You know the saying . . ."

There's no such thing as bad publicity.

Only I don't think that's true.

People get canceled now. So there *are* consequences for bad publicity.

Sometimes. Not often enough.

"What happened between you two?"

Emma makes a slashing movement with her hand against her throat, but I pretend I don't see it.

"Fred?"

"What? Oh, some silly dispute over money. I'm good for it. A gentleman never goes back on his obligations."

I do a mental eye roll. That Oscar that Fred won? It was in a Jane Austen adaptation. And ever since then, he peppers his conversation with garbled quotes from the books or the movies or the SparkNotes.

I haven't figured out which yet.

Not because I haven't read Austen.

I have. I just haven't committed the books to memory the way some people do.

"Why does he think you aren't good for it?"

"I simply asked for more time to pay it off, that's all."

"And this was because of *Julius Caesar*?"

Fred grimaces. "Yes. Though it wasn't my fault the movie failed. You saw those beastly reviews the critics gave it. Like locusts swarming . . . And Tyler's an old friend. I didn't force him to produce the movie. He was *eager* to do so. We all thought it would be a hit."

So Fred and Tyler *are* in a dispute over money. And the wedding schedule is, what? Some kind of revenge? A real threat? Just a stupid accident?

No, there's the note, which I notice Emma is *not* bringing up.

The note is not an accident.

"Can you find out who did this?" Emma asks, tapping the schedule against her hand. "Make sure I'm not in danger?"

"I'm not an investigator."

"You do it in your books all the time."

"That's a fictional version of me."[32]

"But you always solve the case."

"Because I write the mysteries. I know what happens in advance."

"Still," Emma says, "the skills have to be applicable. Putting together a mystery has to be the same as taking it apart. Look at Italy."

"I was almost too late in Italy."

I was too late.

Someone *died*.

"But you solved it in the end. You survived." She shudders and tears spring back to her eyes.

"Why do you think it's directed at you, Emma? Even if the schedule's not a typo, it doesn't mention who the intended victim is."

Emma frowns at me, pissed I'm pushing her to reveal her secret. But if her life is in danger, now is not the time to keep things to herself.

Because that's how people die in these kinds of books.

They hold back a crucial fact, and the next thing you know, they turn up dead.

"I'm sorry, babe," Emma says to Fred. "I should've told you this before, but this isn't the first thing like this that's happened. There have been notes. And a Twitter thing."

"What kind of notes?" Fred says.

"And plural?" I add. "More than one?"

She catches my eye and ducks her head slightly. "Nothing specific. Just vague . . . threats, I guess you'd call them."

"Did you keep them?" I ask.

"I threw them away except for the one I gave you yesterday."

"There was a note yesterday?" Fred says.

---

[32] Everyone always thinks the main characters in books are a thinly disguised version of the author. And okay, I <u>do</u> borrow from life, but after ten books, Cecilia Crane has gotten up to some pretty shady things, including killing someone. Do they think I'm capable of that? Oh, wait, I <u>did</u> kill someone. Fine.

I pull it out and show it to him.

He shakes his head and hands it back to me. "Why didn't you tell me about this, Em?"

"I didn't want to worry you. You know how it is with fans sometimes. It's not the first time I've received weird mail."

Fred frowns. "How was this delivered?"

"It was left in my trailer. The others, too."

"Your *trailer*? That means it was someone who had access to set."

"I know. But there are so many people wandering around all the time. It's not that hard to get access if you want to."

This feels like a lie. Every time I've visited set, I've had to show ID and be on a list. But I understand why she's telling it. She wants to justify why she didn't do anything about it.

Why she didn't tell Fred.

She wants to minimize the possibility that she's in danger.

And who can blame her for that?

"I didn't want to worry you, Fred."

"And the Twitter thing?" I ask.

Emma takes out her phone and opens the app. She taps, then looks up. "I blocked them."

"What's the handle?" I say.

"@Emmaswooden."

"Ouch."

"I don't care about that. It's the other things they know about . . ."

"Like what?"

She meets my eyes, then looks away. *Not here*, she's telling me. *Not in front of Fred.*

"They knew I'd been cast in the movie before I did. Other things they couldn't know unless it was someone very close to me."

"I wish you'd told me about this," Fred says, pouting.

"You had enough going on with Tyler."

"That man has lost his mind. And did you see that karate move he tried to pull last night?" He rubs at his chin. "Maybe *he's* doing the Twitter thing?"

"Doesn't seem like his style," I say.

"It might just be lucky guesses," Emma says tentatively. "You know how it can be with fans on the internet—all their theories. Sometimes they get it right."

"But all of it combined . . ." I say.

"It is concerning," Fred says. "Will you look into it, Eleanor?"

"I will."

"Thank you." He puts his hand on my arm and stares directly into my eyes, and I'm not going to lie: Fred Winter staring into your eyes is a powerful thing.

"You're welcome," I say, feeling foolish.

It's a feeling I'm used to, though.

I'll get over it.

And, like Mr. Bennet, probably sooner than I should.[33,34]

"Darling, I should go check on the next ferry. My parents are arriving on it."

Emma's mouth turns down at the corners. "I thought we said no parents."

"My mother caught wind of it from that stupid Santa Monica Gossip, and she wouldn't be denied, I'm afraid. I figured it was better to have her in the fold than out, you know how she is." He pauses after saying this, a reminder that we all know how his mother is.

She's an actress, too, and was big in the '80s, starring in several soapy television shows where the women had big hair and bigger shoulder pads.

---

[33] See, I have read Austen.

[34] Okay, FINE. I've watched the BBC adaptation of *Pride and Prejudice* more times than I can count. In my defense: Colin Firth.

Her career never recovered after she had Fred, though—something, I gather, that she's made known to him.

"It's not too late to have your parents come, Em," I say in solidarity, though it probably is.

There *is* a storm coming.

And even Hollywood can't keep endless ferries running into a hurricane.

Mrs. Wood isn't going to be happy to have been left out of the wedding, but that's a relationship I don't have to manage.

There are, occasionally, advantages to having dead parents.

Sorry, Mom and Dad! I'm sure you would've been amazing wedding guests.

"I'll think about it. But Fred, let's keep your mother out of the pictures, all right?"

"Not sure we're going to be able to manage that."

"She can't be in the official photos, or my mom will freak. Come to think about it, can you confiscate her phone?"

"I will." Fred plants a kiss on Emma's cheek. "Thanks, darling. You should relax. Go for that soak we talked about. You know you always feel better after a soak."

He tips his head against her forehead and they share a tender moment.

One of those ones TikTokers make endless reels about to heartbreaking songs.

And no, I'm not jealous.

I just sound that way.

Fred leaves, and Emma turns to me after we watch his shadow pass the window. "Did you check the Twitter thread?"

"I left my phone in my room, as per instructions."

"Sorry about that. But you know how it is with these exclusive photo deals."

"It's fine. I'll check when I get back to the villa."

"Thanks."

I twist my hands together. "You really want me to look into this? What if I find something you don't want to know?"

"Fred knows all of my secrets and I know all of his."

"Really?"

Her shoulders slump. "Okay, not *all*, exactly . . ."

"What about Tyler?"

"What about him?"

"There's a rumor that you and him . . ."

She turns away, a blush creeping up her cheek. "I . . ."

"Just tell me. No judgment."

She laughs. "El, come on. There's always judgment."

She's right. I *am* a judgy person.

I've tried to change, but people don't change.

You should remember that.

"I'll dial it down."

"It was a long time ago," Emma says.

"When?"

"Two or three years ago."

Or two *and* three years ago, my judging brain can't help but assume.

"Why didn't you tell me?"

"It was right after your breakup with Oliver. Honestly, I didn't think you could handle it."

"Was I that bad?"

"You were inconsolable. You even said, 'I can't be around happy people right now.'"

"That doesn't sound like me."

"You said it, trust me. You know I have almost perfect recall of dialogue."

"Okay, okay. I'm sorry."

"We've all been there."

"Right," I say. And the truth is, I'm terrified I'll end up back there again. If Oliver and I don't work out this time, I don't know how I'll survive it. Or I do, and that's even worse. That's a hard thing to navigate in a relationship. Tiptoeing around the fact that you're in a panic that your happiness will be taken away at any moment.

"So what happened?" I ask Emma. "How did you and Tyler meet?"

"He's been in my orbit for years. You've met him before."

"Sure, but we always kind of thought he was a jerk, didn't we?"

"He can be. But he has a sweet side . . . Anyway, I was trying to get the funding for that indie Christmas film I wrote, and Tyler was one of the people I approached."

This rings a vague bell. She'd asked me to take a look at the script. It was about a woman returning to her small town at Christmas—one of those Hallmark movies that seems to be on every week. Only this one was . . . "elevated," I think was the word she used. The main character was a singer who'd had a big hit. Her career was slipping away. And she didn't end up staying in the town or re-falling in love with her high school boyfriend.

Ha ha. Of course she did! Have you *seen* these movies?

Had you going there for a minute, though, didn't I?

Anyway, it never got made. Such is Hollywood.

"Tyler was going to finance it?"

"He decided not to. But we had a nice dinner. And then I ran into him again a couple of days later when I was in Malibu."

"What were you doing there?"

"Are you cross-examining me?" Emma asks.

"You want my help. This is how it works."

"It was some promo party thing." She stares off into the distance, remembering. "We talked late by the pool and then went to the beach to watch the sunrise. You want the details?"

I try to hide my shudder. Does one ever want to imagine their best friend having sex?

Besides, I don't have to imagine it.

I've seen her fake it on screen.

"Do I need them to figure out what's going on?"

"Probably not."

"Whatever happened to your no-producers rule?"

"That was for projects I was on. We never did a project together. And he agreed to keep it quiet."

"How long did the relationship last?"

Emma twists her engagement ring around her finger. It's a large square Harry Winston diamond that *People* devoted an entire three-page spread to. "A couple of months, but . . . I think he fell kind of hard."

"Not you?"

"Not me. He was a bit messed-up when I ended it, frankly. Like surprisingly so."

"What did he do?"

She gets a faraway look in her eyes. "A little light stalking. Showing up at my place, leaving messages."

"How long did that last?"

"A couple of months. But this was years ago."

"How did you get him to stop?" I ask.

"I had my security talk to him. I use them sometimes. Around releases. And it seemed to do the trick. We even saw each other a few times after that and it was all good. Or so I thought."

"And then?"

She nods slowly. "And then I got cast in *When in Rome.*"

"You think that was because he wanted you around?"

"I didn't at first, but . . ."

"What?"

She gathers up her hair in her hands, then releases it. "He tried to renew the relationship. I told him no, and I thought that was the end of it, but . . ."

"Then he found out about you and Fred."

Her eyes connect with mine in a way they have so many times before.

I remember the first time we communicated that way. It was the second day of kindergarten and we were playing one of those kids' games involving a ball and minor injuries. We called it murder ball, even though we weren't allowed to.

Anyway, old story: I didn't get picked, but then there Emma was, holding my hand and insisting she couldn't play if I wasn't on her team, and that was it. We were a unit after that.

Eleanor and Emma, murdering everyone in sight on the blacktop playground.

And now we might be bound up in a *real* murder, and the thought of that scares me in a way I haven't been in a long time.

Three months at least.

"What did Tyler do?"

"It wasn't what he did so much as how he was acting. Just angry all the time. And then, when those notes started showing up in my trailer, I thought it was him."

"What did the other notes look like? The same as the one you gave me? Made up of cut-out letters?"

"Yes."

I shudder, thinking of the time it took to do that.

Whoever wrote them went to a lot of trouble not to get caught.

"Did you confront him?"

"How could I? He's the producer."

"What about the studio?"

"*He's* the studio . . . You know he has his own . . . You'd call it an imprint."

"He must have a boss."

"Not really."

"So you did nothing?"

She stands and goes to the window. "I didn't think he was going to do anything, just make my life uncomfortable for a while. It wouldn't be the first time. It's Hollywood, for fuck's sake."

"I'm sorry, Em."

"It's fine. Every job has downsides. Yours, too, right?"

My mind goes to the obvious place. "Downside, your name is Connor Smith."

"All those years that he was needling you . . . how did *you* handle it?"

"Denial, mostly."

She laughs. "The shoot's over and we just have to get through the wedding and then that's it."

"Get through it?"

"You know what I mean."

I walk to her. The view is truly stunning, with the white-sand bay below us and the dark blue water dotted with sailboats and yachts. "What if we postponed the wedding?"

"No, I don't want that."

"I know, Em, but what if someone *is* trying to kill you?"

"No. Like you said, the threats aren't even specific. It's just someone fucking with us."

"Okay, but what about this financial thing between Fred and Tyler . . . You don't want to put your own money at risk."

"Don't worry. We signed a prenup."

"You did?"

"Yes, dearest, we did." She lays her hands on my shoulders. "I keep what's mine and he keeps what's his. We signed the papers at the lawyer's office last week when we updated our wills. It was his idea, even."

I stare at her, impressed with her forethought, which is so different from how I go through life. She's dyed her hair the same color as mine for the shoot, and we *do* look very much alike.

Which is kind of creepy.

How do identical twins deal with this?

"Don't be so surprised," Emma says. "You might not read contracts before you sign them, but I always have."

"Yes, yes."

"He's not after me for my money, he has plenty of his own."

"Why not pay Tyler back, then?"

"Because Tyler is a jerk. He doesn't need the money. He just wants to hurt Fred because I chose him."

"Maybe. But don't be so sure Tyler doesn't care about the money."

"Okay, Mom." She lets me go and checks the time. "All of this is stressing me out."

"Too early for a drink?"

She smiles. "Probably, but there's this amazing series of hot tubs built into the hillside. Why don't you go get changed and meet me there in twenty?"

"Can Harper come, too?"

"Of course. The more the merrier."

I hug her impulsively, and she shoos me away.

I go to the door, and when I get to it, I turn back to watch her. She's staring out the window again, and if I didn't know better, I'd say she was lost in thought.

But I *do* know better.

I know her best.

And so a shiver runs through me when I recognize her expression for what it is.

Fear.

This feels like a good time for a map.
You should know I can't draw.
But here it is:

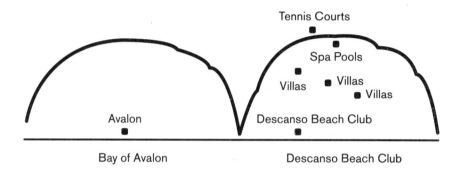

I did warn you.

CHAPTER 7

Doesn't Everyone Know You Shouldn't Drink the Water on Vacation?

"So, let me get this straight," Harper says as we hike up the stone-strewn path to the hot tubs where Emma asked me to meet her. They're near the top of the steep hill above the villas, and I feel more winded than I should as I grip the guide rope and push my calves up, up, up. "Tyler Houston's probably been sending her threatening messages, and that's been going on for a while, including the other day when the last note said someone was going to die at the wedding and then on the agenda a murder is announced?"

I gulp in some air and almost swallow a bug. Gross.

"Yes, but she doesn't know who's sending the messages. We don't know for sure that it's Tyler."

She glances back at me over her shoulder. She seems unbothered by the climb, which shouldn't surprise me but somehow does. "But she *did* sleep with him?"

"Yes. Years ago."

"And he's pissed about her marrying Fred?"

"Yes."

"And Fred owes him money?"

"Yes, but that was from before Emma and Fred got together."

Harper shakes her head, then turns back to the path. Her hair's up in a tight bun, and she's wearing a jungle-print sheer kaftan over her bathing suit. She looks elegantly perfect as always, and if she weren't my sister and my favorite person in the world besides Emma, I'd probably hate her.[35]

"Do you think someone wants to kill her?"

I shudder with a sense of déjà vu. I've been asked this question before, and the answer turned out to be yes.

But the problem when you do what I do for a living is that you're always seeing murder around every corner.

It doesn't mean it's there.

But it's not *not* there either.

"I think we need to take the threats seriously until proven otherwise."

"Good idea." Harper stops to read a sign. It's two white hands—one pointing toward the TENNIS COURTS and one toward the SERENITY POOLS. "And someone's also threatening her on Twitter?"

"Yeah," I say as I pull up next to her. "Give me your phone and we can look together."

She gives me her best *Who, me?* look. "What makes you think I have my phone?"

I put my hands on my hips, resisting the urge to bend over and breathe upside down like I used to do in gym class. "Did I just meet you yesterday?"

"Okay, fine." She pulls it out of her pocket and hands it to me.

I go to the handle Emma told me about and read the posts. I flick through to the oldest, which was the same week we got the green light for the film.

@Emmaswooden Emma Wood has been cast in When in Rome. What a waste. The fandom deserves better!

---

[35] I bet you thought I was going to say that I do hate her sometimes, but I <u>don't</u>. Truly.

@Emmaswooden Who'd she sleep with to get this job? @AnonPLZ you must know!

@Emmaswooden I bet it's Tyler Houston. That guy's a creeper of the first order.

@Emmaswooden Rachel Brosnahan deserved that part, but she would never!

@Emmaswooden Seems like Emma Wood is up to her old tricks on set. Sleeping her way right to the bottom.

@Emmaswooden Fred Winter can do better! Our Connor deserves a *real* Cecilia.

@Emmaswooden I wouldn't marry him if I were you. You'll regret it.

And on and on. None of the tweets are particularly vicious given what Emma normally has to put up with online. But she's right, there's something insidery about them. Something targeted.

"If it wasn't for the other things, I'd say these were lucky guesses," Harper says. "But with the other notes . . ."

"Why would anyone announce that there's going to be a murder, though?"

"To instill fear. Like that Agatha Christie book."

A Murder Is Announced."

"What happened in that one, again?" Harper asks.

"Someone publishes an ad in the local paper saying a murder will take place at a certain time and location, and then it does. Miss Marple is staying in the town for a spa treatment and she gets involved in solving the case."

"Naturally. But spa treatment? That's a little on the nose given where we're headed."

"No one dies at the spa."

"That's *so* reassuring."

"At least we're not the target this time."

Harper taps me on the shoulder. "*I* was never the target."

"Fine." I hand her back her phone. "I wonder, though . . . These messages started *before* it was public that she and Fred were dating. So if it is Tyler, that wasn't what set him off."

"Or he knew about it already."

"That's possible."

"The tweets make him look bad, too, though. 'Sleeping to the bottom'? Would a guy write that about himself?"

"I agree with you. There's something *feminine* about the tweets, as Miss Marple might say."

"Or someone wants it to look that way."

"Right. Well, we're not going to solve it this minute. We should get to the hot tubs."

Harper blows a curl off of her forehead. "I'm not going to want to get into a hot tub after this."

"It's what the bride wants."

"I'm not even in the wedding party."

"That wasn't my decision." I tug on her sleeve. "Come on, let's go. Emma will be annoyed if we don't show soon."

"How much further?"

"Not far now."

"Okay, Papa Smurf."

We give each other a sad smile—this was a thing we'd do with our dad when he forced us to go hiking as kids.[36] Then we continue up the path, my calves protesting, and after a few more minutes of exertion, we get to the outdoor spa.

It's breathtaking—a set of dark wooden pools wedged into the hillside

---

[36] If you know, you know.

with an unobstructed view of the Descanso Beach Club and its private beach. It also feels eerie because there's no one on the beach, just a few boats bobbing in the bay, the blue beach umbrellas snapping in the wind.

We're not alone up here, though. Emma's standing with her hands on her hips, wearing a white cover-up over her white bikini.

All white is the *real* theme of the weekend, not murder.

Ha ha, kidding.

It's murder.

"Took you long enough," she says.

"Please tell me one of those pools is cold," I say, my face burning from the exertion.

"Yes, actually." She points to the one that's farthest away. "You're supposed to do a circuit. Cold, warm, hot, and then the whole circuit again."

"And the purpose of this circuit is?"

"Realigning something."

I smother a laugh. She knows I'm not into all that chi business. "And if I don't want to be realigned?"

She puts out a fake pout. "You'll do it for me."

"What about me?" Harper says.

Emma gives Harper her most charming of smiles. "You'll do it for me, too, won't you?"

Harper melts a little. I can't blame her. Emma's good at this.

She's dazzling.

"Which one are we supposed to start with again?" I ask.

"Oh," Simone says, coming around a corner of the path. "I thought I'd be alone."

"I guess we had the same idea," Emma says, but not in a mean way.

She likes Simone, she's told me, even if she's a bit harsh sometimes. But some women feel like they have to be in this business or they'll be dismissed.

"Is she a bitch, or is she a woman?" Emma likes to ask, and it's a fair question.

The problem is that Simone *isn't* a nice person.

You don't have to take my word for it. There's at least one *Variety* article where she isn't named, but the anonymous complainants are for sure talking about how hard she is to work for.

I mean, it *could* be another South Asian film director who got her start directing a big star's first film,[37] but the odds are low.

"Sure," Simone says, holding on to the ends of the towel she has draped around her neck. She's got a red one-piece on that pops against her dark skin. She looks strong, too, with those long, lean muscles you get from Pilates.

In high school, she was the lead cheerleader *and* the captain of the debate team, and she ran around with a crowd that we called the "glitterati," which was made up exclusively of current and future prom kings and queens. Her crew generated three actors you've heard of and one supermodel. To give you some idea of how extra they were, Simone is probably the least successful of her cohort.

"Hi, Simone," I say.

"Oh, hi, Eleanor. I didn't see you there."

Right, sure, I'm invisible suddenly. Though that *would* be a cool power to have.

Or maybe not. I probably don't want to hear what people have to say about me when they think I'm not there.

Besides, I already have my Amazon reviews for that.

"You remember Harper?"

She looks at her blankly, then nods slowly. "You all getting in?"

---

[37] It was a cheesy rom-com staring Fred. He went on to be a big star, and she lingered in obscurity directing Lifetime movies to pay the rent. I guess I'd be bitter, too.

"I'm starting with the cold pool," I say.

Simone frowns. "I think you're supposed to do hot, medium, cold."

"Emma just said the opposite."

"Your choice."

"*My* choice, I think," Emma says with a bright smile.

"What? Oh, yes, of course. You're the bride."

"Crazy, right?"

Simone takes the towel off her neck. "You think so?"

There's an odd beat of tension I can't place, and then it clears like the clouds racing across the sun. And maybe that's all it was—a shadow.

But—and I know I've said this already—there's a storm coming.

You can feel it in the air like an electric current.

"How do you think the movie will turn out?" I ask Simone.

"What? Oh, great, of course."

"The dailies I saw looked good."

I hate to admit it, but it's true.

Simone's cinematographer has a real eye, and the acting was good.

Not that I *have* admitted it to Simone. Just to you. And you'll keep my secret, right?

"They sent you dailies?" Simone's voice rises an octave.

"I'm an executive producer."

She gives me a hard stare. "And you went to film school?"

"No."

"So you watched the dailies why, exactly?"

"Was I not supposed to watch them?"

"You can do whatever you want, Eleanor, as has always been the case."

I'm about to say something when Harper puts her hand on my arm to stop me.

Which is for the best. It's Emma's wedding, and whatever feud I have with Simone needs to be buried.

At least for this weekend.

Then we can go back to ignoring each other.

"I'd love to cool off," I say, "so I think I'm going in the cold pool first, if you don't mind, Emma?"

"I'm right behind you."

"Suit yourself," Simone says.

I turn my back on Simone's disapproval and Harper follows me to the edge of the pool that is marked as COLD.

We strip off our cover-ups, and then something occurs that feels like it goes in slow motion but has to have happened in real time because we're not in a Marvel movie.

—Harper's holding her cover-up, and the way she folds it releases her phone from her pocket.

—Emma snatches it up from the ground and playfully holds it away from Harper over the water.

—Harper snatches at it, but all she does is bat it from Emma's hand.

—Harper tries to catch it before it hits the water, but doesn't quite make it.

—It lands in the water, floating there before it begins to sink.

—The water starts to spark and smoke, the air filling with an acrid stench.

We stand there staring at the dying phone for a moment, and then Emma lets out a dramatic scream that pierces the quiet day and sends a flock of birds into flight, their wings beating hard against the thickening air.

WHEN IN ROME

ACT 1, SCENE 8

EXT. TREVI FOUNTAIN – NIGHT

Cecilia and Connor are walking arm in arm. Trevi Fountain is lit up, sparkling, and romantic. Other TOURISTS and LOCALS are wandering around, some snapping pictures on their phones or filming themselves with selfie sticks.

                    CECILIA
          It feels like fate that we met, doesn't it?

                    CONNOR
          I feel the same.

He leans down and kisses her, gently at first, then deepening the kiss. They break apart.

                    CECILIA
          I'm so happy.

                    CONNOR
          I'm glad, my dear.

                    CECILIA
          I wish my parents didn't have to die for all
          this to happen.

                    CONNOR
          How so?

                    CECILIA
          It's how I can afford this. My inheritance.

                    CONNOR
          You made something good out of something bad.
          That's a positive thing.

CECILIA
The money makes me feel guilty.

CONNOR
Why? They wanted you to have it.

CECILIA
I know.

She looks at the fountain for a moment.

CECILIA
Should we make a wish?

CONNOR
Ah, but it's three wishes.

CECILIA
Three?

He takes out a handful of COINS and sorts out three.

CONNOR
The legend goes like this. The first coin means
you'll return to Rome, the second means a romance, and the third a wedding.

CECILIA
Oh.

CONNOR
You're disappointed?

CECILIA
In America, we get to choose our wishes.

CONNOR
You'd wish for something different?

CECILIA
I can't tell you or it won't come true.

Connor smiles and hands her the coins.

                    CONNOR
          It's your decision.

She takes them, letting his hand close over hers for a
moment, then releasing it. She walks to the fountain.

                    CONNOR
          Turn around.

                    CECILIA
          What?

He makes a spin gesture with his hand.

                    CONNOR
          You're supposed to throw them with your back to
          the fountain.

                    CECILIA
          Why?

                    CONNOR
          Don't question the gods, my dear.

Cecilia GIGGLES and turns around.

She tosses the first coin over her shoulder. It lands in
the fountain with a SPLASH!

                    CONNOR
          So, you'll return to Rome.

She throws in the second. SPLASH!

                    CONNOR
          A romance!

She's about to throw the third when the air fills with
the wail of SIRENS.

Cecilia and Connor are distracted as a POLICE CAR rushes past and stops at a building on the corner that houses a small bank.

                    CECILIA
        Do you think . . . Is it one of the robberies?

                    CONNOR
        Potentially.

                    CECILIA
        Is it wrong that I'm intensely curious?

                    CONNOR
        It's one of your more attractive qualities.
        Shall we see what it's about?

Cecilia nods enthusiastically, palming the last coin.

CHAPTER 8

Is It Dangerous to Break Bread with Someone Who Wants to Kill You?

As Emma's scream echoes through the day, Harper starts to reach for her smoking phone.

I grab her hand. "Wait, no, you'll get electrocuted."

Emma lets out another bone-chilling scream as Harper's charred phone floats to the surface in a final shower of sparks.

Harper pulls her hand back quickly as two attendants in white uniforms rush toward us.

"Don't touch the water," I say to one of the attendants, a young guy who looks about twenty-five with wiry dark hair. "I think it's electrified somehow."

His eyes go wide while the other attendant bends down and opens a panel on the side of the tub. "I'm going to turn it off," he says.

He flips a switch, and Harper's phone stops buzzing.

We stand in shocked silence, the air, well, *charged*, all of us breathing raggedly.

Holy shit. Did that just happen?

That could've been me, or Harper, or Emma in there.

Or Simone.

She shouldn't be an afterthought, but she is. I know that makes me a bad person, but that's not the relevant point right now.

Someone *is* trying to kill someone at this wedding.

Not good.

When I get my bearings, I bend down next to the attendant, looking into the panel. But I don't know what I'm looking at. I feel like a guy standing over the open hood of a car—I have to pretend I know what I'm doing even though I don't.

"Crossed wire?" I say.

"Maybe. Or a short."

"Has this ever happened before?"

"Not that I know of. José would know."

"José?"

"The electrician."

"Who has access to this panel besides him?"

"It's usually locked,"

"Was it?"

"No . . . Why?" He looks at me. "You think this was on purpose?"

"What?" Emma says. "What do you mean?" Her face is locked in horror.

"I want to make sure this wasn't deliberate."

"Why would it be deliberate?" Simone asks, the calmest of all of us.

"That's a good question."

"You think someone is trying to kill one of the wedding guests?"

I stand slowly. "I didn't say that."

She narrows her eyes at me. She's always been smart—I'll give her that. "And who do you think the victim was supposed to be? You?"

"No."

"Then who?"

"Whoever came to the pool next. It could've been *you*."

"Or Emma."

"Her, too."

Simone scoffs. "Why would anyone want to kill either of us? Or are you saying there's a psycho on the loose?"

"I'm not saying anything, I'm just . . . investigating."

"You're not a private detective, Eleanor. You're a *novelist*."

She doesn't have to say, *Not a very good one.*

It's implied.

"If someone is trying to disrupt the wedding, isn't that something you'd want to know?"

"What's it to me?"

"The movie?"

She laughs. "Is that what this is, Emma? A publicity stunt? The whole wedding?"

"No!"

"That was *not* your most convincing performance. Should we go again?"

"Is this helpful, Simone?" Harper says. "We're all in shock."

"Terrible pun," I say.

Harper shoots me a look that tells me to shove it. "Whether this was done on purpose or not, it's a problem. Look at my phone. That could've been any one of us. Even you, Simone, whether you were the intended victim or not."

Simone stares back at her, then nods slowly. "Yes, of course. You're right. I'm glad no one was harmed." She looks at Emma. "Are you okay, Emma?"

"I'll be all right."

"Good." She turns to the attendant who was on the ground with me. "What's the protocol now?"

"Ma'am?"

"Who are you going to tell about this?"

"My supervisor."

"All right. That good enough, Eleanor?"

"It'd be good to have the electrician take a look and see how it happened. I think his name is José."

"Excellent suggestion. I'll talk to the front desk when I go back up."

She tugs on the ends of her towel again. "If that's all taken care of, I think I'll get lunch."

I check my watch. It's noon.

"That's a good idea. We'll meet you there."

Simone locks eyes with me, and for a moment I think she's not going to take the hint and leave, but then she does. I wait until she's gone back around the bend she came from, then turn to Emma, holding her close to me.

"I could have *died*."

"Yes," I say, stroking her head. "But it could just be a short." I hug her tight. "So let's not freak out, okay? Let's get changed and go to lunch?"

She shudders in my arms but relaxes. "Yes, okay."

"Do you want me to come to your villa with you?"

"No, I'll be all right." She pulls away. "Good thing Harper's phone fell in the water."

I smile at her. "Good thing she broke the rules, you mean."

"Ha. Yes."

"I'll figure out what's going on, I promise."

"I feel like I'm going crazy."

"Harper's right. Terrible pun or not, you've had a shock. Go get changed and we'll see you at lunch. Okay?"

"Okay."

I hug her again; then we separate and she walks down the path Harper and I came up.

Harper stands next to me. "Why does it feel like we're back in Italy?"

A chill runs down my spine. "We're not in Italy. We're in *When in Rome*."[38]

I fill Oliver in on what happened as we get changed for lunch, and we have a few serious moments trying to decide what to do. Because it's becoming

---

[38] This is a clue.

clearer by the minute that there's a killer on the island with us. Or, at the very least, someone who wants to scare Emma out of going through with the wedding and doesn't care if someone gets killed in the process.

Which is pretty much the same thing.

And all of which points to Tyler.

But he doesn't strike me as the type who'd do something like murder.

Not himself, anyway.

He'd get his assistant to do it.

But for now, there's nothing we can do about it other than stick close to Emma and keep our eyes peeled, so the three of us make our way to the Descanso Beach Club.

The club is nestled at the bottom of the hill in a private white-sand bay. Large and white with a gray-tiled roof, it pops against the bright green trees and shrubs surrounding it. Palm trees dot the shore, with sail-covered teak daybeds nestled in between them. There's a beachside restaurant and bar, but the lunch is set up inside, in the same room where the wedding reception will take place tomorrow.

It's a cavernous space with a bank of Pacific-facing windows, papered in paisley wallpaper with crystal chandeliers hanging from the ceiling. The view out the windows is unparalleled—the sea is azure, and the moored boats tip up and down in the sunlight.

For the wedding, Emma told me, it will be filled with flowers and flowing fabric, making it romantic and intimate. It's low-key today, though, with a buffet set up across one end of the room and a dozen eight-tops with white tablecloths and centerpieces made up of local wild-flowers and Catalina poppies.

We check the menu, which is posted on a placard near the entrance. The signature drink is something called Buffalo Milk,[39] and the menu is

---

[39] Made of crème de banana, crème de cacao, Kahlúa, vodka, and half-and-half. Sorry, Catalina, but that sounds disgusting!

heavy on local fish and salads because Hollywood. I doubt there'll be any bread in sight all weekend.

A waiter in black pants and a white shirt with the club's logo on it—two leaping dolphins in a Grecian blue—leads us to our table. I wave to Shawna, who's sitting with Ken, Fred's stand-in.

He's a nice, affable guy who's worked with Fred for much of his career, being patient while shots are being set up so Fred can stay in his trailer and play video games or whatever else he does in there. His physical resemblance to Fred is uncanny—from the back, they're indistinguishable—but there are important differences in their faces; Ken is like the missing link between Fred and Connor.

Shawna gives me a harassed smile. She's wearing headphones similar to the ones she wears on set, and she's got a clipboard with a long checklist next to her.

"Shawna seems stressed," Harper says.

"What else is new?"

"It's not her fault Simone is such a beast, and now with this wedding planner thing . . ."

"What wedding planner thing?"

"The wedding planner refused to come to the island because of the storm. So now Shawna has to do it."

"It *is* supposed to be part of production . . ."

Harper gives me a soft belt in the shoulder, then goes to Shawna and talks to her in a low voice so I can't hear what she has to say. It must help, though, because Shawna smiles at Harper and they share a brief hug.

"Hi, Shawna," I say. "Hi, Ken."

"I was just telling Shawna," Ken says in his high-pitched voice that's completely unlike Fred or Connor, "that she should quit."

"I'll be fine," Shawna says. "Two more days won't kill me."

I give her a bright smile while a shadow passes over my grave, as it always does when I hear that phrase, and then we go to our table.

Unsurprisingly, we're seated with Connor, Allison, David, Tyler, and Simone.

If there *is* murder on the menu, the person behind it knows what they're doing because there are many potentially murderous airings at this table.

It seems hard to believe it, though, in this idyllic setting.

Which is probably the point.

That and the fact that we're essentially alone on this island. Not *And Then There Were None* alone, but not in the middle of a bustling metropolis either.

Not that you need to be in a remote location to pull off a murder. Italy was teeming with people. But still. If we're in the middle of a plan, the location is factored into it.

But whose plan is it?

I search the room, looking for something or someone out of place.

Emma and Fred are sitting at a table with his parents. They're both smiling, and being an actor must be a good asset at a time like this because Fred's mother is a notorious handful, an old-school diva who likes to complain about everyone and everything in a loud, ringing voice.

She was a noted beauty in her youth, with dark hair and startling blue eyes, but now her hair is too obviously dyed black and it floats around her head like an aura. Imagine Marge Simpson as a faded movie star and you'll get the drift.

Her husband is a diminished man who started out acting, too, but once he landed Fred's mother, he faded into the background, becoming her manager and chief apologist. He's still handsome, though, with silver hair and a trim figure. The resemblance between him and Fred is strong, but he doesn't have Fred's charisma.

Right now, the Winters seem to be in some minor fight over a cat— there are a few of them wandering the property that seem feral.[40] This

---

[40] Interesting fact: Catalina Island has a famous feral cat population!

one appears tamer than the others, and its tabby fur is clean and fluffy. Maybe it's been adopted by the club. Either way, it's hungry like us and is hunting the room for scraps. I see Mr. Winter reach down to feed something to it, only to be met with a withering glance from Mrs. Winter.

That cat is probably going hungry now.

But enough about them.

Let's spin the camera back to my table, shall we?

Everyone's dressed like they stepped out of a J.Crew catalog—chinos and striped sweaters from the nautical collection—except for Allison, who's in one of her classic jumpsuits in a creamy fabric.

I'm wearing something similar, but I'm already regretting the choice because (1) I don't look as good as Allison does in it, and (2) I kind of have to pee, and that means I'm going to have to get naked in the bathroom to do it.

Anyways! We spend a few minutes in idle chat before serving ourselves at the buffet.

Mr. and Mrs. Winter are ahead of me in line, as is Simone. She's making friendly conversation with Mr. Winter, who seems like a nice man, but Mrs. Winter gives her a withering gaze over her shoulder, which shuts Simone up, something I didn't think was possible.

What's *that* about?

No point in asking. Simone's not going to tell me.

I fill my plate and return to the table. Allison and David are across from me, and Oliver and Harper are to my left. Tyler and Simone are next to Allison, which leaves . . .

"What's this I hear about someone getting electrocuted?" Connor asks me after he conspicuously sits down in between me and Harper with a full plate of food.[41]

"What?" Allison asks. "Are you serious?"

"No one got electrocuted," I say, trying to hide my annoyance at Connor but failing, as I almost always do.

---

[41] To be accurate, everything Connor does is conspicuous.

"Only my phone," Harper adds.

"Sounds melodramatic," David says with a laugh in his voice. "Like something from a bad movie."

I bite back saying something about how he should know, and instead tell them what happened, with Simone adding in a detail or two, like the sound that Harper's phone made when it hit the water, or the scream Emma gave that brought the staff running.

She gets the laughs she's looking for, and I'm grateful to her, grudgingly, for doing so.

Because listening to her, it sounds scary, but silly, too.

Then again, I left out the threatening notes, the Twitter feed, and the murder that's going to be served at midnight. But I watch Tyler for a reaction while we're catching everyone up. He's listening but seems unconcerned as he methodically cuts through his steak.

Like a surgeon, I can't help thinking.

Like he doesn't care that it used to be a living thing.

"Sounds as if you had a close escape," David says. "Glad I skipped a soak this morning."

"Seriously," Allison says. "We talked about it! I didn't think there'd be time before lunch."

"How did you know it was there?" I ask. "It wasn't on the schedule."

"I researched the property before we came—why?"

"You think someone did it on purpose?" Connor asks.

"Interesting question," David says.

"I don't see how it could be targeted at anyone specific," Simone says. "It wasn't like they'd know who was going to be there or when."

"That's true," I say. "The decision Emma and I made to go there was spontaneous. Certainly not enough time to set anything like that up."

"But if they wanted to disrupt the wedding," Connor says, "... a dead person in a hot tub might be a good way. It wouldn't matter who."

"Why would anyone want to disrupt the wedding?" Allison asks.

Tyler frowns but says nothing. He just reaches for his red wine and takes a large gulp.

"Perhaps someone doesn't want them to get married," I say.

"And they're willing to kill someone to keep it from happening?" Tyler says, looking up and meeting me in the eye.

"I admit it's a bit of an extreme solution."

"It was probably an accident," David says officiously. "As I'm sure we'll learn. We're lucky no one got hurt."

Connor leans closer. "If it had been Fred who was in danger . . ."

"Are you saying your client is capable of murder?" I say under my breath.

"He's pretty pissed off."

"That's not the same as trying to murder an innocent person."

"Is Fred innocent?"

"I don't know yet."

I feel Oliver stir and lean away from Connor. I reach for Oliver's hand under the table and squeeze it, then turn my body away from Connor for emphasis.

"Only two days," I say to Oliver, my eyes trying to convey that this is as much a torture for me as it is for him.

"Yes."

"It *could* have been a coincidence."

"There are no coincidences," David says, and I realize I was speaking louder than I should've been. "That's the first rule of screenwriting."[42]

"But this isn't a script," Allison says gently, touching his arm. "Life doesn't follow a beat sheet."[43]

"Of course, darling."

---

[42] It isn't, actually, but WHATEVER.

[43] A beat sheet is a document that outlines the beats in a screenplay. There are different theories about how many beats there should be. I'm not sure which theory David subscribes to. Probably none because a beat sheet is supposed to keep your screenplay from being <u>bad</u>.

They kiss, and it's one of those *aww* moments you usually see at weddings between the bride and groom.

Everyone is smiling at them, though it feels like Connor flinches next to me.

But that can't be right. He doesn't still have feelings for Allison. They've been divorced for almost ten years. And he's moved on—numerous times, including, much to my chagrin, with Harper. It must be man-jealousy—he doesn't want her, but he doesn't want anyone else to have her either.

"If I was writing this," David says when they pull apart, "then something else would happen to tip the scales toward it being deliberate."

"Like what?"

"Something deadly. One of those moments that ends an act."

"Some kind of twist that takes the story in a new direction," I say.

"Yes, exactly. Like a body dropping or a more serious attempt on someone's life." David checks his watch. "It should happen right about now . . ."

Everyone freezes.

A clock ticks down in my brain like it's hanging over the scene.

Three, two, one . . .

Then the moment passes, and we all start to laugh.

"I guess we're not caught in one of your screenplays," Harper says.

Thank goodness.

And amen to that.

I reach for my wine, but before it gets to my lips—

"Mother, please calm down." Fred's voice breaches the din of the party.

"Do not tell me to calm down. There *is* something in my food."

"Don't be so theatrical."

"You know I hate it when you say that!" She takes her plate and puts it down on the floor. "Here, I'll show you."

The cat that was looking for scraps takes its cue and races across the room toward her plate. It dips its head and starts to eat, purring deeply.

Everyone is watching now, like it's a car crash, and nothing happens for a minute, but then the cat goes rigid, and starts to shudder, then falls to the ground stiff as a board.

Dead.[44]

---

[44] Don't worry. No actual cats were harmed in the making of this scene.

CHAPTER 9

Is There Only One Detective in This Series?

"Oh, no, no, no, what have you done to Crystal?" a man I later learn is the hotel manager says in distress as he runs up with a waiter. He's in his forties, with bleached-blond hair and red cheeks that give him a boyish look in his tailored light gray suit and tie.

Failed actor, probably, but I only guess that because it's true for half of the people you meet in Southern California.

Even in Avalon.

"I think it's moving," Emma says, pointing. "Look, there, wasn't that a twitch?"

"Crystal? Baby, are you okay?" The manager crouches by the cat and starts to stroke it.

Everyone else takes a step closer, holding their breath, as the cat twitches, then springs to life like a cartoon, hissing, with its feet splayed out.

The manager tries to pet Crystal, but she bites him and runs away with a growl that sounds more mountain lion than cat.

The manager holds his bitten hand to his chest and stands.

"Will you look at that?" David says, watching Crystal bound through the room and out of view. "It's not dead."

"It must've been a seizure," Allison says. "That happened to my cat once. It's quite scary."

"It was a poisoning," Mrs. Winter says in a voice she learned to project off-off-Broadway.

"What did you do to Crystal?" The manager's eyes accuse Mrs. Winter.

"I should ask *you* that. I could taste it in my food. A good thing I tested it on that beast."

"There are signs everywhere that say *not* to feed the cats."

"Oh, please, do not be so . . . What is it my husband is always calling me?"

"Over-the-top?"

She glares at Mr. Winter. "We need to get that food tested for poison before anyone else is put at risk." She looks down at the floor. "Where did my plate go?"

I search the room. The waiter who arrived with the manager is standing next to the door to the kitchen, scrapping a plate into the waste bucket.

I point toward him. "We won't be able to test it now."

"Tomas was simply doing his job," the manager says.

"What's your name?"

He straightens his shoulders. "I am Mr. Prentice."

How formal.

"Well, Mr. Prentice, it seems that there was something potentially poisonous in Mrs. Winter's lunch."

"Impossible."

"How do you explain what happened to Crystal, then?"

"We'll check everything, of course. But as I said, madam, you should not be feeding anyone but yourself."

"I won't be eating another thing with a poisoner on the loose!"

"Now, Mother. Let's not scare the guests."

Mrs. Winter pulls her kaftan tighter across her shoulders. "You don't care about my welfare. No one does."

"Of course I do," Fred says. He looks exasperated and not one bit scared.

Maybe his mother frequently thinks she's being poisoned.

But *why* and by who?

And why isn't Mrs. Winter asking that question? It would be the first thing on *my* mind if I thought I almost ate something that could kill me.

"Not enough to tell me about your wedding!"

"Please keep your voice down, dear. Everyone is staring."

"Let them stare." Mrs. Winter flings her arms out, the large rings on her fingers flashing in the chandelier light. "Are you enjoying the show?"

Fred turns red to the roots, and I exchange a glance with Emma. I can tell she's more than glad her parents aren't here. Unlike the Winters, they're the furthest thing from show business, more like hippies out of their time who run a wellness store, and they wouldn't be into all of this drama.[45]

"Mrs. Winter, why don't you come sit by me and tell me all about it," Emma says in a soothing voice, patting her on the arm like she used to do to the horses at our summer camp in the High Sierras. "I'm sure we can get to the bottom of it."

Mrs. Winter huffs. "We need the police, that's what we need."

"I don't think that's called for, Mother, I—"

"Perhaps I can be of some assistance," a voice says behind me, and I stiffen.

What?

No. It can't be.

A man in his sixties with a bald head and a linen suit steps forward. He's holding a crushed fedora, his shoulders a bit slumped. He's speaking in an Italian accent covered over by a British one.

He gives a deep bow. "Inspector Tucci at your service, madam."

"What the hell is *he* doing here?" Connor asks.[46]

---

[45] Emma's parents actively tried to persuade Emma from going into show business, but since when has anyone ever listened to their parents about something like that?

[46] How many times is someone going to ask themselves that question in this book? Just once more, I promise.

"It's not him, Connor," Allison says, laughing. "It's—"

He puts up a hand. "As I have told you repeatedly, Ms. Smith, I prefer to stay in character throughout the shoot. Please address me as Inspector Tucci."

"What's he talking about?" Oliver asks. "Is this *not* the guy from Italy?"[47]

"This is the guy *playing* Inspector Tucci," I say. "He's a method actor, you know, who stays in character the whole time?"[48]

"But the shoot's over."

"There might be reshoots," Inspector Tucci says.[49] "I don't want to presume anything."

"Give me a fucking break," Fred says.

"Is this for real?" Simone asks. "Or is it part of that thing that was on the wedding schedule? The murder that will be served at midnight?"

"What?" Connor says.

Emma looks panicked, then recovers quickly. "How clever of you to pick up on that, Simone. Yes, we're doing a murder mystery theme. To go with the movie, of course."

"And was this part of it?" Simone gestures around her. "An almost-cat-poisoning?"

"No, of course not. It will be in much better taste than that."

"What about him?" She points at Inspector Tucci. "Have you hired *him* to be in it?"

Inspector Tucci looks hopeful.

"If I told you that, I'd be ruining the surprise."

---

[47] Don't judge Oliver too harshly here for not recognizing that it wasn't the real Inspector Tucci. The man playing him is <u>very</u> good casting, and Oliver spent way less time with Inspector Tucci than I did.

[48] In case you missed this from context, the real Inspector Tucci investigated the murders in Italy recently and ten years ago.

[49] For ease of reference, I'm just going to call him Inspector Tucci.

"Well, it's all a bit unusual."

"It's her wedding, isn't it?" I say. "If she wants to have a theme, she'll have a theme."

"Did you clear this with *People*?" Tyler asks, the sarcasm dripping from his voice.

Fred joins the conversation. "We can do what we want, Tyler. Bad enough that we can't even have *who* we want at the wedding."

"You're unbelievable, you know that? You don't want to pay for your wedding, you go back on a deal with your oldest friend, and now you're complaining that I'm here? What the fuck, Fred? What. The. Fuck."

"Keep your voice down. My parents are here."

"I'm supposed to care about that?"

"You don't care about anything anymore."

"Or anyone," Emma adds.

Tyler stares at her like he wants to correct her assertion, to profess his undying love maybe, but he clamps his jaw shut.

"What about the cat?" Inspector Tucci says. "Shouldn't we be talking about that? Taking samples of the food? Sending things, how do you say, to the lab?"

"He is, how do you say . . . totally nuts," Harper says to me, sotto voce.

"We should eat our lunch," Oliver says, making a placating motion with his hands. "Before we ruin the rest of this day for everyone."

"Too late," Fred says, through his teeth.

"Fredrick Hubert Winter! Come sit down right this minute."

My heart sinks in empathy for Fred, but her command has the impact Mrs. Winter wanted: We start to disperse back to our seats.

We can't shake Inspector Tucci, though, as he follows us to our table and pulls a chair up to join us.

"Where shall we begin?" He pulls the bread basket toward him and plucks out a breadstick. "Who would want to kill Mrs. Winter?"

"No one wants to kill Mrs. Winter," I say.

"Someone else at the table, then?" He looks around, his bald head shining in the overhead lighting. "Does *Mr.* Winter have any enemies?"

"You know you're bad at this, right?" Connor says with his trademark sneer.

"What do you mean?"

"If someone is trying to kill someone at that table, it's not Mr. and Mrs. Winter."

"You mean it's Cecilia or Connor?"

"Their names are Emma and Fred," I say. "And no one's trying to kill anyone. Mrs. Winter was being melodramatic."

"That is possible, yes." Inspector Tucci rubs his chin. "And the cat. Perhaps it ate something it was allergic to. There is a long list of foods cats cannot eat."

"Yes, but . . ." I stop.

"Yes, Ms. Dash?"

I glance at Connor. He's watching me with his mouth in a thin line, and I can feel Oliver's body tighten in response. "It's nothing."

"As I have been saying. All a big overreaction to the momentous events at hand. Not hard to believe with all of these dramatic types around, no?"

"That's preposterous," Tyler says. "This whole weekend is—"

"Enough!" I say. "Enough." I look around the table. "We're *all* here for a nice wedding and some slightly terrifying outdoor activities, and then we'll take the ferry back on Sunday, and that will be that, all right?"

Ugh, I just heard how that sounded.

But I want to celebrate my best friend's wedding without also having to try to stop a murder.

Is that too much to ask?[50]

---

[50] You know it is, right? I don't actually need this footnote.

CHAPTER 10

Does Writing a Mystery Mean You Can Investigate a Mystery?

"Where's Harper?" Oliver asks me as we pick our way over a path toward the maintenance building.

"She's doing that glass-bottomed boat thing, I think."

Oliver makes a face. "Didn't I hear that Connor was going on that?"

"Not sure."

"He was making all those Jacques Cousteau jokes at lunch?"

"Oh, right."

I stop at a fork in the path. The undergrowth is fuller here, palm fronds growing into the path. One sign points toward the beach, and another says "Staff Only Beyond This Point" in neat white lettering.

"This way," I say, pointing toward the staff sign.

"Not even our first full day here, and we're already breaking the rules," Oliver says.

"I'd expect nothing less." I shoot him a glance over my shoulder, grinning wide, and he grins back. "Why did you ask about Harper?"

"You won't like it."

"Tell me."

"Are you sure everything is over between her and Connor?"

My heart starts hammering in my chest. "Um, yes."

"So convincing."

I push a low-lying branch out of my way. "What do you know?"

"Nothing specific, it's just . . . I think I heard her on the phone with him the other day."

"That doesn't mean anything. She does have to talk to him about work sometimes."

"This didn't sound like work."

"What did it sound like?"

"Honestly? Phone sex."

I stop. "I think I just threw up in my mouth."

"Sorry."

"Are you sure?"

"They were talking about sex."

"Oh my God." I feel dizzy *and* seasick. Not a good combo.

"I shouldn't have told you."

"No, I'm glad you did." I shake myself. Harper's a grown-up. She can sleep with who she wants to. And she *has* been acting secretive recently. Around less, and lit up in a way that, now that I think about it, could indicate that she's in a relationship. "I wish she'd told me."

Oliver lifts his eyebrows. "Because you took it so well the last time."

"Why does everyone in my life lie to me about who they're dating?"

"I think you know the answer to that question."

"Fine. FINE. Whatever. I can handle it."

"You're not jealous, are you?"

"What?"

"Excuse me, what are you doing here?"

I turn around. There's a man in his mid-thirties in a pair of brown coveralls walking toward us. He looks like he works outdoors—his hands roughened, the ridge of a tan around the edge of his hat. His complexion is darkened by the sun, his black hair in an unruly mop that partially covers his eyes.

"We're looking for José."

"That's me. But you can't be back here. This is a staff-only area."

"Yes, we know, but we need to talk to you."

His eyes shift left, then right, but there's no one here but us. "What about?"

"That electrical short that happened at the pools today."

"That was . . . unfortunate. Thankfully no one was hurt."

"Yes, that is good news, but was it unfortunate?"

He frowns. "I don't get your meaning."

"We have reason to believe that it might've been done deliberately."

"Who is 'we'?"

I point to me and Oliver.

"And who are you?"

"Oh, sorry. I'm Eleanor Dash and this is Oliver Forrest. We're guests at the wedding that's taking place tomorrow."

"Are you the police?"

"No, we write detective fiction."

"So I don't have to answer your questions?"

"Why wouldn't you want to answer them?" Oliver asks. "Do you have something to hide?"

"Of course not."

"Well, then."

José looks back and forth between us. "Are you doing research for your next book?"

"No," I say. "Why do you ask that?"

"Because that other guy was here earlier asking the same thing."

"What other guy?"

"He said his name was Inspector Tucci. *He* said it was research for a part."

My heart sinks. We were beaten to the punch by an actor pretending to be a detective.

Of course we're *authors* pretending to be detectives.

Is that better or worse?

"What did you tell him?"

"The wiring was loose and that's what caused the short."

"Could that have been done on purpose?"

"Impossible to say. The wiring is old and was on the maintenance list to be replaced."

"Why didn't you replace it, then?" Oliver asks.

"Management didn't approve it. I'm sure they will now." A phone *beeps!* in José's pocket. "Is that all?"

"Who has access to the panel?"

"Anyone with keys. It's locked."

"It wasn't locked this morning."

"That doesn't mean anything," José says. "The person who turned it on this morning likely simply forgot to lock it."

"Who turned it on?"

He shifts uncomfortably.

"Was it you?"

"Yes, it was. But I didn't notice anything out of sorts."

"We're not accusing you of anything," Oliver says. "We just want to know what happened."

"Where are the keys kept?" I ask. "Maybe someone tampered with the wiring yesterday."

"I have a set. One is kept in the maintenance shed back there." He points over his shoulder as his phone *beeps!* again.

"Do you need to get that?" I ask.

"I'm good."

"Has anyone been in the shed who shouldn't be?"

"Not that I've noticed."

"And the extra keys?"

"Are right on the hook where they should be."

"Is the hook labeled?" Oliver asks.

"Yes."

"That's not very secure," I say.

Oliver puts a hand on my shoulder. "Thank you for your time, José."

The radio on his hip crackles.

"You're a popular man."

He picks it up. "No rest for the wicked."

He puts it to his ear and walks past us. I try to eavesdrop, but he's speaking in rapid Spanish.

"What do you think?" Oliver asks.

"If someone wanted to get into the maintenance shed, it probably wouldn't be that hard. And the panel was unlocked . . . so anyone could access it."

"But they couldn't count on that. More likely they had the key and forgot to lock it after themselves."

"Right."

Oliver's eyes dance with interest. "You want to try to break into the shed?"

I step back in surprise. "Oliver Forrest, what's gotten into you?"

"Better than being on a glass-bottomed boat with Connor Clouseau."

"You mean Cousteau."

"I said what I said."

"Okay then, let's go."

I check over my shoulder for José, but he's out of sight. We walk down the path, and after a minute we arrive at a white maintenance shed. It has a black shingled roof and is about twelve-by-twelve in size. Oliver tries the handle. It's locked.

"You're leaving fingerprints."

"I don't think anyone's going to be dusting for prints. But I'll wipe the handle down after if that will make you feel better."

"It will." I look at the lock. It's a standard one, the kind that comes from Lowe's or Home Depot on prefabricated doors. "What now?"

"We pick it."

"You know how to do that?"

He winks at me and pulls out his wallet. He takes out a credit card and slips it into the crack, wiggling it into place. He fiddles for a moment, then turns the handle and the door opens. "Ta-da!"

"I'm impressed."

He holds out his hand. "After you."

I walk into the space as he snaps on the light. It looks like every maintenance shed I've ever been in, which isn't many, but you get the idea. Tools on hooks on the wall, a workbench, leftover pieces of wood, a bare lightbulb hanging from the ceiling. Everything is tidy and tucked away where it should be. The air smells like sawdust and linseed oil.

"Here are the keys," Oliver says, pointing to the farthest wall. There are twenty different keys on hooks, each labeled by a label maker.

"He's organized, I'll give him that."

"I think he'd notice if one was missing. Seems like the type."

"I agree."

"Dead end, then?" Oliver says.

"Ugh, do not use that expression."

"Sorry, sorry." He taps me on the arm. "On a scale of one to panic, how worried are you?"

"Six? You?"

"I know there are no coincidences, but it would seem a bit cruel for us to be involved in back-to-back murder plots."

"At least we're not the target this time?"

He smiles. "You mean you're not."

"Yeah, yeah." I loop my arms around his neck. "Watching you pick that lock was kind of hot."

"What are you two doing in here?"

We spring apart.

José is standing in the doorway with his hands on his hips, a look of fury on his face.

"The door was open," I say.

"It was *not*."

"We'll just be on our way," Oliver says.

"I'm calling management." José takes his radio off his hip.

"There's no need to do that," I say. "We haven't done anything. We promise. We just wanted to see the keys for ourselves."

He holds the radio to his ear, his eyes narrowed.

"What if I make it worth your while to forget you ever saw us in here?" Oliver says, reaching into his pocket. He takes out his wallet and removes a couple of hundreds.

José eyes them.

Oliver takes out a third.

José nods, and Oliver passes him the money, then grabs me by the arm and leads me back out into the sunlight.

When we hit the path, we start running, the palm fronds slapping our faces as we push them out of the way. The effort hurts my lungs and my calves, but it feels safer to run than to stop.

Life is like that sometimes.

You run away from danger.

But that doesn't mean there aren't monsters up ahead.

CHAPTER 11

Can You Do a Dress Rehearsal for Murder?

"Can you zip me up?" I ask Oliver, turning my back to him and gathering my hair up.

He steps toward me and takes the zipper in his hands. He pulls it up gently, then plants a kiss on my bare shoulder. "You know this is a romance trope, yes?"

"It is?"

"Mmmm-hmmm." His breath is warm on my neck. "Usually deployed when things are still platonic between the two main characters, but about to get spicy."

I turn around. He's wearing a light gray suit and matching tie with a white dress shirt. His hair is curling in the right way, and his freckles are popping because of the sun we got today on the boat and walking around Avalon after our near miss with José. "Are things about to get spicy?"

"Do we have time?"

I sigh. "No."

"And yet you tempt me."

"Good. But wait. Why do you know about romance tropes? *You're* not thinking of writing a romance novel, are you?"

"I might need to if Vicki turns down my latest manuscript." Vicki is our common editor and the reason we met in the first place.

"She won't."

He leans his forehead against mine. "She might."

"I don't know what you want me to say."

"You don't have to say anything."

"I feel bad. Your new book is fantastic. They all are."

"Thank you." He brushes his lips against mine and runs his hands down my arms raising gooseflesh. "I've always liked this dress."

It's a pink halter with a deep *V* in the front that hugs my curves in all the right ways.

That makes two compliments from Oliver on my appearance in as many days. Maybe because my usual wardrobe consists of leggings and oversized sweatshirts.

But I hate how my brain is cataloging his compliments.

Like I need to gather evidence that he loves me.

Like I'm building a case to prove to myself we'll work out this time.

"You don't look so bad yourself."

"Why, thank you."

We kiss, slow and lingering. I start to think about taking off the dress he's just zipped up as the heat builds between us, but . . . "We have to go."

He smiles against my lips. "Who says?"

"The schedule."

"The one that has a murder on it? I'm thinking we shouldn't be following that one."

I sigh and release him. "Poor Emma."

"It's not great."

"Understatement."

He smiles. "Certainly not what I hope for my wedding."

My heart starts to beat faster. "You've thought of your wedding?"

His eyes meet mine. "As one does."

"And?"

"I've always liked the month of May."

May. It's October now.

And I know—because I'm a woman—that seven months is not enough time to plan a wedding unless you have Emma-level resources, which I do not.

"El?"

"Yeah?"

"Are you calculating whether there's enough time to plan a wedding in May?"

"Maybe?"

"I haven't even asked you yet."

Yet. That means he's going to, right?

Right?

"I know."

"It doesn't have to be May."

"Sure. Any month will do."

"Hey, hey." He puts his finger under my chin, lifting it. "You should know I think proposing at someone else's wedding is tacky."

I force a smile. "Especially when there might be a murderer on the loose."

"Especially then."

"So, no proposal this weekend is what you're saying."

"Don't you want to be surprised?"

"Not sure. I've never been proposed to before." I say this as gently as I can because even though we were together for four years last time, marriage never came up. Not this specifically, anyway, and that was a sore spot between us.

For me, anyway.

I don't know how Oliver felt about it.

I never addressed it with him because I was young and stupid, and I thought if I told him what I wanted, then he'd never give it to me, which was unfair to him.

Because how can you give someone something you don't know they want?

And also: He's not Connor.

By which I mean, if I'd told him I wanted to get married, we could've had a normal conversation about it. Instead, I'd probably done something stupid like crap on everyone we knew who was getting married and talked about how it was a patriarchal institution that wasn't good for women.[51,52]

And then I'd gone and done something extremely stupid that ended us.

So all this talk of weddings and wedding dates is scary and nerve-racking, and we should move on to other things.

Like preventing someone from dying at *this* wedding.

That felt like a remote possibility as we wandered around Avalon after our encounter with José. It was a nice respite to take in some of the island's history, hold Oliver's hand, and forget about all the drama. The sun was shining, and the little shops on the main street were brightly painted in a rainbow of colors, and the air smelled like the ocean and flowers.

It was eerie, though. It feels like we're the only people left on this island.

Because, of course, we are.

Hurricane Isabella is building steam in the Pacific off the coast of Baja California. If it makes landfall here, it will be only the second time that's happened this century.

As the afternoon wound on, the wind picked up, making the ocean choppy as the palm trees rustled above us.

Nature was telling us something.

We shouldn't be here.

It was a message that was hard to miss as we passed shops whose windows had been boarded up with plywood and crews filling sandbags

---

[51] I definitely did this.

[52] It's true, by the way. Men are happier married; women are not. Married men live longer; married women do not. You do the math.

on the beach. There was a long line for the ferry—scared-looking people pulling large suitcases and holding their dogs tight against their bodies.

It was still a beautiful day, and so we chose to ignore the red-and-black hurricane warning flag whipping against the wind and put our feet in the ocean, letting the warmish water tickle our toes, and the hours ticked away without any friction between us.

But now we're about to go back into the lion's den, so potential murder feels like something we should talk about.

Somehow there are fewer minefields in that than in our relationship.

"You guys coming or what?" Harper calls through the door. She came back from her boat tour an hour ago with a ridge of sunburn on her nose. I wanted to ask her about the Connor thing, but instead, I've added it to the list of things I've shoved down and hope never to have to think about again.

"Yes!" I open our door. She's wearing a flowing dress in a deep teal blue, and her hair is in an updo. She looks, for a change (ha ha), better than me.

She's also holding a phone.

"Where did you get that?"

"It's your work phone."

"I have a work phone?"

"It's where your work emails come to. You know this."

"And you brought it this weekend?"

"Good thing I did."

"Is there some publishing emergency I don't know about?"

I feel a beat of panic because, despite my joke, there *is* a publishing emergency. I've owed chapters to my editor for weeks. If it goes too much longer, she could cancel my book deal.

The problem is that the idea I pitched to her has floated away from me the way ideas sometimes do. They feel so strong in the moment, and then, *poof*, when you try to flesh them out, they're not there.

I have to find it again *or* come up with some new fabulous adventure for Cecilia and Connor to go on, or the series might be over.

Which is ironic, given that I wanted to end it three months ago.

That's what ironic means, right?[53]

"No, dummy," Harper says. "Me having your phone means I can text since mine got fried."

"Who do you need to text?"

"No one."

I reach for the phone and she holds it away from me.

Ugh. It must be Connor.

Wasn't I just saying I didn't want to know this??

I never learn from my mistakes.

"You look nice," I say to Harper.

"Flattery will get you somewhere."

"Good."

The phone bleats. She looks down and frowns at it. "That person is tweeting again."

"Who?"

"@Emmaswooden. I put an alert on it."

"What did they say?"

She shows me. It's a short thread.

@Emmaswooden Maybe the soak didn't get you all wet but you haven't got nine lives left now . . .

@Emmaswooden I wouldn't go high flying, you're always lying, just stop trying.

@Emmaswooden And hold on to your man real tight, if you can't treat him right, you wouldn't want to lose him in the night.

---

[53] Yes! The definition of ironic is something "happening in the opposite way to what is expected, and typically causing wry amusement because of this." Phew.

"Song lyrics?"

"Not from any song I know."

"But the 'all wet,' that must refer to the hot tubs, and the 'nine lives' . . . that refers to cats."

"Yeah."

That frisson of fear I pushed away rises into my throat. "It's someone who's here."

"Or who has contact with someone here."

"Right. Shit."

"Should we tell Emma?"

"We definitely should," Oliver says.

"I agree," Harper says. "But here's some good news: I looked into it and cats are allergic to chocolate and grapes . . . those were in the dessert Mrs. Winter gave it."

"So, not poison."

"Not for humans. But that's probably why the cat seized."

Ugh. Inspector Tucci was *right*? That's almost never happens.

"We did some investigating of our own," I say, then fill her in on our conversations with José.

"So he took hush money?" Harper says.

"He did."

"Did you, at any point in your conversation, say, 'No way, José'?"

"Why would I say that?"

"Come on, you definitely thought it at least."

Harper's right. This does sound like me.

But it's kind of annoying to be called out on my shit, and by my own sister at that.

Not that this hasn't happened before.

I just can't get her back for it because if I do, the Connor thing is definitely popping out.

And I'm saving that information for an emergency.

Oliver checks his watch. "We should get to dinner. But first, everyone put their cell phones on the table."

"Why?" Harper asks.

"You know the rules."

"That doesn't seem prudent given everything going on, does it?"

"It won't kill you to give up your phone for a couple of hours, Harper," Oliver says.

"Everyone keeps saying that," I say. "But yeah, things *can* kill us. Like your phone. Which almost *did*."

"Okay, okay." Harper looks at the phone in her hand. "Goodbye, Rebecca."

"You named your phone?"

"No, I named *your* work phone. She's the one who answers Crazy Cathy when she starts to email me incessantly."

I start to laugh. "You're the best."

"I know." She puts the phone down on the table and pats it. I put mine next to it; then Oliver does the same.

We're ready.

For what, remains to be seen.

Cocktails are on the veranda, which faces the club's private beach. Everyone is dressed up and happy under the setting sun, and I wave hello to those I know as I search for Emma.

Like the night before at Shutters, I find her in the middle of the crowd.

She's dressed in white but not a wedding dress, and she's talking to Simone and Tyler with her jaw clenched.

Which means she's in trouble.

Not that they can tell. I've just known her long enough to know.

Once, when we were small, we ended up at some grown-up party her parents were throwing. Our parents had put us in matching sundresses, and we were expected to "use our manners" and answer questions politely. Emma had gotten caught in a conversation with an older guy who was saying how beautiful she was—she was ten!—and he could help her go places. Her jaw was clenched in that same way. I ran up and saved her by being rude, and we laughed and laughed while our parents looked on disapprovingly.

Later, when we were older and she was going to lavish parties for meetings with producers, she always used to bring me along, and I'd watch her face, and when her jaw got tight, I'd sweep in and ask some stupid question, and maybe she wouldn't get the part, but she also never ended up as one of those terrible stories in a documentary about young women in Hollywood.

So I know what I have to do now.

I kiss Oliver on the cheek and I walk up to her.

"This is my cue," I say, and she turns to me, startled, with a kind of wild look in her eyes, and then she laughs.

She leans closer to me. "You always know. How do you always know?"

"What's going on?"

"Fred's missing."

Ah, *shit.*

SANTA MONICA GOSSIP

@SMGossip

#BREAKING: Sources tell me Fred Winters has potentially done a runner from his wedding to Emma Wood, which is taking place this weekend on Catalina Island. Attendees are rumored to include the cast of "When in Rome," an assortment of stars, and musical guest Bob Dylan. Maybe it was the choice of music?

6:55 PM · October 23 · Twitter for iPhone
712 Retweets 40 Quote Tweets 4,578 Likes

CHAPTER 12

Can We Have a Wedding If We Can't Find the Groom?

"When was the last time you saw Fred?" I ask Emma after I've pulled her aside into a small room that has a distinct *Great Gatsby* vibe.

We're alone, and I can hear the din of the party in the background—music, talking, laughter, the clink of glasses. The rehearsal is scheduled to start shortly, and people are going to notice if the groom and bride don't appear.

And by "notice," I mean start posting on social media about it on the cell phones they were supposed to leave in their rooms.

"Two hours ago," Emma says. Her hair is in a bridal updo with a small tiara of what I assume are real diamonds. On someone else, it would look overdone and fussy. But on Emma, it serves as an added touch of elegance.

"Where?"

"In our room. He was, um, consoling me after this morning."

I smile at her. She's never been that comfortable talking about sex, which is kind of adorable given that she sometimes gets naked on camera. "Then what?"

"I had to finish getting ready for the party, and then do a photo shoot before with the photographer from *People*."

"Where was the photo shoot?"

"On Descanso Beach."

"What about Fred?"

"He's only going to be in the photos at the dress rehearsal. He offered to come, but I told him it would be boring for him. He said he was going to find Tyler to try to clear things up."

"That's great of him."

"Yes, but now I'm worried. Because Tyler's here and Fred isn't."

"You think Tyler did something to Fred?"

Her hands twist together. Her engagement ring twinkles under the muted lighting. It's a bit ostentatious, and for the first time, I wonder who paid for it.

"I feel like I'm going crazy. All this stuff with the cat and the hot tub and the schedule . . . Normally, I'd think it was Fred being Fred, that he was late like he always is, but it feels different. Do you get it?"

"Instinct can be powerful. You should listen to it."

Tears pool in her eyes. "So something's happened to Fred?"

"I'm not saying that. But I'm sure he's not simply blowing you off."

"What do I do?"

"Did you speak to Tyler about it?"

"I didn't want to ask him. You understand."

"Did you try calling Fred?"

"He left his phone in the safe in our room."

"Ah."

Her mouth twists. "Say it."

"I'm not saying it."

"I can literally *hear* you saying it."

I hug her. "Okay, okay, I'm thinking it, but that's not helpful, so let's go and see if we can find Fred, all right?"

She sniffs against my shoulder. "Why is this happening? Who would want to hurt me? Or Fred?"

"I don't know, Em."

"I just want to marry the man I love. Why does it feel like that's too much to ask?"

I pull away. Her eyes are red, but no tears have fallen; they're just gathered in the corners of her big blue eyes. "If I knew the answer to that, then *my* boyfriend wouldn't have told me he's not proposing this weekend."

She sniff-laughs. "He said that?"

"He thinks it's tacky to propose at someone else's wedding."

"It *is* tacky."

"I know, I know."

"Is this the universe telling me I shouldn't marry Fred?"

"No. You should marry him."

She uses her thumb to wipe the moisture out of the corner of her eye. "Aren't you the one always telling me you have terrible romantic instincts?"

"Where *I'm* concerned. But I've matched a bunch of people and they're still together."

"Like who?"

"The details aren't important."

"Uh-huh. What about Harper?"

"I haven't had any luck there, I admit, but I think she *is* dating someone, only she won't say who. Which worries me."

"Why?"

"Because what if it's Connor? Again?"

She shakes her head. "I think you need to let her make her own mistakes."

"You're right."

Her face falls. "I'm scared, El. Really scared."

"I know, sweetheart. Let's go find Tyler."

We locate Tyler off to one side of the party in conversation with Simone, David, and Allison. They're all dressed in chic party clothes—the men in summer suits without ties, and Allison in a pink dress covered in flowers. Simone is wearing a saffron-colored jumpsuit that resembles the ones she wore on set but dressier, with heels and a statement necklace.

The sun is sinking through the horizon behind them, glinting off the water as the boats bob up and down. It looks picture-perfect, despite the strong wind, and it's hard to imagine a storm is coming.

But I should know better than to judge the severity of a situation by its appearance.

"—should come out next spring to time with the next book," Tyler is saying in his authoritative voice.

Simone frowns. "But that's not *When in Rome*."

"No, it's . . . Ah, Eleanor, good, good, you can help us."

"With what?"

"When's your next book coming out?" Simone asks. "*When in Rome 2* or whatever?"

"It's called *Amalfi Made Me Do It*, and it's releasing in March."

"And it's about you and Connor in Italy, yes?" Tyler asks. "All that recent kerfuffle."

"Connor and *Cecilia*, yes."

"Can it be considered a sequel to the first book?"

I don't like where these questions are going. I glance around for a waiter. I could use at least one alcohol drink. But there aren't any around.

Why is there never alcohol when you need it?

Sigh. I should probably keep my wits about me, anyway.

Oh, I definitely should.

"It's about many of the same players, why?"

"You see, Simone, it's the perfect time to release the movie. There will be buzz about the book, and it will set up a sequel nicely."

"A sequel?" Simone says, her tone as unhappy as I feel.

"Yes, David's working on the script already, aren't you?"

David gives us all a wide grin. "I did five pages this morning."

"Wait," I say. "Have you even read *Amalfi Made Me Do It?*"

"Unnecessary."

"*Unnecessary?*"

"I've read the media accounts and conducted some interviews with the key players."

"Interviews?"

"He means me," Allison says with her trademark laugh that turns every situation, no matter how serious, into a joke. "Don't be so formal, honey."

"Well, regardless, aren't we getting ahead of ourselves?" Simone says. "Perhaps David isn't the best person to write the sequel."

"Pardon me?"

"I *did* have to do extensive rewrites."

"They weren't *that* extensive," David says.

Simone looks down at him. "Is that so."

"I've been meaning to speak to you about that . . . I'll be taking you to mediation."

"I'm not afraid of the WGA."[54,55]

"What's she talking about?" I say to Allison. As an actress, I assume she knows more about these things than I do.

"Not sure."

"A director doesn't get credit for writing a script unless they contributed at least 50 percent," David says.

"So," I say to Simone, "you changed 50 percent of it?"

"I did."

"She did *not.*"

"Are *you* the one responsible for the terrible dialogue?"

---

[54] Will it surprise you to learn that there are often disputes over who wrote a movie? No, right?

[55] The WGA is the Writers Guild of America, the union that protects writers against producers and directors.

"The dialogue is *good*," David says. "And all Simone did is a polish—"[56]

"So you're *both* responsible is what I'm hearing?"

Emma gives me a tap on the small of my back and makes a small pleading sound.

I'm a terrible friend.

"I'm sorry, Em. Um, have any of you seen Fred?"

"Missing, is he?"

"Did you do something, Tyler?" Emma says.

A slow, satisfied smile breaks on his face. "So he *is* missing."

"We're looking for him," I say. "What do you know?"

"I know he isn't to be trusted. I'm sorry, Emma, but it's true. If I thought bringing you together on this movie was going to lead to this . . ."

"But where's Fred?" Emma says. "This isn't funny, Tyler."

"I am *not* amused. You can be *certain* of that."

"What's all this about Fred?" Mrs. Winter says, arriving in a cloud of Chanel with Mr. Winter in tow. She's wearing a bright yellow kaftan with a matching headpiece.

Which tracks.

I mean, what mother *wouldn't* want to outshine her son at his wedding rehearsal?

"He was supposed to come to us for a drink before *these* drinks, and he didn't show up. Is that your fault, girl?" She glares at Emma, which I'm proud to say Emma doesn't shrink under.

Emma always rises to every occasion, especially a challenge.

"No, Mrs. Winter. We're looking for him."

"By standing around bickering?"

---

[56] "Polish" is an industry term that means they changed up to 10 percent of the script. TL;DR: When you see a screenwriter's name on a movie, that means they wrote some of it, but there's anywhere from one to an infinite number of other people who had their hands in the final draft, including the director.

"We're trying to find out if anyone saw him," I say. "Has anyone seen Fred in the last hour?"

"Fred's missing?" Oliver says, walking up with Connor in tow. "Are you sure?"

"Yes," Emma says. "Do you know anything?"

"I might," Connor says, raising his hand like he's being called on in class.

"Excuse me?" I say.

He glances at Tyler, who nods his head imperceptibly. "I have a tracker on his phone."

"You *what?*"

"Standard operating procedure."

"Standard operating procedure for what?" Oliver asks, his voice as stiff as his posture.

"That's none of your business."

They glare at each other.

"Connor," I say, "if you know something, please tell us. Emma's worried."

"If you insist." He takes out his phone and taps at it. "He's in the building."

"No," Emma says. "His phone is in our room."

Connor gives her a sad shake of the head. "Maybe *one* of his phones is."

"What does *that* mean?"

I put a hand on her arm. "Let's figure that out later, okay? Where is he, Connor?"

Connor opens an app, which shows a glowing dot. "It looks like he's below us."

"In the basement?"

"If there is one?" He glances around and spots the hotel manager. "You. Sir. Is there a basement in this establishment?"

Mr. Prentice walks up. He's wearing a baby-blue suit like you might see at a gender-reveal party. "Why do you ask?"

"We need to see it."

"Why don't you just call Fred?" I say.

"I'll do it," Emma says.

Connor looks at her with some pity. "No, you can't."

Emma pales and shrinks away. I pull her to me. "Just call him, Connor."

Connor dials a number. We can all hear it *ring, ring, ring* through his phone. But no one answers. And there's no voicemail; it just goes, um, *dead*.

"The basement?" Connor says to Mr. Prentice.

"There isn't one. Just a furnace room."

"We'll go there, then."

Connor holds his phone in front of him like a divining rod as we follow Mr. Prentice to a side door, where there's a dark staircase leading down into the ground. He snaps on a light, but it's still gloomy and damp.

It looks like one of those stairs in a horror movie.

You know, the ones where people go down and never come up again?

And you want to yell, *Don't go down there!*

But it looks like we're going down there, so . . .

"Why would he go to the furnace room?" Oliver asks.

"An excellent question for Fred once we find him," I say.

"Are you saying that my son is down there? Whatever for?"

I feel Emma shiver behind me. "You should stay here, Em. Stay here with the Winters. Just in case."

She goes even paler, but she does as I ask, leading Mrs. Winter away from the rest of us, with Mr. Winter following along behind.

Now it's just me, Connor, Tyler, Simone, Oliver, Allison, David, and Mr. Prentice. We walk down the rickety stairs, and my feeling of unease grows.

This is why I don't watch horror movies.

I don't like jump scares.

Or that ominous music they play before something bad happens.

But that music's playing in my head right now. *Duh-duh . . . Duh-duh . . .*

Oh, wait. That's the *Jaws* music.

You get the idea.

"Watch your head," Mr. Prentice says. "The ceiling is low."

We've reached the cellar floor. It's dirt, with blackened beams overhead holding up the building, built into ledge rock. The walls drip with moisture, and the air reeks of mold and wet wood. It smells like something might've died down here a long time ago.

It's exactly the sort of space you'd use if you were space-casting this type of scene.

And the hotel manager's right, the ceiling is *low*. I reach a hand up and touch it. It comes away wet, and I rub my hands together, trying to warm them.

Why would Fred come down here?

Maybe it's just his phone?

A *second* phone.

That's never a good sign.

"Which way?" I ask.

"This way," Connor says. His phone glows in the dark, lighting up his face.

I know his expressions well enough to recognize what he's feeling.

Excitement.

The jerk.

I take Oliver's hand. "What if . . ."

"Don't go there," Oliver says. "Maybe it's just his phone."

"I thought that, too, but why? And that would still mean he's missing."

"We should add this to the script," David says behind me. "It could make a really dramatic scene at the midpoint, don't you think, Simone?"

"Not the time, David," Allison says gently.

"Oh, yes, of course. It would be better in the sequel, anyway."

"There isn't going to be a sequel," I hiss.

"We'll see."

We shuffle along the corridor. There are red lights up near the ceiling, the kind that might come on in an emergency, even though the power's not out.

Not yet, my brain can't help but think.

Because it's just a matter of time before that complication arises.

"Just up here," Mr. Prentice says. He reaches up and snaps on a light, another bare single bulb hanging from the ceiling. There's a metal door in front of us, closed tight and covered in rust. "It's in there."

"Aren't you going to open it?" Connor says.

Mr. Prentice shivers. "I don't . . . You should."

"Oh, for heaven's sake." Connor hands me the phone. "Hold this." I take it, and he puts his hand on the door handle and pushes it down. "It's stuck."

"Is it locked?" Oliver asks.

"No," Mr. Prentice says.

"Put your shoulder into it, then."

Connor steps back. "I'm wearing my good suit."

"Seriously?" I say. "This was your idea."

"I'll do it," Oliver says, stepping forward. He takes the handle, puts his shoulder against the dusty door, and pushes. "It's stuck."

"I just said that."

Oliver pushes again, coming up on his toes. "A little help here?"

"Fine."

He and Connor start to push, counting together. "One, two, and . . ."

The door gives, and they both tumble into the room, almost losing their footing. I follow them in, but it's dark and hard to see anything.

A light snaps on.

Fred's splayed out on the floor on his stomach with his arms extended.

And from this angle, it looks like he's . . . wait for it . . . *dead*.

CHAPTER 13

Is a Dead Body Ever Going to Show Up?

"Fred! Fred, are you all right?"

Oliver is crouching by Fred on the floor of the furnace room while the rest of us crowd around him. Fred's pale and still. He's dressed for the rehearsal dinner in a cream linen suit, with a streak of dirt across the back and crumpled creases at the knees, like he sat down too long.

"Fred. Come on, Fred. Talk to me."

A groan escapes Fred's mouth, low and frightening, and I breathe a sigh of relief.

Fred's alive. Something bad happened down here, but not that.

He didn't die.

He didn't walk out on Emma.

Oliver puts an arm around Fred and gets him onto his back. Then he tips him up slowly into a sitting position. Fred moans at the effort, but the color is returning to his face as his eyes flutter open.

"Shouldn't we wait till the doctor gets here?" David says. "I always thought you weren't supposed to move people in these kinds of situations."

"You've been in this kind of situation before?" I say.

"Well, no, but . . . it seems like common sense."

"Is a doctor coming? Did you call one?"

I'm not sure why I'm feeling so hostile to David, besides the usual.
But his bad dialogue didn't make Fred pass out in a basement.

Did it?

"What . . ." Fred says.

"Yes, Fred?" I say moving closer. "Are you okay?"

He reaches up and touches the back of his head. "Someone . . . Something hit me."

"Did you see who it was?" Oliver asks. He's still crouched behind
Fred, helping him stay upright.

"I . . . no . . ."

"There's a doctor on staff," Mr. Prentice says, "but he didn't come to
work today because of the storm."

"Is there a hospital or a clinic we could call?"

"There's a medical practice, but I'd wager they aren't here either, because of the—"

"Storm, I get it."

"We did warn your party."

"Okay."

"And you signed a waiver."

"I did?"

"He did." Mr. Prentice points to Fred, now sitting on his own but
with his eyes only half open.

"He *what?*" Tyler says.

"Signed a waiver of liability. For being here during the storm. It was
the only way we'd agree to proceed with the event. I believe it was on
behalf of the film's production company? When in Rome, Inc.?"

Tyler's anger is simmering close to the surface. "He doesn't have the
authority to do that."

"That will be a question for another day, presumably."

I reach around the back of Fred's head gently. I'm not an EMT, but I
did have lifeguard training as a teenager. Which qualifies me for almost
nothing, but it's better than nothing, isn't it?

I know enough to feel a big lump back there, which I touch gingerly as he winces.

"There's evidence of blunt force trauma," I say.

"You sound so official," Allison says.

I lean in front of Fred and hold up my hand. "How many fingers?"

"Two."

"That's right. And now?"

"Four."

"Good. I don't think he has a concussion."

"Probably shouldn't take *your* word for that, though," Connor says. He's standing behind David and Allison, looking unfazed.

It takes a lot to rumple Connor—I'll give him that.

Is it possible Tyler asked him to take Fred out?

No, no. Connor's shady AF, but he's not a *murderer.*

"You have a better idea?" I ask.

"There must be *someone* with medical training on this island," Allison says. "Or surely we can bring someone over on a boat?"

"All boats have been canceled because of the—"

"Storm, we get it!"

It feels like a funny moment, except for the fact that Fred really might need a doctor.

And what about the rest of us?

What if one of *us* needs a doctor?

Coming here was irresponsible.

You've probably already arrived at that conclusion.

"No need to take that tone," Mr. Prentice says. "We are *all* here putting our lives at risk to accomodate the vagaries of some overpaid actors and—"

"Tell us how you really feel," Allison says dryly.

David produces a notepad and a pen from his back pocket. He clicks the pen open.

"What are you doing?" I ask.

"Taking notes. This is good stuff."

"For what?"

"The sequel."

"I already told you, there isn't going to be a sequel."

"I don't think that's up to you, Eleanor," Tyler says.

"It's *my* book."

"Where's Emma?" Fred says slowly, stopping our childish argument in its tracks.

I snap my attention back to him. He's got dirt across his nose and his eyes look exhausted.

"She's upstairs. We should let her know you're okay." I look at the collection of men and women around me. "Simone, can you tell Emma we found Fred and he's all right? And Mr. and Mrs. Winter, too? They'll be worried."

Simone folds her arms across her chest. "Why should it be me?"

"Just go, Simone."

She wants to fight me, but she has no good excuse to refuse. So instead, she shrugs and then leaves.

"Can you at least check if anyone here has medical training?" I say to Mr. Prentice.

"Yes, of course." He takes out his phone. "There's no signal."

"Well, go find one," I make a *move on* motion with my hand, then turn to Fred again while the manager is bustling through the crowd. "Give me your phone," I say quietly.

"What phone?"

"The burner. Quickly, Fred. It has a tracker on it."

He reaches into his pocket and pulls it out. I palm it and put it in the pocket of my skirt, checking over my shoulder if anyone noticed what I was doing.

Great.

Everyone did.

Whatever.

Oliver's even laughing at me, though he's trying to mask it behind a serious expression.

I can't blame him. I realized a while ago that I was bad at subterfuge, and I'm too old to change that now.

Not that I'm *that* old.

Good Lord, it's like *I'm* the one who's been hit on the head.

"What were you doing down here, Fred?" Oliver asks.

Fred moves his head slowly from side to side like he might be able to figure it out if he can shake the memories back into place. "I got a text."

"From who?"

"He said his name was José. He wanted to talk about what happened at the hot tubs today."

"José the electrician? Why would he call you?" I ask.

"You'd have to ask him that."

"I will. Why did he want to meet down here?"

"He said he had something to show me and that it was easier to explain in person."

"You didn't find that suspicious?"

"I didn't think . . . I didn't believe anyone was truly targeting Emma."

Plus, *he's* not Emma.

"What happened when you got down here?" Connor asks.

"There wasn't anyone. I tried to call José, but I had no reception. And then, the next thing I knew, there was this *thunk*, and I passed out."

"What time did you come down here?" I ask.

"What time is it now?"

"Just past seven," Allison says.

"It was around five. And . . . Oh." Fred looks around at all of us, taking in our attire. "The wedding rehearsal . . . I missed it."

"It's fine, Fred," I say. "Don't worry."

"Emma will be so disappointed."

As if this was her cue, Emma rushes into the room and drops by Fred's side. "Fred! You're okay."

He hugs her to him. "I'm fine. I'm so sorry."

"What happened?"

"I was trying to figure out what happened to those hot tubs."

"Oh, Fred! You should've let El do that."

"I have a question," David says, his hand hovering above his pad of paper and a devilish glint in his eye. "What was the number that called you? Or texted you, is that right?"

Fred shrugs.

"Why don't you check your phone?"

I narrow my eyes at David, and he gives a little shrug of his shoulders. I should've seen this coming, it implies.

And also, he's going to use this in his next work.

I should know. I'm going to do it, too.

Fred pats himself down, then stops. "My phone's in the room."

Both Allison and Tyler look like they want to say something, but I stop them with my eyes.

They can be quite expressive when I want them to be.

"We'll check it later," I say.

"But Fred," Emma says, "Connor said he was tracking you to some other phone?"

"I don't have another phone. He must've slipped it into my pocket," Fred says, daring Connor with *his* eyes to contradict him.

"Why, Connor? Why were you tracking Fred?" Emma searches Connor's face in a way that's hard to resist.

"That's confidential," Connor says, puffing out his chest.

"Yes, yes," Tyler says. "And not important right now, I'm sure."

"How can you say that, Tyler?"

"I think the most important thing is to get him some medical attention. And then contact the authorities to file a complaint."

"The police?" Fred says. "No."

"Why not, honey?"

"It will be in all the tabloids. I'll look like an idiot."

"But if someone hurt you . . ."

"El can figure it out, right, El?"

Six pairs of eyes turn toward me. "I can try."

"Thank you."

"But I do think we should call in the police."

"I doubt you can," David says.

"Why not?"

He raises his hands like he's conducting an orchestra, clicking his pen for emphasis. "Because of the storm."

CHAPTER 14

You Don't Have to Do the Dress Rehearsal the Night Before the Wedding, Do You?

Mrs. and Mr. Winter are happy to see their son safe and sound but don't agree with his insistence on not going to the police.

But it turns out our chorus of guesses in the basement were right. Most of the police force—such as it is[57]—is off island, and so even if Fred wanted to call them in, it likely wouldn't do much good until a couple of days from now when it probably won't matter.

I'm saying that like I know something.

I don't.

Not at this point.

But no one's feeling like doing a wedding rehearsal after all of this, that's for sure.

"We don't need to rehearse, darling, do we? We know our lines," Emma says, walking arm in arm with Fred in a way that looks romantic but is really her half propping him up.

Fred insists that he's fine, and they leave together to go back to their room.

---

[57] Catalina Island has a small contingent of police, but no real detectives. Which seems like a mistake given all of the tourists and wealthy visitors. I mean, it's just setting itself up as a murder location, isn't it?

"What's that about?" Harper asks, coming up to me with Shawna, who looks stressed for a change.

Ha ha.

Stressed is her resting face.

"They're skipping the rehearsal. Fred bumped his head and needs to lie down for a bit."

"Oh, no!" Shawna says. "But I need them in their places."

"Don't think that's going to happen."

"Is he okay?" Harper says, as Shawna says, "Is the wedding canceled?"

Was that a note of hope in her voice?

I mean, it probably was.

Because she has no interest in planning this wedding.

Not because she's the one who hit Fred on the head.

"Wedding is still on," I say with a confidence I don't feel.

What I *do* feel is the weight of that cell phone in my pocket. The one everyone let me take from Fred, the one we're all pretending doesn't exist.

Fred has a burner phone like a drug dealer.

What does that mean?

I almost don't want to check, but let's be honest, you know I'm going to.

In a minute.

"What am I going to do?" Shawna says, twisting her hands in front of her. "Everything's all arranged. We *need* to rehearse."

"Hey, now, don't worry," Harper says, putting her arm around Shawna's shoulders and hugging her close. "We can think of something."

"But the photographer from *People*, and everyone . . . We need to do a dress."

Harper gets a look on her face I don't like. "Could we use stand-ins? Like on set. When they're setting up a shot. We could even use Ken— that would work, wouldn't it?"

"I guess?" Shawna says.

"But who's playing Emma?" I ask, but I know who it's going to be.

Me.

I have foresight like that sometimes.

Sounds cool, right?

It isn't.

"I think we all know who's playing Emma," Harper says.

"No."

"Why not?"

"Because I can't do a fake wedding ceremony with someone who looks that much like Connor. Not in front of Oliver."

"He doesn't look *that* much like him, does he?"

"Yeah, he does. I mean, look at them."

Our heads swivel to where Ken and Connor are standing at the bar, ordering drinks. They're both wearing jackets and dress pants, and their hair is cut the same.

They'd struck up a bit of a friendship on set, which I chalked up to Connor's ego. Because, let's be honest, who wants to be close friends with someone who looks enough like you that they can be confused for you?

A narcissist, that's who.

But we all see it: From behind, they're nearly identical. Same broad shoulders, sandy hair, and an agility that might be athletic but might also be from years of training as a cat burglar.

"It's for Emma," Harper says. "Your best friend."

"Why do *you* care if the dress rehearsal happens or not?"

Harper nods slightly toward Shawna. "She needs your help."

"You'd be doing me a huge solid, Eleanor," Shawna says with a note of desperation in her voice.

"I mean . . ."

"Oliver will be fine with it," Harper says.

"There's no way he's going to be fine with it."

"Have a little faith."

I *should* have faith. But I lost that a long time ago.

I search out Oliver in the crowd. He's standing off to the side, glaring at Connor. Or at least that's what it looks like to me. The girl who *definitely* doesn't want to be pretending to marry a man who looks like Connor.

But that's what I end up doing. The collective guilt trip from my sister and Emma and even Shawna finds me, twenty minutes later, walking down the aisle with a bouquet of fake flowers in my hands while Ken stands in for Fred. The cast and crew watch us from either side of the aisle, as I do that old half-step advance to "Here Comes the Bride."

You're allowed to laugh at this image.

I want to cry.

But it's fine. FINE.

Oliver won't look me in the eye, though.

Bad enough that the cover for this whole weekend was a fake wedding between Connor and Cecilia. To see it enacted out in front of him is a lot to ask.

I hope not too much.

I get to the head of the aisle, and it's then that I realize who's "marrying" us.

Inspector Tucci.

"Shawna, what the hell?"

"The minister couldn't make it because of the—"

"Storm, okay, I get it, but him?"

Inspector Tucci glares at me. "I'm an ordained minister."

"Come on."

"He has one of those certificates to marry people in California you can get on the internet," Shawna says.

"Why?"

"Something to do in between gigs, I assume."

"I'll have you know—"

"*Stai zitto*, Tucci!" Shawna says with more aggression than I thought she had in her.

"No need to take that tone with me."

Shawna turns to me. "Just go with it, okay? Five more minutes."

I nod and step to Ken. He's a nice guy who wanted more out of his acting life than being the stand-in. But he's good-natured about it. He makes a nice living.

And sure, maybe sometimes people mistake him for Fred and he gets seats at restaurants he wouldn't normally be able to get into.

You'd say yes to that, too.

"Ladies and gentlemen, we are, as we say, gathered here today for the union of Emma Wood and Fred Winter."

Someone in the audience laughs, and it's contagious, spreading through the room like a yawn. Even *I* laugh as I turn to look at the audience and make eye contact with Oliver. His smile is strained, but he gives me a return smile nonetheless.

I gaze into his eyes, trying to let him know everything that's in my heart in this moment.

That I love him.

That I don't want to be walking down this aisle with anyone but him.

That I'm *not* wishing this was my real wedding to Connor, despite the appearances.

I think he gets it.

But it's hard for me to know because as the laughter ripples through the room and then starts to die like a wave on the shore, the photographer from *People* stands in front of me and snaps a series of pictures with a flash that almost blinds me.

I blink the flashes away.

And when I can see properly again, Oliver's gone.

WHEN IN ROME

ACT 1, SCENE 12

INT. HOTEL ROOM - DAY

Cecilia and Connor are curled up in bed in the early morning, luxuriating in a night spent together.

Connor gathers Cecilia close and kisses her.

> CONNOR
>
> Happy?

> CECILIA
>
> So happy. You?

> CONNOR
>
> How could I be anything but?

> CECILIA
>
> I can't believe we almost didn't meet.

> CONNOR
>
> How's that?

> CECILIA
>
> I almost didn't come on this trip . . . my sister . . . it was hard to leave her.

> CONNOR
>
> Isn't she in college?

> CECILIA
>
> Yes, but . . .

> CONNOR
>
> You can let her fly the nest now.

> CECILIA
>
> I know. I'm trying to.

Connor gazes at her.

                    CONNOR
     It's one of the things I love about you. Your
     dedication to your family.

Cecilia thrills to the word "love."

                    CECILIA
     I want you to meet her.

                    CONNOR
     Can't wait.

                    CECILIA
     And your family?

                    CONNOR
     No one to meet, I'm afraid.

There's a KNOCK on the door.

                    CONNOR
     That'll be the breakfast I ordered.

He goes to get it while Cecilia stretches in bed. He
comes back, wheeling in a food cart with two plates covered in silver domes and a newspaper folded in between
them.

Cecilia plucks up the newspaper while Connor places the
food on a table by the window.

                    CECILIA
     It was another robbery last night! That's what
     the police were there for.

                    CONNOR
     Oh?

                    CECILIA
     We were right there.

Cecilia stands and walks to Connor, looping her arms
around his neck.

                              CECILIA
          I wonder how they're getting away with it.

                              CONNOR
          Planning, guile, bravado.

                              CECILIA
          You sound like you admire them.

                              CONNOR
          I do, in a way. It's all very cinematic, no?

                              CECILIA
          Like "To Catch a Thief," with Cary Grant? My dad
          loved that movie.

                              CONNOR
          You'd make an excellent Grace Kelly.

                              CECILIA
          Ha!

          Cecilia releases him and then looks at the paper again.

                              CECILIA
          I feel like there's a pattern to these robber-
          ies, but I can't put my finger on it.

                              CONNOR
          My little detective.

                              CECILIA
          I'm good at things like that. I told you I al-
          ways know who the murderer is in books before
          it's revealed.

                              CONNOR
          The least likely person?

                              CECILIA
          Not always . . .

SATURDAY

Storm Warning From Saturday 8 AM PDT until Sunday 1 PM PDT

Action Recommended An **EVACUATION ORDER** has been issued

Affected Area The Channel Islands, including Santa Catalina and San Clemente

Description STORM WARNING REMAINS IN EFFECT FROM 8 AM PDT THROUGH SUNDAY AFTERNOON . . . The storm has intensified and is expected to make landfall Saturday evening with significant rainfall and wind which will cause mudslides and generalized flooding.

PRECAUTIONARY/PREPAREDNESS ACTIONS . . . You should monitor latest forecasts and be prepared to take action should Flash Flood Warnings be issued. **Anyone who has not yet evacuated should SHELTER IN PLACE.**

CHAPTER 15

If You Don't Go to Sleep, Can You Still Wake Up Angry?

I have a rough night as the wind beats against the building and howls like a wolf. When we got back to our room, I saw the evacuation order on my phone, but there wasn't anything we could do about it. There wouldn't be another ferry until the morning, assuming it could actually get to the island.

We had no choice but to shelter in place.

Which felt like a metaphor.

But for what?

I don't get an answer to that question; instead, I toss and turn, wanting to wake a peacefully sleeping Oliver to make up for the fight I'm not quite sure we're having.

He didn't say anything while we ate dinner with Harper or on the way back to our room when we all decided to have an early night. But I know him. I know what his silences mean and what his laughs mean and what *he* means, except for when I don't.

But the chaste peck he gave on my forehead after we got into bed was words enough.

You know that kiss.

The one the man gives the woman right before he's about to say, *We need to talk.*

The last time someone said that between us, it was me. I said it after we'd had a bad fight—one that was so bad, I'd thought we'd broken up. And then I slept with Connor.

Oliver, understandably, didn't take *that* news well, and we spent too many years apart.

Turns out, like Ross and Rachel, we weren't on a break, just in a fight, one I picked.

And maybe that's why I didn't say anything last night. I'm the screwup in this relationship, and I don't want to do or say anything that drives him away a second time.

So we went to bed in silence, and I couldn't fall into a deep sleep. I was just skimming along its surface, and then I tumbled into *When in Rome.*

Not even *When in Rome* the book, but *When in Rome* the movie, bad dialogue and all.

I was Cecilia, and Connor was Connor, and we were in the first act, which meant I was reliving our beginning, those heady days in Rome where we were trying to solve the mystery of the bank robberies and the mystery of us.

But the story has changed. And it isn't *just* the dialogue. Now there is a narrator, in voice-over, involved, too, making quippy/snarky remarks and casual asides, and breaking the fourth wall.[58,59]

It takes me a minute, but I figure out who the narrator is: *me.* Or, more specifically, it's my inner voice telling me not to trust Connor, not to trust any of it, to look for the hidden meaning in everything he says and does.

To look over my shoulder.

---

[58] Breaking the fourth wall is when a character speaks directly to the audience. Like I'm doing now.

[59] I have no idea what the first, second, and third walls are. The walls of a set? And the fourth is the camera? That's probably it. But how does that apply to books? Hmmmm.

To see what—*who*—is standing behind me, just out of view. The person who's behind everything.

I can't see them, but I can sense them.

I can feel their eyes on me.

And right when they're about to come into view, I wake up, my heart hammering, the sheets around me hot and sweaty and the glow of the bedside clock too bright in this dark room.

I try to go back to sleep, to forget, but the whole night is like that—a carousel of memories and regrets—and when the dawn starts to break, I decide that, come what may, I need to talk it out with Oliver.

I shake him gently and say his name.

His eyes flutter open.

And then he smiles. Thank God, he smiles.

"What time is it?" he asks, rubbing at his eyes with his fists.

"Early."

"Define 'early.'"

I prop myself up on an elbow and look down at him. His hair is rumpled and his eyes are still filled with sleep and I love this man so much it scares me.

"I'm thinking about going for a swim."

"That doesn't answer the question."

"Sure it does. You know what time I go swimming."

"You're an infuriating woman, you know that, right?"

I smile. "Part of my charm."

He reaches up and kisses me. Our mouths are raw from sleeping, but I don't care. It feels good to be close to him and erase the weird images the night brought.

He pulls away. "I thought you were going for a swim?"

"I could be persuaded to do something else."

"What about Harper?"

"I can be quiet."

"Can you, though?"

I rest my head on his chest, listening to the thump of his heart. "Yesterday was a lot."

"It was."

"Do you want to talk about it?"

"Don't worry so much," Oliver says, his voice a low rumble underneath me.

"Impossible."

"We're fine, I promise. Not so sure about Emma and Fred."

I sit up. "Ugh. Yeah."

"Have you talked to Emma?"

"I thought I'd give them some time alone."

Oliver takes a pillow and folds it under his head. "Should we be worried?"

"We should."

"You think someone's trying to kill Emma *and* Fred?"

"Not Fred. They had him incapacitated, so they could've done it then. Instead, they just hit him on the head and left."

I realize I never asked Fred if he was missing anything. Like on his person. Maybe it was a robbery, because those happen in mysteries, too, when the killer wants something they can't get otherwise. Or maybe it was a warning.

I probably forgot to ask him a lot of things.

Because I'm not a detective. I just play one in my books.

And I'll be honest about something: I've given myself all kinds of skills in there that I do not have.

"What then? Why do that?" Oliver asks.

I click my teeth together. "I think it's clear someone doesn't want this wedding to happen. And they think that if they apply enough pressure, it will be called off."

"Tyler?"

"He's the most likely suspect."

"What about that cat thing?"

"Mrs. Winter shouldn't have given it food. And why would anyone poison *her*? There wasn't any suggestion the plate was meant for Fred, right?"

Another question I never asked.

And maybe Mrs. Winter *was* the intended victim. If we're dealing with a sociopath, he wouldn't care who he hurt just as long as the wedding didn't happen.

But he's not going to get Emma back like that.

Then again, does logic apply to sociopaths?

Oliver sits up with an idea. "What about Fred's phone? The one you took?"

"I haven't looked at it yet."

"That's not like you."

I pull a face at him and then get up, pulling his T-shirt over my head from where it lies at the end of the bed. "I was distracted last night. Let's look at it now."

I go to the chair in the corner where I put my dress, and fish the phone out of its pocket.

It *is* a burner phone, one of those low-tech, pay-as-you-go devices that look like cell phones from the 1990s or the ones drug dealers use in the movies. Black, with a keypad and a small gray screen. No one's watching a TV show on this device.

It has a password on it, but something tells me Fred didn't put much thought into setting that up, and this assumption proves to be right.

I punch in 0000, the factory setting, and the phone unlocks.

"I got it opened," I say to Oliver, waving it at him with pride.

"What's in there?"

I navigate through it. He's received texts from three people. The most recent one is the one from José that he mentioned yesterday, but there are two other numbers that he's received regular messages from.

The texts from José say: *This is José, the electrician. I heard you wanted to discuss what happened at the hot tubs? I can meet you at 5 in my office.* And then there's a photo of a hand-drawn map to the basement on a napkin. Fred had responded with a thumbs-up emoji.

"What are you doing?" Oliver asks.

"Calling José." I dial the number, and it rings twice, then cuts off. "No answer."

"It's, like, six in the morning."

"Aren't electricians up early?"

"Okay, weirdo. What else is in there?"

I check the other texts. The ones from a 209 area code are just a series of times and locations, like *11AM VB* and *6PM Pier*, with Fred once again responding with a—you guessed it—thumbs-up emoji.

The texts from the third number are a conversation about money, and as I read it, it becomes apparent that it's between him and Tyler.

I tell Oliver what I found. "That's one mystery solved, anyway."

"What's that?"

"How Connor knew the number to Fred's burner. He was texting with Tyler from this phone."

"Why?"

"No idea. Maybe he didn't want Emma to know."

Emma is totally someone who'd check her boyfriend's texts.

"Trust but verify" has always been her motto.

"Are they fighting in the texts?"

"Yeah, it's all about money. Looks like Tyler has him on some payment plan, but he's missed a bunch of installments . . ." I keep reading.

The first text to that number is from Fred and says "new number." Tyler had responded with an amount that made my eyebrows rise to my hairline. Fred had agreed, but more recently, he'd been asking for more time, and saying he'd have it soon. And then in the last couple of messages, he shifted to saying that he just didn't have it and didn't know when he would.

Tyler responded with a string of expletives.

And then.

Fred: *Tyler, if you don't stop harassing me about this I'm going to have to tell everyone what you're doing.*

Tyler: *You wouldn't dare.*

Fred: *Watch me.*

Tyler: *You're doing the film for scale.*[60]

Fred: *You'll be hearing from my agents about that. You can't offset a personal debt against what production owes me.*

Tyler: *Just watch me.*

Fred: *Why are you being such an asshole?*

Tyler: *Pay me now or you'll regret it.*

That was the last message, sent a couple of days before filming started. A threat? A statement of fact?

None of it is good, and it raises a lot of questions.

Like why the hell won't Fred just pay him?

And what happened between then and now?

"How did José get the number?" Oliver asks. "And why did he call Fred, of all people?"

"I have no idea."

"If it even was José."

"Right. Plus, there's the other messages." I show him the ones with the dates and locations. "Was he having an affair?"

Oliver's forehead creases. "He was meeting with someone. But look, not for a while."

"When was the last one?"

He scrolls through the texts. "Four weeks ago?"

I purse my mouth. "When he got engaged to Emma."

Our eyes meet.

"It doesn't have to be that," Oliver says.

---

[60] Scale is the basic minimum that an actor can be paid depending on a film's budget.

"I know. But . . . he doesn't have the money he owes Tyler, and he says he's going to get the money, but then he doesn't . . . It doesn't look good."

"You think he's marrying Emma for the money?"

"It's possible. But why does he need it?"

I pick up my phone and google "Fred Winter net worth." "It says he's worth fifty million dollars."

"Those sites aren't always accurate."

"I know, but . . . even if it's half that, he's clearly in some sort of money trouble. What did he spend it all on?"

"All excellent questions," Oliver says. "But if this is about paying Tyler back, and he's going to get his money from Emma, then why the threats to the wedding?" Oliver runs his hands through his hair, then mats it down.

"You're right. Tyler should want the wedding to take place."

"Except he's in love with Emma."

"Maybe Fred owes money to someone else? Maybe that's what those texts are about? They're pretty dry for an affair."

"But smart if you don't want to get caught because then you can make that exact point," I say.

"We could just ask him, I suppose."

"Does that ever work?"

"Isn't that what Connor does in your books?" Oliver says. "Ask questions?"

I don't take the bait. We've just made up.

"Maybe I'll ask him over tennis this morning," I say.

"Gah, is that still happening?"

"It's on the schedule."

"Before or after the murder?"

I pick up a pillow and toss it at him. He catches it without effort. "If someone is going to get murdered today, we should make hay while the sun shines."

"That's a terrible mixed metaphor."

I climb onto the bed and push him back. "Let's save the editing for later, shall we?"

He smiles at me and I cover his mouth with mine, and the few clothes we have on peel away as the day breaks.

But you don't need to hear about all of that.

So I'll just say:

And, scene.

Later, ahem, but not *that* much later, I slip into my swimsuit and head down the steep path to the beach. It's eerily quiet, only the birds in the trees greeting the day, and the clank of halyards on the boats that are still anchored here as they rock against the increasing surf. The umbrellas I spotted yesterday have been tucked away, and the beach is empty of beach chairs. The sky is still clear and blue, but there are dark clouds on the horizon, pregnant with rain. I can't smell it yet, but I can feel like it's coming, like I felt in my dream last night.

Like someone's watching me.

Maybe someone is.

I check over my shoulder.

There isn't anyone behind me but a cat. It might be the same one from yesterday that almost died.

Sprinkles? Sparkles? I wish I were better with names.

We stare at each other for a moment, and then it darts off into the bush.

If it *was* the cat that almost died, it seems to have bounced back.

But cats have nine lives.

People only get one.

I put my towel down on the sand and do a running start into the water. I don't like to get in by inches if I can help it.

The water's cool, but I'm used to that. I swim straight through the chop out into the bay, passing the boats, getting my rhythm, four strokes and a breath, four strokes and a breath. I do ten minutes out and then stop, treading water. I take in my surroundings. The beach already looks far away. And the current's taken me toward Avalon Bay. I can see the dock we landed on yesterday, and the high street. There's a small clutch of people on the dock and a ferry pulled up next to it, but the rest of the town seems deserted.

Given how all of this is going, that's probably the last ferry before the storm hits. And the smart people on this island are taking advantage of it and getting the hell out of Dodge.

Not me, though. But I'm having my doubts.

I feel very alone out here.

I don't usually feel that way on the water, but I can't help it this morning.

The texts, the threats, the odd series of events all jumble through my mind.

And then there's that word: "murder."

It's one thing to write about it. Another to be its object.

I know. I almost was.

And I recognize the feeling I have now as an echo of what I had then. Like having a sixth sense for danger. Like a metal detector for black thoughts.

It's all around me and I'm alone out here.

Someone could grab my foot and pull me under, and no one would be the wiser.

I freeze, doing that countdown in my head that I did yesterday at lunch.

Because one thing David and I have in common is that our thoughts tend toward writing.

And if I were writing this, it *is* the moment when something terrible would happen.

Right about . . .

"What the *fuck* is wrong with you?"

The shouts carry over the water from the dock. I wipe the water from my eyes to see who's speaking. Tyler is there with Fred. They're waving their arms at each other, but I don't hear any other words. I try to swim closer, but I'm too far away, the words I heard a fluke of an air pocket.

Fred reaches for Tyler's arm, and he tugs it away.

But while Tyler is unsteady on his feet, Fred shoves him so that he tumbles over backward and falls into the water with a loud splash.

There's a shocked circle of onlookers around them, and then the ferry blasts its horn, and everyone rushes to get on.

Fred's standing over Tyler on the high ground of the dock, while Tyler struggles to pull himself onto the dock. He says something that's swallowed by the breeze.

And then the world quiets down and I can hear what he says next.

"If you come near me again, you're dead."

CHAPTER 16

No One's Ever Been Murdered on a Tennis Court, Right?

"Are you sure that's what you heard?" Harper asks me as we walk up the path to the tennis courts later that morning. "You were pretty far away from the docks."

I put my hand on the black metal railing that leads the way up the steep stairs. I stopped counting at twenty. "You think my mind's playing tricks on me?"

She glances over her shoulder. "It's possible. Or it's just filling in the blanks. There's a lot of threats going around . . ."

"What do you think, Oli?" I look back at him. He's red in the face, which makes him look cuter, especially since he's in tennis whites.

We're climbing these stairs because we're going to the exhibition tennis match Emma arranged between us. The courts are above the villas and the spa pool/hot tub thingies that maybe tried to kill us yesterday.

What's trying to kill us *right now* are these stairs. My calves are screaming and I've got a cramp in my right shin, which is a pain I've never experienced before.

This game is going to go great![61]

---

[61] I want to make sure that my sarcasm is pulling through here. Yes, right? You get the vibe.

Especially since we're all dressed like we're about to play at Wimbledon.

When Emma had suggested this match—she and I were on the tennis team in high school—I'd made a joke about doing it in our "dress whites" to be on theme for the wedding, and she'd cooed and said this was a great idea and she was going to make it mandatory.

Oliver hadn't been too pleased when we'd gotten the wedding invitation with the list of clothes we were supposed to bring, like one of those lists you get when you go away to summer camp. He'd hated wearing tennis whites at the snotty New England country club he'd had to attend as a kid, and said he felt like a six-year-old when he put on the shorts and polo shirt I'd found him on Amazon.

"I don't know what to think, honestly," Oliver says with a note of strain in his voice. "Seems like a lot is going on here that we don't have a handle on."

"That, I agree with."

He lifts his foot over a rock and grunts.

"You okay back there?"

"Yes, yes."

"We can't lose this match."

"So you've told me."

"El's super competitive at tennis," Harper says.

"I'm aware."

"No, Oli, like I mean *seriously* competitive. Like I stopped playing the entire sport because if I played one more match with her, we probably wouldn't be speaking today."

"I'm not that bad, guys."

"Oh, really? Have you seen the dance, Oli?"

"The dance?"

Harper stops in front of me and spins around on the stairs so she's facing us. Then she does some version of what I think is now called the backpack kid dance, but back in the day, it was just the dance I did to celebrate a good point on court during a match.

I *want* very badly to be able to tell you Harper's version is an exaggeration, but that would be a lie. And though I might be a liar in certain circumstances—have I told you that yet?—I'm choosing the truth in this moment.

I did do that dance.

And I *loved* it.

"I was trying to teach you resilience," I say to Harper.

"Uh-huh."

"Don't blame quitting tennis on me. You hated it from the beginning."

"You say so. All I know is, it's a shame I quit because I look fabulous in this outfit." She does a twirl, and the skirt on her white tennis dress flares out. Like everything about us, our matching outfits look *slightly* better on her.

Plus, wait, is she wearing more makeup than usual?

Is this for Connor?

Harper's never dated anyone I thought was good enough for her. I wish she had higher standards for herself. But she seems okay with coasting along in her romantic life.

That's probably my fault.

It's definitely my fault she knows Connor.

"So, you're saying I shouldn't play with her today?" Oliver asks.

"I wouldn't."

"Hey! It's not up for negotiation. It's for *Emma*. And it's just for fun."

"You've never played tennis *just for fun* in your life." She puts air quotes around those last words to drive her point home.

Sisters can be the *worst*.

"I'll have you know that—"

"Is this the way?" Allison says coming up behind us. She's wearing a cute Lululemon tennis dress and looks like she should be starring in a movie about a woman making a tennis comeback in her forties.

"Almost there, I think," Harper says. "Hey, Allison. Hey, David."

"Why is it up here, anyway?" David asks, out of breath and redder in the face than all of us. I guess he doesn't work out that much, what with the (re)writing and all.

"Only flat area, I guess," I say, but my tone says, well, *duh*.

"Ah, yes. Even so . . ."

"There you all are!" Emma says, appearing at what I pray is the top of the path with her hands on her hips. "Let's get a move on!"

"And you think *I'm* the bossy one," I say to Harper under my breath.

"I heard that! And that dance is *banned*, El. Like, seriously, the umpire is docking you a point if you do it."

"What umpire?"

"Get up here and see for yourself."

I take a few more steps and get to the landing. In front of us is a beautiful tennis complex, with two red clay courts surrounded by a green chain-link fence. There's stadium seating to one side that must have an incredible view of the ocean. Much of the cast and crew are seated there, all in some version of white tennis clothes, and it's a bit blinding.

Simone's sitting in the front row with Shawna and Mr. and Mrs. Winter, and Ken the stand-in is sitting just behind them. The photographer from *People* is off to the side with his camera aimed at the stands, taking shots. Fred's on the court, holding a racquet and bouncing a ball up and down on it.

There's a white umpire chair up on a platform like a lifeguard sits on in between the two courts, just like at a professional tennis match.

And I should've seen this coming, and you should've, too.

Because Connor's sitting in the chair looking down on us with a devilish grin. He's wearing a white bucket hat and a whistle around his neck.

He picks it up and blows a short, shrill bleat. "Let's get this show on the road!"

Oliver shoots me a look, and I hope my tennis shoes can grip this surface well because if I know one thing it's this: I'm skating on thin ice.

There's a saying that football is life. Okay, it comes from *Ted Lasso*. Whatever. But I think the better analogy to life is tennis. And not just because I think soccer is boring, because, *hello*, that's just watching people run back and forth on a grass field pretending they're going to kick the ball into that enormous net.

Tennis covers all the *phases*. When you're single, I mean playing singles, everything is on you. You have to make each shot and cover the entire court. There's no backup. If you win, you did it. If you lost, you did that, too. No excuses. But when you play doubles, it's like being in a couple. You have to work together. You have to share the court. You have to consider the other player and be there for them. You can't make all the shots, but you have to be ready to. You can share your wins and console each other over your losses.

You get the idea.

And *if* this wedding happens, that's what I'm going to say to Fred and Emma during my speech.

I'm going to tell them to treat their marriage like a doubles match. And even if it sounds corny to you right now, I promise there won't be a dry eye in the house.

But right this minute, I'm not sure I'm going to need this speech. I mean, is this wedding even going to happen?

And not just because of the potential murder.

Let me set the scene:

We're halfway into the first set. The cast and crew are into it—cheering and waving these little placards on popsicle sticks of Fred and Emma's faces that got passed out by Shawna. Some friendly wagers are going on, too—a few twenties changing hands over who's going to come out on top—and you can tell who's gambling by the groans and cheers depending on who wins a point. The sky is mostly still clear and blue, the sunlight washed out and warm enough to be comfortable but not hot. It's windy, and the ocean is sparkling but choppier than it was this morning, and with us in our whites, surrounded by the lush greenery, it all looks like a postcard.

Which should make you feel like something bad is about to happen.

You'd be right about that.

We're tied at three games apiece. Only the score really should be 5–1 for Oliver and me. But Connor, out of some perverse pleasure of his own, which he's calling "being kind to the newlyweds," keeps ruling against us. Every ball that touches a line is out. Serves that are clearly in the box are out, too. Oliver and I have to make our winning so obvious he can't call the game against us. Which is hard while the wind is swirling the ball around every time I toss it up to serve, but not as hard as Connor's making it.

And while I'm frustrated and upset—which I assume is the point of what Connor's doing—Fred is *losing* it. Maybe it's the residue of whatever happened on the dock this morning with him and Tyler, but it feels like something more than that.

That or he's just psycho on a tennis court, like some people are behind the wheel. Which happens. And no, I don't mean me.

Emma keeps asking him what's wrong, but he shakes her off and tells her to focus. I'm not sure anyone else is picking up on it. They're too busy cheering for every point like it's a US Open night match.

All but Simone.

She looks like she'd rather be anywhere but here. She's not even wearing white, just one of her director's jumpsuits in Barbie pink with her name embroidered over her left breast.

But her attitude is nothing new. I bet she can't wait till this whole shit show is over.

And me? Well, I just want to win this game.

So I can do my backpack kid dance in my head, of course.

Not in front of this crowd.

I mean, probably not.

"Out!" Connor yells as Oliver's beautiful serve hits the service line and bounces into Fred's chest. He adds a burst of whistle for emphasis.

"It was in!" I yell.

"Are you challenging the call?"

"Yes!"

"It was out, Eleanor," Fred says.

I glance at Emma. She looks embarrassed. Emma was and always has been the fairest person on court. I can't remember the number of times she overruled my line calls if she thought there was any chance the ball was in during our matches.

Oh, wait. Yes, I can.

Every. Single. Time.

ANYWAY.

"What do you think, Emma?"

She struggles, but she can't bring herself to lie. "It was in, hon."

"It was out."

"I was looking right at the line . . ."

Connor blows his whistle again. "I saw it out."

"Why do you even have that whistle, Connor?" I say. "This isn't basketball."

"The umpire makes the rules."

"No, the umpire *enforces* the rules."

We glare at each other. Connor's wearing white pants and a white cable-knit sweater with the Wimbledon logo on it, because of course he is. He probably ordered away for them special the minute he got his invitation.

"Perhaps I could be of assistance," Inspector Tucci says, shuffling out of his seat and onto the court. His white pants are ballooning around him, two sizes too big. "I have an innate sense of, how do you say, fairness."

"No!" Connor and I say in unison.

Inspector Tucci backs up with his hands in the air.

"Fred," I say, "let's play fair, all right? You know Emma always tells the truth."

"What a reputation!" Simone says from the sidelines.

"It's true, Simone. Right, Fred?"

He nods grudgingly.

"What's up, mate?" Connor says with a laugh. "You have money riding on this game or something?"

Fred's face turns very red.

"Oh, no, Fred," Emma says. "You promised me you'd stopped all that."

Connor sits up straight in his umpire chair as David leans in to make sure he doesn't miss a beat of this conversation. "Stopped all what?"

"It's none of your business," I say.

"Oh!" David says with anticipation. "That's what it is, right? It makes sense."

"What do you mean, David?" Allison says.

David turns to Allison with an excited look in his eyes. "He was asking me about Connor's motivation. You know, for *When in Rome*. Like what the backstory was about why he got involved with Cecilia in the first place, and he wondered if it might be because he had a gambling problem, and—"

Fred's making a slashing motion at his throat, but it's too late. David's got Mrs. Winter's attention now.

"What's this? Fred? Is it true? Are you gambling again?" She's wrapped in head-to-toe white cashmere including a massive wide-brimmed hat that has flowers around the rim.

Fred's face dissolves into panic. He looks to Mr. Winter for help, but he just shrugs his shoulders and pats Mrs. Winter on the arm gently.

The chatter in the stands has stopped. Some of the cast and crew look uncomfortable, but most of them are reacting the way you'd expect.

Like they've stumbled into a live taping of their favorite TV show.

But the person who I care about here is Emma. And she's not doing well.

"Fred?" she says, her voice shaking.

He wheels around. "Just a friendly wager on the game, that's all, sweetheart, I swear."

"With who?"

"Some of the cast and crew . . . You know, just the guys."

"But you promised."

He steps toward her, letting his racquet drop to the ground. He takes her hands. "It's okay, I promise it's going to be okay."

"Is that why you won't repay Tyler? Because you don't have the money?"

"No, I told you, it's not that. He's just being a jerk. Look at the way he's treating you."

"Speaking of which . . . Where *is* Tyler?" Connor asks.

"I think he got on the ferry," I say. "Took the last boat out of here."

"Sounds like a Taylor Swift song," Allison says, humming a little. "We took the last boat out before the perfect sto-or-mmm . . ."

"Should we be recording this?" Simone says.

Allison raises her left shoulder to her ear, then laughs. Maybe someday Allison will take serious situations seriously, but not today.

And she and David are a perfect match because: "I can see it, Alli. A montage, over the sea . . ." He stands, holding his hands out like a camera. "The storm is on the horizon, and he's standing on the prow of the boat looking melancholy. Meanwhile, the wedding is in full preparation, quick cuts—"

"Why would you be cross-cutting him with the wedding?" Simone says with disdain. "You should stick to writing."

David drops his hands. "It was just a suggestion."

"Are we playing this match or what?" I say.

"Yes!" Fred says emphatically.

I point my racquet at him. "You're going down, Winter."

"El, you promised you'd play nice."

"Sorry, Em!"

I walk back to the baseline and get ready for Fred's serve.

It has a wicked twist on it that looks like it's going wide but then spins unpredictably, and it's hard to prepare for even when you know what's coming.

I told you tennis was like life.

CHAPTER 17

Is My Fear of Heights Going to Come Back to Haunt Me on This Ropes Course?

Lunch is a calorific and boozy affair. There's a bison burger bar where your burger is cooked to your liking with the toppings of your choice. After my defeat, ugh, at tennis, I treat myself to one with all the fixings—cheese, bacon, caramelized onions, a creamy spicy sauce, and lettuce and tomatoes. It's so big I have to eat it with a fork, but every bite is worth it.

There's also a large drink dispenser full of Buffalo Milk, and what the hell? When in Rome, right?

Have you been waiting for me to use that?

I've had it in my drafts folder for years.

Anyway, the first couple of sips are disgusting, but it's alcohol, and it goes down surprisingly easily.

I'm about to have a second when Oliver reminds me that we're doing a ropes course after lunch. This doesn't dissuade me, though. Because I'm afraid of heights, and frankly I'd rather be slightly hammered if I'm going to go up above the tree line.

That's my logic, anyway.

Flawed, I know, in light of recent events.

But everyone else is drinking, too. It is a party, after all. And at the center of it is Fred, celebrating his ill-gotten gains from his tennis win over me and Oliver. Emma's smiling at him indulgently, all forgiven, apparently, after the revelation that he'd been gambling.

If I were a real detective, I'd be questioning Fred about his financial situation, but I'm not, so bottoms up!

Oooh, boy, these are *strong*.

The other "real" detective isn't talking to Fred either. Instead, he's cracking jokes with Harper, and I don't know, but fuck it, I guess? If he makes her happy, who am I to judge?

Ha ha ha ha.

Come on, Eleanor. We all know you're just biding your time until you can put a stop to it.

I am. I am.

But in the meantime, there's a slightly terrifying group activity on the schedule, so as Inspector Tucci might say, *Andiamo!*

We're doing the ropes course in shifts. The first one includes the usual suspects—me, Oliver, Harper, Allison, David, Emma, Fred, Connor, Simone, Shawna, and Inspector Tucci.

We load into a series of dune buggies to go to the ropes course. Harper, Oliver, and I gravitate to one of them, Harper up front and me and Oliver in the back.

The ropes course is set into the hillside above the Casino, a landmark that seems to be visible from everywhere on this island. It was built by the Wrigleys in 1929, our driver reminds us, in the Art Deco and Mediterranean-revival style, and is twelve stories high.

But here's some new information. *Casino* is an Italian word that means "gathering place," and—wait for it—there's *never* been gambling at the Casino. Instead, it has a twenty-thousand-square-foot ballroom and a theater.

I'm not sure why this gives me goose bumps. Maybe it's the misdirection or the use of Italian, but it feels like a warning.

Or these drinks are just super strong.

Either is possible.

We turn away from the Casino and start to climb up the hill. The track is bumpy and we get jostled up and down, which is not allaying my fear of heights and ropes and anything to do with ropes and heights.

"I thought the ropes course was optional?" Harper says. She's changed into a pair of black leggings and a crop top that looks like it comes from the Olivia Newton-John videos my mother used to work out to. I'm wearing leggings, too, and a long-sleeved shirt I bought when I was going through a running phase.

"That was yesterday. Today, there's no opting out," I say. "How was the glass-bottomed boat, by the way? You never said."

"It was cool."

"Cool?"

"Yeah, you know, colorful fish, et cetera."

"And Connor?"

"What about him?"

"He was on the boat, right?"

She gives me a look. "So?"

"That must've been annoying."

"You should cut him some slack."

Um, what?

"Why?"

"He's been turning over a new leaf."

I glance at Oliver. He's looking out at the scenery, his baseball cap pulled low.

"I could tell on the tennis court when he was deliberately making me lose."

"Maybe he just didn't want to see the backpack kid dance."

"Ha ha."

"Seriously, El. He's not the devil."

My stomach churns with unease. "He blackmailed me for ten years."

"Well, he's stopped now, hasn't he?"

"Yes, but—"

"And he's got some other things going on, too, so maybe let it go."

I look at Oliver again, but he's not going to help me out here. Besides, what can he do about this?

At least he knows I didn't bring it up.

Small mercies.

"Other things like?" I ask.

"It's not for me to say."

"Are you guys dating?"

She arches an eyebrow. "Wouldn't you like to know?"

"We're here," Oliver says as the dune buggy lurches to a stop on a small flat plain in front of a thick clutch of cherry and scrub oak trees with a thick jungle undergrowth beneath it. "Let's try not to die on this ropes course, shall we?"

"Why would you say something like that!"

He shrugs. "Just stating the obvious."

"Honey, I love you, but sometimes you don't think before you speak."

He gives me a wide grin. "We *both* do that."

"Okay, fair." I touch his arm. "Is this a mistake, you think?"

"Going up into the trees where a fall would mean certain death with a potential murderer among us? Nah."

"Oliver is funny," Harper says with an indulgent smile. She had a couple of drinks at lunch, too. "Did you know Oliver is funny, El?"

"I did, in fact. And do *not* tell me that Connor can be funny, too."

"Well, sometimes."

I climb out of the buggy, my legs protesting after the workout from the tennis game. Even though I knew I was going to lose, my competitive spirit didn't stop me from pushing myself harder than I should have.

And if that's not a metaphor for many things about me, I don't know what is.

"Enough," I say. "If this is going to be my last act on this earth, I don't want to be wondering what Connor Smith said that made you think he has a sense of humor."

"She's so easy to goad, isn't she?" Harper says.

"Totally," Oliver agrees.

"Don't you two gang up on me."

He winks at me and takes my hand. "Come on, I'll watch out for you."

Oliver means it. While the instructor, Andre, a tall guy with dark hair and a deep tan, explains the course, Oliver moves among us, checking that everyone is in their harnesses properly and that all of the safety ropes are secured.

Speaking of which, I should be doing my own safety checks.

"You okay, Em?" I say, catching her at a moment when she's a bit apart from Fred. Her hair is pulled back by a light blue headband, and her makeup is light. She looks like she did when we were in high school, fresh-faced and vulnerable.

"I'm good."

"And earlier? The stuff about the money?"

"We talked it out," Emma says.

"Hey, you can tell me."

She turns to me with a remote look in her eyes. "Tell you what, El? That someone wants to kill me or scare me out of marrying Fred and I just learned that he's been lying to me?"

"I'm sorry, I—"

"I know you mean well, okay? But you don't have to solve this."

"You asked me to look into it."

"That was before. I don't want to know anything more. I know enough."

"This isn't my fault."

She catches my hand. "I'm not blaming you. But you can leave it now. Tyler's left and Fred's happy and I'm happy, too."

"You sure?"

"Yes."

She hugs me, then walks to Fred and kisses him, maybe for emphasis, maybe just because she's in love and it's her wedding day and it's easier to concentrate on the task ahead than the wind whipping through the trees and the undercurrents pulling against the group.

Andre finishes his instructions, and we get separated into groups of four—Fred, Emma, Harper, and Connor in one; me, Oliver, David, and Allison in another. Inspector Tucci, Simone, and Shawna get lumped in with a member of the crew. I feel a moment of sympathy for Simone as Inspector Tucci starts rattling off statistics about how many people have a fear of heights and how the top of the ropes course is the same height as the Leaning Tower of Pisa.[62] Then we flip a coin for who is going first, and it's tails, we lose.

"I'm not sure I can do this," I say to Oliver as I look up above me. The first platform is very high—not Leaning Tower of Pisa high, that's ridiculous, but high enough.

Oliver checks his harness again. "So, don't."

"What? No pep talk? No 'you can do this'?"

"I'm not a greeting card."

Allison laughs. She's dressed in a black Lycra bodysuit, and if they are looking to cast the next Catwoman, she's in for sure. "Come on, El. It will be good to build the team."

"What team?"

"*When in Rome, Part II.*"

I'm about to say something I'll probably regret when I realize Allison's joking. "Ha, right. Good one."

"You're a little stress case today, aren't you?"

"I'm always a stress case."

"Oh, wait, I remember. You're afraid of heights."

"Thanks for reminding me."

David walks up in his harness. He's wearing it high on his waist,

---

[62] It isn't.

which makes his white shorts bunch up like they're a diaper. "Everyone ready to rumble?"

"What?"

"You know, bond, or whatever."

I sigh internally. "Sure."

Oliver reaches out and squeezes my hand. "Deep breaths."

I squeeze back, and we follow Andre to the rope ladder that leads up to a platform where the course begins. He goes first, and I follow behind him because if I'm going to go up here, I want to get it over with. Oliver is behind me, murmuring reassuring words, but I don't look down. I just put one foot in front of the other and move my hands up and climb, climb, climb until I get to the platform. Andre gives me a hand onto it, and I lie on my back, staring at the clouds racing against the sky as the palm trees rustle around us, trying to steady my breathing.

"You all right there, Eleanor?" David asks as he climbs onto the platform after Oliver. Andre is busying himself checking the clips we'll use to attach to the guide ropes above the course.

"I'll live."

I regret the words the minute they leave my mouth because it feels like a stupid thing to assume.

Because Emma might be reassured by Tyler's absence, but I'm not.

Instead, I've got a feeling like someone's watching me, but there's no one up here but us.

"Do you mind if I run something by you?" David says.

I sit up. "What?"

"There's always something that bothered me about the script, but I couldn't quite put my finger on it."

"What's that?"

"Well, you know how you—I mean Cecilia—helped Connor solve the robberies, right?"

"Yes."

"And then Connor gets a finder's fee, right?"

"He does."

"Why doesn't he share it with Cecilia?"

"I . . ."

"Is it because she doesn't need the money? Because I had another theory."

"Oh?" I stand up. Don't look down, El. Just don't look down.

"I wondered if maybe they were in on it together?"

"In on what?"

"The robberies. Like maybe Connor had planned them and Cecilia knew, and that's why she didn't claim part of the fee."

I look down at my harness, checking it again as Allison climbs onto the platform looking calm and assured, like always.

"What do you think, Allison?" I ask.

"About?"

"Whether Connor could be behind the original robberies in Rome."

A smile curls onto Allison's mouth. "Was I not supposed to tell people that?"

"Pretty sure that was a secret."

"Oops."

I start to seethe. "You know *you're* in on it with Connor in this version, right?"

"So?"

"You don't find it weird that your boyfriend changed the original story to make it so that Connor and Allison are scamming Cecilia the whole time?"

She walks to the edge of the platform. "It's very high up here, isn't it?"

"Don't try to distract me."

"From what?"

"Were you in on it with Connor? It never occurred to me before, but it would make sense."

"*What* would make sense?"

"Where David got the idea from. Because I don't think he could think that up on his own."

"Hey!"

Allison steps toward me. She's calm, but there's a hint of menace underneath. "I'm not quite sure what you're talking about, Eleanor. David wrote the movie long before he met me and—"

"Okay, people, focus up!" Andre says. "You, Miss Talk-a-Lot." He points to me. "You're up first."

"You don't have to," Oliver says.

"It's fine. Let's just get this over with."

"You can do it, El!" Emma calls up from below.

"Thanks, Em!"

I step to the edge of the platform. There's a bridge made of rope to another platform. Andre hooks my harness to the guide rope above, and I take a step out onto the bridge. It starts to sway.

"Is this normal?"

"Normal!" Andre barks. Maybe he was a drill sergeant before he did this.

I take a few more steps. It's much windier up here than on the ground, but through the trees, I can see a glimpse of the ocean, the surf white-capped now.

And then I make a mistake.

I look down.

"I feel dizzy!"

"You're okay, El," Oliver says. "Just keep going to the other side."

"Why am I doing this again?"

"It builds character," Emma calls from below.

"My character was fine!"

"That's what everyone thinks, but it's not true!"

"Thanks a lot!" I take a tentative step, and then another as the group down below watches me. I try not to look down, but you probably won't be surprised to learn that I'm not good at working against my impulses.

But this time—ha!—I master them. I force myself to look straight ahead, up even, at the platform I'm heading to.

But—ha!—joke's on me because that's why I don't see it. A gap in the ropes that's bigger than it should be. My foot falls through, and I go down on one knee, my heart hammering.

"Stand back up!" Andre barks.

I grasp the edge above me and try to pull myself up, but upper-body strength has never been my strong suit.

"I can't."

"You can do it, El," Oliver says.

I grasp the rope again and pull myself up. I get halfway there, then fall back down. The bridge sways underneath me, back and forth.

Don't look down. Don't look down.

"I can't do it."

"Stay there, I'm coming out," Oliver says.

"Okay."

I lie half propped up, trying to free my foot from the hole. The rope is scratchy and thick, and it's rubbing against my neck and a spot on my back where my shirt has ridden up.

"I'm blaming you for this, Em!"

"I'd expect nothing less!"

"Almost to you," Oliver says.

"Can't happen soon enough."

I feel the bridge sway under me, Oliver's weight pushing it down. He gets to me and hefts me up from behind, and it's not the most elegant thing, but it works.

I turn around slowly.

"There you are," Oliver says, smiling at me. "All better now."

"All b— Oh, shit!"

The ropes we're standing on give way beneath us and we fall rapidly toward the earth, clinging to each other, and are stopped with a jerk five feet from the ground.

"Are you okay, El?" Emma says.

"What the hell happened?"

"I knew we shouldn't have come here."

"Stay there! I'll be down in a moment to cut you out."

I start to shake.

We just fell thirty feet.

We were five feet from slamming into the ground.

Someone's trying to kill me.

Again.

"Are you okay?" Oliver asks.

"Yeah, you?"

"Okay. But man, that was close."

I rest my head against his chest. His heart is beating as fast as mine.

"Do not say 'I told you so,'" Oliver says.

"I won't."

I'll just say it in my head.

Only you can hear me in here, right?

"I literally hear you saying it," Oliver says.

"No, no. Your brain hearing is off today."

He hugs me tight and I look down between my legs.

And it's then that I see it. Something in the undergrowth beneath us.

"Something's down there," I say.

"Where?" Oliver asks.

"Right below us."

"I'll look," Connor says.

"I don't think that's a . . ."

But Connor doesn't listen to me. He never has.

He pushes into the bushes and stops.

"It's a body."

"What!?" Fred says.

"Are you sure?" I ask.

"I'm not an idiot, for Christ's sake, Eleanor."

So much for Connor changing.

"Who is it?"

"He's wearing a maintenance uniform . . ."

Oh, shit.

It can't be.

Wait for it.

No way, José.[63]

---

[63] Come on, you <u>knew</u> I was going to say that, right?

CHAPTER 18

Can You Get Away with Murder by Making It Look Like an Accident?

"Have you called the police?" Oliver asks Mr. Prentice twenty minutes later.

Andre had radioed for him to come while we all stood around in a stressed circle because dead body, and he arrived in a paisley suit and a flop sweat. "I have, but . . ."

"Everyone left because of the storm?" I say.

"There's one officer still on the island. She'll be here as soon as possible. She was attending to something on the other side of the island in Two Harbors. She'll want to talk to everyone, I assume."

I glance at Emma. She has her fist in her mouth to keep herself from losing it, a habit she's kept from childhood. She got a look at the body before I could get down from the tangle of ropes. Fred pulled her away, and Andre covered it with a tarp, then cut us out of our harnesses. But I didn't get the same consideration as Emma. I had an aerial view, as did Oliver.

It's definitely José. He's on his back, in a ropes course harness, with his neck at an odd angle. Like Oliver and I might've been if the safety ropes hadn't arrested our fall.

We're alive, but José is dead.

Fuck.

"In the meantime," Mr. Prentice continues, "everyone should return to their rooms and await the arrival of the police officer. She'll decide how she wants to proceed." His radio crackles on his hip. "Excuse me." He walks away with it to his ear.

"Should I start canceling things?" Shawna asks. "I mean, everything is here already, but if there isn't going to be a wedding, I should let everyone know."

"We're going ahead with the wedding," Fred says with authority. "This has nothing to do with us."

"How can you say that, Fred?" Emma says. "It's happening at our wedding. Oliver and Eleanor . . . they almost died, too."

"I'm sure it was simply an accident. This ropes course isn't safe, and we'll be speaking to an attorney about it as soon as we get back to the mainland."

"The electrician wasn't using the ropes course, surely," Connor says.

Fred blinks slowly. "Well, I don't know. The police will look into it and that will be that."

"What do you think, Em?" I ask.

She looks uncertain and I know that look.

Emma is a lot of things—strong and beautiful, a great actress, and kind. But one thing she's never been good at is standing up for herself in her relationships.

It was something I'd raised to her, back in that conversation we had when I told her that getting married this quickly was too soon—didn't the fact that she'd had a massive crush on Fred since she was a teenager concern her?

"Why would it?" she'd asked.

"It could set up a bad power dynamic."

"That was forever ago," she'd said.

"Right, but he knew about it, didn't he? You told a bunch of people in interviews."

She'd smiled at me indulgently. "And we've laughed about that. Everyone has had a crush on him at some point."

"I know, but . . ."

"But what?"

I'd held back what I wanted to say. About it all being too much—becoming a star, marrying another one. Marrying your co-star. It wasn't my life; it was hers. And it's not like I'm any role model in the relationship department.

But now I wish I'd been more forceful.

Because it feels like I could've kept this from taking place.

From my best friend being in danger.

If I'm taking credit for the wedding, I have to take credit for the bad that's come with it.

And while that doesn't quite make me a murderer, it *does* make me murderer-adjacent.

Connor puts his hands on his waist. "Well, this is a clusterfuck."

"You don't say," Oliver drawls.

"I say," Inspector Tucci says, bustling up, still in his harness. "Perhaps I can be of assistance? Murder is my business, after all."

"Knock it off, Corey," Simone says. "You're taking this method business much too far."

"It's *Inspector Tucci*."

"I'll call you whatever I want," Simone says.

"I do not answer to you."

"I'm the director!"

"I do not recognize your jurisdiction!"

"Enough!" I say.

Simone glares at me, but Inspector Tucci shrinks back.

"I think Tucci's right. We should investigate," Connor says.

"Shouldn't we wait for the police?"

His mouth twists into a half smile. "When has that ever stopped us before?"

"And look how well that turned out for us."

"Bestselling book series."

"Almost getting murdered."

He smirks. "There is that."

And oh, no.

Oh, shit.

We're *bantering*.

I can feel Oliver stiffening beside me, but I can't seem to make it stop.

"I, for one, think Tyler is behind this," Fred says.

"How?"

"I saw him on the dock this morning. He was getting ready to take the last ferry before the body was discovered. That's suspicious, isn't it?"

"We don't even know what time José died," Allison points out.

"Well, no, but it has to be Tyler."

"Why?" Oliver asks.

"Because of what happened yesterday. How else would José have gotten my number?"

"You mean your *second* number?" Connor says.

Fred glances at Emma, the two bright spots on his cheeks betraying his mistake.

But this confirms something I assumed before.

Fred only gave that number to a few people—Tyler and whoever he was meeting up with. So the list of people who could've given it to José is small.

But wait. Connor's on it, too. *He* had Fred's number.

"Fred," I say, "what's going on with you and Tyler? All of it. Someone's dead. It's not time to keep secrets anymore."

Fred runs his hands through his hair, which is a classic stalling tactic.

But then Emma puts her hand on his waist and stares into his eyes. "It's okay, Fred. You can tell me. You can tell us. Whatever it is, I love you."

And now, finally, Fred looks vulnerable. "I'm broke."

"Seriously?" I say.

"How?" Harper says. "You've made so much money."

"You don't understand. All you see is the big numbers they announce in the trades, but it's not like that in real life. My agent and manager and lawyer—they take 25 percent right off the top. And then there's taxes. That's another 50 percent."

His math is wrong, but now's not the time to point that out.

Or that 25 percent of $20 million is still $5 million.

A picture!

He's made *ten*.

"And then there's all the expenses no one tells you about—a money manager and the glam squad and having to travel in a private jet because you can't go commercial anymore, and so it makes sense to have your own jet, or at least time-share in one. And someone else convinces you that you should buy this enormous house that costs a fortune to run and you need actual *servants* to do it, and the taxes are nuts, and so then you have to take roles just to pay for all these things you didn't even want in the first place."

"So that's how you lost your money? Overspending?"

"I'm getting to that. So yeah, I had all that going on, but it was fine, I was managing, and then I started going to Vegas with some guys who are big gamblers, and I got into some situations that weren't good. But I did stop. I stopped like I told you, Emma, I promise. But now the government's saying I owe them some insane amount of money in back taxes that I don't have, and they're going to take the house."

I sigh. No point in counting up all the money he's blown through. It's not like it's mine.

But it *is* honestly perfect casting that he's playing Connor.[64]

"Why didn't you tell Tyler you didn't have it?" Oliver asks.

"I tried to, but . . . I couldn't tell him about all of it. I . . ." He hangs

---

[64] Connor blew through most of the finder's fee he got when we solved the original case we worked on in Rome ten years ago at the baccarat tables in Monte Carlo, and the money he got from my books God knows where.

his head in shame. "He put me on a payment plan. Like I was some . . . some criminal."

"Did you make the payments?" I ask.

"I did what I could. And Tyler's not paying me for the film—he's only paying scale. That's one of the things we were fighting about."

"What were you supposed to get for the film?"

"It's a bit complicated because I co-own the option and have executive producer credits, but my acting fee was supposed to be ten million."

I guess his quote went down after the disaster that was *Julius Caesar*.

"So why was he still after you?" Oliver asks. "If he's getting his money back?"

"And this morning?" I ask. "On the dock? What else was going on there?"

Fred's eyes shift from Oliver to me. "He's been extra pissed ever since he found out we were using the production as a decoy for the wedding. But it was the least he could do after everything. He told me he was going to rat me out to TMZ. I was . . . trying to convince him to keep it in the family, so to speak."

"Did he threaten you?" I ask. "Say he was going to kill you?"

"How did you know that?"

"I heard him."

"So you see? He's lost it. Clearly."

"Is that everything?"

His eyes rove around the group and rest on Emma. "Yes. That's everything. Do you forgive me, Em?"

Emma's standing very still, the way she does when she's trying to absorb information. I know she's struggling; we can all see it. But she also loves Fred; I know that, too.

"I don't care about the money, Fred. I have enough for both of us."

"You don't need to pay my debts. I don't want that."

"I know. It's . . . It's you keeping things from me. That's what I'm having trouble with."

"Don't we all have secrets? Things that knock about our hearts deep in the night. Things we can't even admit to ourselves?"

Wow, that was eloquent. But wait, I recognize that . . . Oh.

He's quoting from the movie he won an Oscar for.

Hmmm. I wonder if Emma will notice.

"Yes, that's true."

And now Fred is down on one knee, holding a hand to his heart. "I love you, Emma. Truly. I only kept all of this secret to shield you from it. I never meant to hurt you, and if you don't want to marry me anymore, I understand. But it's the thing I want most in the world. Not your money. *You.* Will you still marry me?"

I watch Emma melt and then she's down on the ground next to him. "Oh, Fred, of course I will."

They kiss with passion, then cling to each other, not seeming to care that they're doing it in front of us.

Allison and David are smiling and indulgent. Harper looks wary. Oliver raises his eyebrows at me and smiles. Connor is watching them like this reunion might hold clues to José's death, while Simone snorts again in disgust.

And as for me?

I still have a lot of questions.

But maybe I can get the answer to at least one of them. I walk away from the group to where I left my backpack earlier. I search around in it and pull out the phone I got from Fred yesterday.

"What are you doing?" Oliver asks, coming up behind me.

"I thought I might make a call."

"Maybe we should turn that over to the police."

"I will. Just let me do a couple of things first." I pull out my phone—which, yes, I *did* bring with me because it feels like walking around on this island without a phone is a bad idea—and take screenshots of the text messages and the numbers on Fred's phone.

And then I dial a number.

"Is that a phone ringing?" Emma asks, her head poking up.

"I think it's coming from there." Fred points to the thickest part of the undergrowth near where we found José's body.

The phone stops ringing, and everyone pauses. I push the call button again.

"There!" Connor says, pointing in the opposite direction from Emma.

"No, it's over here, I do believe," Inspector Tucci says.

"You're both idiots," Simone says. "It's this way."

The ringing stops.

"Are you having fun?" Oliver asks me.

"You have to admit, it's a bit funny."

"Can you ever be serious?"

Ouch.

"Of course I can. Sorry. Last time." I make another phone call and follow the ringing sound myself with Oliver close behind me as the others close in around us in a ring.

"You're the one making the phone ring?" Allison says, nodding toward the phone in my hand. "How?"

"I have José's number."

We stop and peer into the thicket in front of us. José's in front of us, covered by the tarp Andre put on him.

I take a step forward. You're supposed to leave the body in situ until the police arrive to process the scene. Even *I* know that. And if I do what I'm thinking of doing, I'm going to be contaminating the scene, which is a crime in and of itself, isn't it?

Whoopsie.

I'm a novelist, not the police.

There's a reason for that.

I'm not fit for anything else.

I drop to my knees. I get the phone to ring one more time and reach out my hand; when I come into contact with a phone case, I rip a leaf off a palm frond and pick the phone up with it, then stand.

"So, it *is* his phone," I say to Oliver.

"What's the relevance of that?" Connor asks.

"It means José was the one who wrote to Fred to get him into that basement yesterday."

"Or someone used José's phone," Harper says.

"Why would someone use José's phone to get Fred into a basement?" Shawna asks, gnawing at her bottom lip.

"Misdirection, indubitably," Inspector Tucci says.

"Don't be ridiculous," Connor says. "A man doesn't just give up his phone like that. He's clearly involved."

"So," David says, "*José* lured Fred to the basement and hit him on the head, then left him down there?"

"Maybe," I say.

"At the behest of someone else?"

"Stands to reason. I don't think he just randomly decided to hit a major movie star on the head the night before his wedding and lock him in a half basement without there being a fairly good reason. It's not how *I'd* write it, anyway."

"*Was* that door locked?" Connor says, ignoring my sarcasm. "I don't remember that."

"Jammed, whatever. Don't edit me, Connor."

"But why would anyone lure Fred to the basement?" David says, pressing the issue. "What for?"

Emma looks down at the ground. "Because he was in love with me."

"José was in love with you?"

"No, Tyler."

"Emma," I warn.

"It's okay, El. I told Fred everything last night." She raises her eyes to his. He nods twice but doesn't seem happy about it.

I mean, who would be?

"Love," Inspector Tucci says with a nod of the head that I assume he thinks makes him look wise. "It's a powerful emotion."

"Either motive would do, honestly. Or both," Connor says. "But I must defend my client. His intelligence at least."

"What's that got to do with it?" Oliver says.

"Why would he hire me to find Fred's assets when he was planning on killing Fred?"

"Or Emma," I add.

"Maybe it's a smoke screen," Oliver says. "So you could make this exact point."

"Does Tyler strike you as a murderer?" David says. "Not me."

"Me neither," Simone says. "Not one bit."

"What do you know about it?" I bite.

"I wouldn't cast him in the part, that's for sure."

"We're not casting parts."

"Aren't we?" Simone puts her hands on her hips. "You'd be surprised how accurate casting can be. Typecasting exists for a reason. When you watch thousands of self-tapes[65] . . . you get a sense of a person is all I'm saying."

"What would you cast me for?"

"A woman who feels like she lucked into her fame but also kind of thinks she deserves it."

Well, that's a *little* too accurate.

"Easy guess. Plus, you know me."

"I knew high school Eleanor. Are you the same person?"

"Are you?"

She gives a little shrug of her shoulders. "That's irrelevant."

"I wouldn't be so sure that Tyler isn't capable of this," Allison says.

---

[65] When people audition now, they put themselves on tape reading lines from the script—it's called a self-tape.

"He's a self-starter. He built his company himself. He's not a nepo baby. And he's okay with getting his hands dirty. Trust me."

"How do you know that?" I ask.

She shrugs. "I've been in this business for twenty years. I've heard all kinds of things."

"So he thinks that by leaving the island he'll just get away with it?"

"It makes sense to create an alibi."

"Not if José was killed yesterday."

"But it's only luck that we found him," Simone points out. "He could've been missing for days or weeks, especially with the storm."

"True, but wait . . ." I think it over. "Me and Oliver falling through the ropes . . . that had to be deliberate. That's why José is in a harness. Someone wanted to make it look like he had an accident on the ropes course. And so they made that hole my foot went through, and maybe they frayed some of the ropes and that's why they gave out."

"But everyone knew we were coming here this morning," Oliver says. "It's on the schedule."

"Maybe they forgot that. Or maybe if the body was found today it doesn't matter, because it would be long after the murder happened."

"We saw José yesterday after lunch. Anyone see him since then?"

"He texted Fred around five last night," Harper says.

"Right. And it's eleven thirty now. That's a big gap."

"We should ask Mr. Prentice when the last time anyone saw José was," Oliver says.

"Agreed."

"So, we are saying Tyler killed José?" Inspector Tucci says, making a note in a notebook that he's pulled from somewhere.

Maybe his ass.

But it *does* make me think of something.

"Maybe Tyler communicated with José?" I look down at the phone I'm still holding. The screen is locked. What are the chances his password is as easy to crack as Fred's?

Won't know unless I try.

"What are you doing?" Connor asks.

"Seeing if I can unlock this phone."

"We should leave that for the police," Harper says.

"Just give me a second." I tap in 000000 and get nothing. Then
111111. Nothing again. I try 123456 and it works. "Oh, I'm in. Let me
see if—"

"Freeze! All of you! Hands in the air!"

I drop the phone and wince as it hits a rock and cracks, the screen
shattering into spiderwebs.

CHAPTER 19

If Your Hands Are Up, Are You Under Arrest?

"What are you still doing here?" Mr. Prentice splutters at us. "Why are you not in your rooms as you were instructed?"

"Can we put our hands down?" Oliver asks.

"Slowly," the police officer says. She's wearing an LA County Sheriff's Department uniform—forest-green trousers, a long-sleeved khaki shirt with a green-and-gold patch over the breast—and looks to be in her late twenties. Her reddish-blond hair is in two braids, one over each shoulder, and she's holding her arms out straight with her gun pointed right at us.

She looks deadly serious.

I mean, the gun kind of gives it away.

"What did you drop?"

She's looking right at me.

Which means the gun is pointing at me, too.

Right at my heart.

"It's José's cell phone." I nod behind me. "The victim. I found it on the ground."

"Give that to me."

I pick it up and walk it to her slowly, my eyes on the gun, and give it to her in the palm frond. She takes one hand off her gun and takes it, palm frond and all, then lowers her gun arm slowly.

"There's an evidence bag in my pocket. Reach in and take it out."

I do as she asks and pull out a folded piece of plastic with an orange seal on it. She instructs me to open it and deposit the phone inside. I do it, then hand it back to her. She slips the gun into a pouch that she's wearing like a cross-body bag.

"Return to your friends."

"They're not . . . Yes, of course."

She holsters her gun, then puts her hands on her hips. "Who are you?"

"We're here for a wedding," I say.

"Why didn't you evacuate?"

"Seemed unnecessary," Fred says. "After all the planning."

"There was an evacuation order issued."

"Yes, but that happened last time, didn't it? Hurricane Hilary? And then it was all for nothing. Just some rain."

The officer shakes her head like she's swatting away a fly. I'm not sure if she recognizes Fred. I'm going to go with no because she's treating him like a regular person rather than a movie star.

"And what are you doing *here*, exactly? This isn't the wedding venue."

Oliver speaks into the silence, always the good student who never got into trouble. "We were doing the ropes course and then we found José."

"And whose idea was it to look for evidence?"

"Connor," I say as he says, "Eleanor."

The fink.

But, oh!

Was *that* the point? Is he working for Tyler, even now? Is he smart enough to have used reverse psychology on me?

I'm not sure he is. But I've underestimated him before.

"Why would you do such a thing?" the police officer asks.

"I . . . Who are you?"

"I'm Officer Anderson of the Avalon division of the LA County Sheriff's Department." She speaks robotically, like Mr. Anderson from the

Matrix movies, though they look nothing alike. I'm not sure who'd play her in the movie—some ingenue, I guess, in her first starring role. "Who are you?"

"Eleanor Dash." I pause to see if she's heard of me.

She hasn't. Fine. Moving on.

"And you've been assigned to this case?"

"I'm the only officer on the island."

"Are others . . . en route?"

"All ferry service has been canceled—the last ferry went out this morning when the evacuation order got issued. I'm to ascertain if this is an emergency and advise before they send a boat. The sea is already rising, and the storm can come in fast. We don't want to risk lives."

"Where is it now?"

"It's touched land in Baja and is making its way up the coast. Heavy rain is already flooding coastal towns. You all should have evacuated."

Or never come here in the first place.

"Did you find anything else near the body?" Officer Anderson asks.

"No."

"What were you looking for, exactly?"

"I was looking for his phone."

"I say." Inspector Tucci comes forward with his hand extended. "Inspector Tucci of the Roman police force. May I be of assistance?"

Officer Anderson creases her brow in confusion, or maybe that's recognition? "Are you . . ."

"He's not a policeman!" Simone says. "Just an actor."

"Oh, I . . ."

"Ignore him."

"All right. You're here for a wedding?"

"Yes," Emma says, her voice anxious but hopeful. "It's ours. Mine and Fred's. We're—"

"I know who you are."

Of course she does.

Good for her for not fawning all over them.

Not that I'm jealous or anything.

"Okay, well, yes," Emma says. "We're here for our wedding. And I'm sorry we didn't evacuate, we didn't mean to be a bother, but everything was all arranged. And . . . anyway, that doesn't matter. But you need to find Tyler."

"Who?"

"Tyler Houston. Our producer. He left this morning on the last ferry."

"Why are you telling me this?"

"Because it's suspicious," Fred says. "Especially given the call I received yesterday."

"What call?"

"To come see José in the basement of the hotel."

"I don't understand."

"There was an almost-electrocution yesterday morning," Emma says. "At the soaking pools? They're up the hill above the villas, below the tennis courts. Anyway, if it wasn't for Harper's phone falling in, I might've been electrocuted. Or Eleanor."

"Or me," Simone says dryly.

"Oh, yes, you too, Simone. And Harper. We were all there. But it was very upsetting, so we told the administration."

"Oliver and I spoke to him," I say. "He said the wiring was old, and that was the most likely reason."

I leave out the part about Oliver and I doing our own investigation in his work shed.

Seems like the wrong time to bring that up.

"And then he called Fred yesterday afternoon," Emma says, warming to her story. "And asked to meet him."

"He called you?" Officer Anderson says. "How?"

"On my, um, cell phone. Doesn't matter. I went to meet him, naturally.

Wanted to know what had happened. But I got a cosh on the head for my troubles."

He mimics someone hitting him on the back of the head, and then him reacting to it.

It's quite a good reenactment.

"And then Fred was missing," Emma says.

"Knocked on the head, you see?"

The group laughs, and this seems to unstick something in everyone as they each leap in to add something to the story, everyone contributing something so fast that it's hard to know who's saying what.

See if you can tell.

"We were in a panic. But there was a tracker on his phone."

"My fault, I'm afraid."

"And then we found him in the basement. In the furnace room."

"So the wedding was back on."

"And then the rehearsal dinner was canceled."

"Because of the cat almost dying!"

"No, the cat was at lunch."

"Right, right."

"So we all went to bed, and then, this morning, we played tennis."

"First there was your fight with Tyler on the docks."

"Ah, yes. He was attempting to blackmail me. Well, not blackmail exactly, but I owe him money and he was making threats. Saying he would tell the press about it."

"He said he'd kill you, didn't he?"

"Yes, yes, he did."

"So, Tyler left, and then we went to tennis."

"And we were winning—"

"Connor was making terrible calls."

"We won fair and square."

"Think that if you want to."

"And then we came to do the ropes course and Eleanor saw the body after she and Oliver fell."

"It was awful."

"And then the hotel manager left to take a call and we decided to investigate. Not sure it *was* Eleanor who suggested it. Maybe it was Connor?"

"I say, throwing me under the bus like that."

"And then Eleanor had José's number—you'll want to ask her about that—and she rang it and rang it and then she found the phone."

"And then she was looking at the phone and then you arrived and said 'Hands up.'"

Officer Anderson's head is swerving from left to right and back to front trying to follow all of us as we download what happened over the last twenty-four hours.

"What is Mr. Houston's connection to the victim?" Officer Anderson asks.

"We're not sure," I say. "But they could've been working together. That's why I was checking his phone—to see if they'd had any contact."

Officer Anderson fishes the phone out of her pouch. She puts on a pair of latex gloves, then takes the phone out of the evidence bag.

I tell her the code.

"Not very original."

"Right?"

She gives me a look, then punches it in. "There are texts on here."

"From what number?"

She reads it out.

"That's Tyler's number," Emma says.

"Are you sure?" Officer Anderson asks.

"Yes. If I had my phone, I could show you, but yes."

"What do the texts say?" I ask.

"He's asking the owner of the phone to meet him."

"Where?"

She looks up. "Here."

A murmur goes through the group.

"So he *is* the murderer," Inspector Tucci says. "It is all clear now. The spurned man, and money! Both are excellent motives, no? And he's here, right on the spot. He tries to disrupt the wedding, to scare the bride out of going through with it, and when that doesn't work, to cause an accident, and he has, how do you say, the inside man, to help him. But then, the inside man doesn't want to go along with it anymore. He will tell on Mr. Houston.

"So, Mr. Houston must act. He lures José to this location, kills him in such a way that he can make it look like an accident. He puts him in the climbing harness, cuts the ropes above, then buries him in the brush, and then he leaves the island so he is not here when the body is discovered. If he is lucky, the body won't be found until today at the earliest, when it is much more difficult to tell how long ago he died. He looks for the phone to take it, but it has slipped from the body and he cannot find it. He is careless, maybe, and does not think to make a call to find it . . .

"Ah, no. He is *not careless*. He does not bring his phone to the scene of the crime so he cannot be tracked here, but now that means he cannot find the phone. So! He is nervous. He leaves, worried. He sees Fred on the dock and makes threats. This is also a distraction. If he has acted, why threaten? And now he is waiting somewhere. But he will have an excuse for these messages, mark my words. Now, is that everything? Yes. Yes. I believe it is." Inspector Tucci's eyes come back into focus and a smile breaks out on his face.

"By George, I think he's solved it," Allison says with an air of surprise.

"I did, didn't I?'

Connor and I make eye contact. Neither of us can believe it.

I can tell that we're both cycling through the facts he recited and double-checking them for accuracy and logic. We complete the task at the same time and nod at each other.

I feel a blush creep up the back of my neck at this familiar feeling.

The attraction of being right with someone.

Of solving a mystery together.

It's a high. I write about it in my books, funneling that feeling into Connor and Cecilia's romance.

But I haven't felt it myself in a long time.

I break eye contact. Connor and I aren't right together. Not in any way but this.

I feel bad for this moment of weakness. But also: Oliver saw it.

Fuck.

"I . . ." I stop and turn my face to Officer Anderson. "It all makes sense."

"We will have to verify everything."

"I can give you Mr. Houston's address," Connor says.

"He shouldn't be hard to find."

"Does this mean we can have the wedding?" Emma asks with a note of hope.

"I'm not sure. I'd ask you to return to your rooms. I have to call all of this in. And we need to secure the body."

"Are you going to leave him out here?" Harper asks, and shudders.

"We have no choice until a tech team can get here. But we'll cover him with tarps to preserve whatever evidence you lot have not already ruined."

"I'm sorry," I say.

"Let's hope this is the solution and we won't have to worry about that. If it isn't, you all may be looking at an obstruction charge."

"Do you need anything else from us?" I say.

"I think you've all done enough for one day."

"Yes, yes, of course. Come on, everyone, let's go. Connor, give her that information about Tyler. The rest of you, follow me."

I reach out my hand for Oliver. He doesn't look happy, but he takes it and I give it a squeeze.

Seems like I've had to communicate with hand-holding and looks too much on this trip.

As I've mentioned, I get a sixth sense about things sometimes. I can tell what someone's going to say before they say it. And Oliver has something to say.

Something I don't think I want to hear.

And maybe it's just the malaise that comes with being involved in a death.

Or maybe what's coming next is the end of me and Oliver.

That we're as dead as José.

SANTA MONICA GOSSIP

@SMGossip

#BREAKING: Sources tell me that a BODY has been found at Emma Wood and Fred Winter's wedding on Catalina Island, and it's NOT Fred Winter. No word yet on whether foul play is involved. Catalina is under an evacuation order because of the #CASTORM. No word on when authorities can reach the island. #HURRICANEISABELLA

3:14 PM · October 24 · Twitter for iPhone
899 Retweets 40 Quote Tweets 7,567 Likes

CHAPTER 20

Does "We Have to Talk" Always Mean "We're Breaking Up"?

"We have to talk," Oliver says after we get back to our villa. We stopped by the Beach Club to get some lunch first, but it was a somber affair. Everyone was whispering and talking in small groups. It felt like high school when something big happened on the weekend, and it was filtering through the ecosystem on a Monday morning.

A man is dead. There have been threats and mishaps. It feels like Italy all over again, and not in a good way.

Is it worse or better that I'm just an observer this time, and not the target?

I'm not sure.

If I were the target, I might have some clue as to the motivations and secrets that drove someone to this desperate act.

But despite what I told Connor yesterday, I don't know the players here. I could tell you who wanted to kill Emma in high school, but not now. Fred was a poster on Emma's wall. The others I met on set, but that was an environment where I was more preoccupied with vacillating between being blown over that my book was coming to life and being horrified with how it was changing.

All this to say, I'm not the author here. I'm not plotting all this out in advance and watching it unfold.

I'm the reader, trying to see around corners and parse out what the characters are saying. Whether their words mean more than one thing. Whether there are gaps to fill in. What's a clue and what isn't.

I know what it's like to be in the middle of a plot.

I don't like it.

Especially not at my best friend's wedding.[66]

Harper doesn't come back with us to the room, instead going off with Shawna to help plan the remaining details of the wedding in case it's still happening. I watch them go with a bit of dread because I know what's coming once Oliver and I get back to the villa.

"We don't have to talk, though," I say to Oliver, trying to keep my tone light. "We can not talk."

His eyes cloud with confusion and maybe also hurt. "Eleanor."

"Oliver." I sigh. "Our names rhyme."

"I . . . what?"

"Nothing, it's stupid." I step to him and take his hands, twining my fingers through his. "Don't break up with me. Please."

"I don't want to."

"Then why did you say that? 'We have to talk.' That's what it means."

The corner of his mouth lifts. "So, what do you say if you just have to talk?"

"I don't know."

He holds our arms out to the side, then brings them back together. "Two authors, at a loss for words."

"How many authors does it take to screw in a lightbulb?"

"How many?"

"Three. One to blame their agent, one to blame their publisher, and one to blame writer's block."

"Who screws in the lightbulb, then?"

"It doesn't get screwed in. Not unless there's a deadline."

---

[66] Which is a <u>great</u> movie, by the way.

"What are we even talking about?"

"I'm distracting you."

He lets my hands drop. "That won't work forever."

"For today, though?"

"Is that wise?"

"I don't want to be wise. I want to be with you. Wait. That's not what I meant. It *is* wise to be with you. Very wise."

I have become a blathering idiot.

Do you think Oliver will notice?

Maybe that's why he's breaking up with me. Because I'm a *moron*.

"Are you sure about that?" he asks, and I worry for a moment I was speaking the last part out loud instead of in my head, which is a thing that happens sometimes.

But no, not this time.

"I'm sure being with you is what I want," I say.

"Then why have you been flirting with Connor?"

Excellent question.

How come, Eleanor?

Don't we hate Connor?

"I haven't."

"Eleanor."

"Okay, I get it. We banter. It's a thing we do. It's an extension of the pattern we've developed on tour. You know how it is. Getting asked the same questions by a million people—it's a defense mechanism. It doesn't mean anything more than that. And it certainly doesn't mean I want to be with him because I don't. I swear to you. It's the last thing on my mind."

"It hurts to see you like that with him."

"And you have trouble trusting me."

He nods slowly. "And I have trouble trusting you."

"I know I haven't given you any reason to. Not historically. But everything that happened with him was when I was scared. I'm not scared now. I know what I want and it's you."

I reach up on my toes and kiss him for all I've got. Not with passion but with ferocity, holding the side of his face, willing my lips to convince him of what my words can't.

I pull back and stare into his eyes.

Which is difficult for me. I'm working on my emotional intimacy issues.

But you try it. Try *really* looking someone in the eyes for more than a moment.

It's *hard*.

"You're very seductive when you want to be," Oliver says, staring right back because *he* doesn't have intimacy issues.

"That's a good thing, right?"

He smiles. "That's a good thing."

"But?"

"But I don't know if I can watch you with him. It hurts too much."

My heart squeezes. A physical pain that might take me to the ER if we weren't trapped on this island, and I hadn't been here before. "We just have to get through today and tomorrow and then that's it."

"It's not it, though. He's in your life. He's always going to be."

"You knew that when we got back together in Italy."

"You said you were ending the series."

I *had* said that. When I was desperate to get him back and it was the only way I saw forward.

Not that I hadn't plotted Connor's death. Many times.

But it was only a fantasy, me taking him out of the picture. It wasn't going to happen in real life.

"I can still kill him off," I say anyway, because I feel desperate again, and maybe repeating myself will work like it did last time.

"You tried that, remember?"

I'd plotted out a whole book where he died. But that wasn't what I ended up writing.

In the book I turned in after Italy, Connor lives.[67]

"I know, I just . . . I'll do whatever it takes. I haven't been writing anyway, so that will be easy."

"Don't use writer's block against me."

"I'm not."

He leans his head against my forehead. "Eleanor, you love writing those books. And I'm not going to take them away from you."

"Then what do we do?"

"I don't know."

I breathe in his scent—a mix of soap and the light spice of his after-shave. "What about therapy? That might help."

"I thought you hated therapy."

"I only went once. I didn't give it a real chance. Plus, I love you more than I hate therapy."

He tips his head back and laughs, but it's not the usual sound I love. "That's a lot."

"It is a lot. It's everything. You're everything." I look away from him to the window. There are clouds on the horizon now, not just metaphorical ones. "You chose to get back with me. Please don't break my heart."

"I don't want to."

"You're doing it, though."

"I'm sorry."

My mind cycles and I face him again. "Can we try something?"

"What's that?"

"Can we pretend everything is normal for the rest of the weekend?"

"Despite the murderer on the loose?"

"The murderer fled the coop."

"Did he?"

---

[67] Why didn't I end the series as I had planned? Well, like Taylor Swift confesses to in "You're on Your Own, Kid," I took the money. Don't judge. You would, too.

"I think so. It stands to reason that it's Tyler. Who else would want to kill Emma or Fred or disrupt their wedding?"

"I don't know."

"Sometimes the simple solutions are correct."

"Almost never, though."

"That's in books, not in real life." I bring his hands to my waist. "I know it's hard to see us together. I get it. But I don't feel like that about him anymore. I haven't in a long time. And I never felt with him what I feel with you."

"Oh, yeah?"

"*Yes.* I'm not going to lie and say I didn't love him. I did. But he was never accessible to me in the way you are. He was always playing a part, and I was just part of his scam. And I think I felt that deep down the whole time I was with him. But with you, it's different. I can give my whole heart to you. I don't have to worry. I know you're there for me no matter what. And I don't want to lose that. I can't."

"What if it's too hard?"

"You sound like me."

"Ha."

"I don't think it's supposed to be easy. I think it's supposed to be work. Good work. And we're still learning how to be back together. It's only been three months. Maybe we both thought things would go right back to how they were. That would've been too easy. Let's give ourselves a break."

Oliver's eyebrows raise to his hairline. "*You* want to go on a break?"

"I don't mean that. I just meant, let's stop expecting too much from each other. From us. All that talk of marriage and proposing yesterday. Let's take that off the table for now. We don't have to decide anything until we're ready."

"Isn't it what you want?"

"Of course it is. But only when we're both ready."

He pulls me closer to him. "No clock ticking?"

"I have no idea if there is or isn't. I don't even know if I want kids. I mean, can two writers have kids and not fuck them up totally? Plus, who gets to write in that scenario?"

"I'm not sure I'm even going to be a writer anymore."

"You will."

He steps away and I shiver like it's cold.

"Are you a writer if you don't have a book deal?"

"Of course you are, Oli. And you'll get a deal. If not with our current publisher, then with someone else."

"And if I don't?"

"Is that what this is about?"

The corner of his mouth turns up. "It's hard when everything in your life is up in the air."

"I know."

"You don't. It's all come so easily for you. Write a book by accident, it blows up. Get this long-running series. Try to quit, and that's a new bestseller."

"Almost get killed . . ."

"Okay, there's that."

I take his hands again. I need to be connected to him. "The book business isn't a meritocracy."

"I know."

"And you can't want me not to succeed so we can be together."

"I know that, too."

"So, can we work this out? Can we try?"

"I want to."

"That's something."

He pulls me into his arms and holds me close. I can't tell if this feels like a beginning or a goodbye, and sadness wells up in my chest as tears spring to my eyes.

"Hey," Oliver says, tipping his head back and looking down at me. "Hey."

"Hi."

"I love you."

"You do?"

"Very, very much." He dips his head down, and we kiss, a slow build that starts soft and then turns into hunger, our mouths open, our tongues intertwined, our bodies pressed close. And right when I'm about to pull him into the bedroom, to seal us together instead of pulling us apart, there's a loud knock at the villa door.

"Do we need to get that?" Oliver asks, slightly out of breath.

"I was thinking we could ignore it."

He kisses me once more, then lets me go and walks to the door. When he opens it, Officer Anderson is standing there.

"Can I come in?" she asks.

"Yes, of course."

Oliver steps back and she enters. She looks even younger, up close, with a lot of responsibility resting on her shoulders, her two red braids falling over them.

"How can we help you?" Oliver says.

"I have some questions about the events of today."

"Let's sit over here," I say, pointing to the dated, tile-covered table near the window. "And you can ask us anything you like."

We sit at the table, and she takes out a notebook like the one Inspector Tucci was using and clicks a pen after turning up a fresh page. She takes down our details—names, addresses, occupations—and then goes through our timing over the course of the weekend. The party on Thursday, when we got on the boat, what we did since then, mapping out the last two days.

We're thorough in our explanations, both good at remembering the details of plots.

"And then you contaminated a crime scene," Officer Anderson says with a cluck of the tongue.

"Right. Sorry about that."

"I would've thought you'd know better, being crime writers and all."

"Yes, well, we weren't thinking, clearly, but no harm, no foul, right?"

"We'll see about that."

"What does that mean?"

She puts her pen down. "Just seems convenient. All these people on this island who have a motive to harm Mr. Winter and Ms. Wood."

"All these people? Who besides Tyler?"

"Mr. Smith, for one."

"Connor?" I glance at Oliver. "Why would he want to harm them?"

"He's a hired gun, he told me that himself."

"He doesn't own a gun that I'm aware of. Was José shot?"

"No, his neck was broken. And Mr. Smith told me the same thing," Officer Anderson says. "However, I'm not sure he was telling the truth."

"He does tend to lie," Oliver says.

I shoot him a look.

Even though he's right.

Fuck. Maybe I *do* have unresolved feelings for Connor?

No. No. Absolutely not.

"That's true," I say. "He can be less than truthful . . . But he's not a murderer."

"He killed someone in your book *Drowned in Porto*, didn't he?"

"Oh, you read that?"

"I've read all your books."

"You have?"

She taps herself in the chest. "Big detective fiction reader."

"You didn't give any indication when we met earlier."

"You have to keep it close to the vest, don't you, while you're getting the lay of the land?"

"I guess that makes sense. Anyway, that was fiction."

"Who else is a suspect?" Oliver asks, his mouth in a frown. I don't think he's about to ask if she's read *his* books, but it's possible.

Oliver has an ego, too, even if his is better hidden than mine.

"That Mr. Liu is an interesting fellow, don't you find?"

"David the screenwriter? How so?"

"Seems like he might be behind those notes being left for Ms. Wood."

"I thought Tyler left those?"

"Cutting out of the pages of a script? That screams scriptwriter to me."

"How did you know it was from a script?"

"It's that Final Draft font, isn't it?"

"You know Final Draft?"

"Doesn't everyone in LA?"

"I . . ."

She gives me a broad smile. "I write screenplays in my spare time."

Of course she does.

Because only in LA would a cop also be a screenwriter.

Heck, a few more years in the force and she'll probably be able to get a series green-lit with the reductive former-cop-turns-to-writing-about-cops pitch line alone.

Don't ever let anyone tell you that Hollywood is full of imagination.

They take "write what you know" literally.

"So it stands to reason that it could be Mr. Liu who'd do that."

"But why?" I ask.

"I've heard that Mr. Liu believes that Ms. Wood had him fired off an earlier movie?"

"But that was years ago."

"And there was also an issue with rewrites in this film, too, wasn't there?"

"Surely you don't try to murder someone because of changes in a script," Oliver says.

I bite my tongue. I *was* feeling murderous about that very thing.

Not that I did anything about it.

I swear.

"I agree with Oliver. That's not enough of a motive," I say. "It happens all the time in the business. David's a professional. He knows how to roll with the punches."

"There's a sequel, though, I understand. And some doubt about who'll get to write it?"

"But if Emma and/or Fred is killed, wouldn't that end hopes of a sequel?"

"Hmmm. You might be right there."

"Anyone else?" Oliver presses. He always has liked summing up a list of suspects. When we used to watch crime shows together, we always tried to guess who it was before the third act. We kept score and everything.

Do I need to tell you Oliver had a winning record?

No, right?

"We have to examine the possibility that it's Mr. Winter and/or Ms. Wood themselves."

"What? Why?"

"To get out of his money troubles. To get out of the wedding. To drum up some publicity for the movie. Take your pick."

"I don't think they'd do that. Certainly not Emma."

"But Mr. Winter?"

"No, no, I . . ."

She squints at me like she needs glasses. "You're keeping something from me."

I'm impressed she can tell.

Then again, maybe she learned everything she knows from my books?

I *am* full of myself, aren't I?

"Only that he had a second phone. I'm sorry I forgot to mention it. I meant to turn it over to you." I rise and go to get it from my backpack.

But it's not in there.

"I thought it was in here . . ."

"Where did you see it last?" Oliver asks.

"I took it out to get the number to call José."

I replay the events at the murder scene in my mind. And yes, I had it then. That's how I found José. But what did I do with it then? I could've sworn I put it back in my bag, but I have no memory of doing so.

Shit.

"What was on the phone?" Office Anderson asks.

"There are texts on there between him and someone else . . . It looks like he might've been having an affair."

"Ah. Now there's a motive."

"But there's any number of possible explanations for all of it."

"Such as?"

"The texts aren't romantic, just a series of meeting times. Maybe it had to do with his money thing. Or it's some friend he's helping out. Or his trainer. Or his dealer."

"He has a dealer?"

"Not that I know of. I'm just saying there's lots of possibilities."

"We shall see. The last time you saw it was at the crime scene?"

"Yes." I gnaw on the inside of my cheek. Sometimes I have to learn to shut the hell up.

Not today, apparently.

I don't have to tell her that I took screenshots of the texts, though.

But I should, right?

Only, one thing I know is that secrets never stay buried. If I give the texts to Officer Anderson, they'll get released, even if they were innocent, and I don't want to do that to Emma.

"Can you do me a favor?" I say.

"What's that?"

"Please don't ask about this in front of Emma. She's been through enough."

"I will follow proper police procedure." She cocks her head to the side. "Haven't you found that there are certain instances where it's good to apply pressure?"

"How so?" Oliver asks.

"People under stress say things they wouldn't under normal circumstances. They disclose secrets."

"You think if you ask Fred about the texts in front of Emma, she'll
help you solve the case?"

She blinks at me.

"That doesn't . . . I know we always write about gathering all of the
suspects and getting them together to get a confession, but I have no idea
if that works in real life. It's just a tool that we use in books and movies
for dramatic effect."[68]

"We shall see."

"Please don't."

She looks ready to say something when her phone bleats with a text
alert. She reads it, looks disappointed, then smooths out her features.

"We've located Mr. Houston."

"That was fast," Oliver says.

"Does this mean we can have the wedding?"

"If Ms. Wood wishes to, I don't see the harm."

"Why wouldn't she want to?"

Officer Anderson gives a small shrug of her shoulders. "We can be
trapped in things sometimes, can't we? And if a solution presents itself,
then we're happy to get out of it."

"Emma loves Fred."

"You'd know better than me."

"I do, yes."

Oliver walks her to the door. "Out of curiosity, where did they find
Mr. Houston?"

"Oh, he was right here, the whole time. On the island."

---

[68] I <u>definitely</u> do this in my books.

WHEN IN ROME

ACT 2, SCENE 8

EXT. ROME - NIGHT

Connor and Cecilia are staking out a bank, dressed in black, hiding behind a stone wall. Connor has a pair of binoculars. Cecilia has a camera. It's late. Very quiet.

                    CECILIA
     Why do you think this is the one?

                    CONNOR
     It's a pattern. I'm sure of it.

                    CECILIA
     No one's showed up yet.

                    CONNOR
     They will.

                    CECILIA
     Maybe we should've gone to the police. Someone's
     died . . .

                    CONNOR
     That Inspector Tucci—I know him. He's incompe-
     tent and he certainly won't listen to me. We
     have to bring him irrefutable proof.

                    CECILIA
     Catch them in the act.

                    CONNOR
     Precisely.

There's a SOUND that startles them. They freeze. But it's just a CAT.

                    CECILIA
     Is this what your life is like all the time?

                    CONNOR
     Scared?

                    CECILIA
A little.

                    CONNOR
Doesn't it make you feel alive, though?

                    CECILIA
You do.

They kiss and smile at each other.

                    CONNOR
You should remember this when you go home.

                    CECILIA
The kiss?

                    CONNOR
No, this feeling. You like it, I can tell. Don't
go back and do something boring.

                    CECILIA
Like work in advertising.

                    CONNOR
Precisely. Don't do that.

                    CECILIA
Where did you come from?

                    CONNOR
It doesn't matter.

                    CECILIA
No, I want to know.

                    CONNOR
And I want to know what you're going to do when
you get home.

                    CECILIA
Go to work.

                    CONNOR
No, please. What have you always dreamed of?
There must be something.

                           CECILIA
          Writing.

                           CONNOR
          So do that.

                           CECILIA
          I can't.

                           CONNOR
          Why not?

                           CECILIA
          It's what my sister wants to do.

                           CONNOR
          Why should that stop you? You have to live <u>your</u>
          life.

Cecilia smiles and goes back to looking at the bank
through her camera. CHARLES GUY walks up (40s, beefy,
bald).

                           CONNOR
          Get down. They'll see you.

                           CHARLES GUY
          There isn't anyone.

                           CONNOR
          There must be.

                           CHARLES GUY
          Check for yourself.

Connor looks at Charles, then at Cecilia.

                           CONNOR
          I'll be right back.

He and Charles exchange another look, which Cecilia
doesn't see.

Connor leaves and Charles takes his place next to Cecilia. He picks up the binoculars.

                    CHARLES GUY
Interesting date night.

                    CECILIA
Not your cup of tea?

                    CHARLES GUY
Not how I'd spend my Roman vacation if it wasn't
my job.

                    CECILIA
It's good to feel like you're helping.

                    CHARLES GUY
Is that what you're doing?

                    CECILIA
I'm not?

                    CHARLES GUY
How much has Connor told you?

                    CECILIA
About the case?

                    CHARLES GUY
About him.

                    CECILIA
I . . .

                    CHARLES GUY
You should be careful.

                    CECILIA
Why?

                    CHARLES GUY
He's not . . . You don't know him, Cecilia.

                    CECILIA
I do, though.

                    CHARLES GUY
No. You don't. And I'll give you some advice. You
should walk away. Walk away and don't look back.

CHAPTER 21

Is Murder Usually Served at Midnight?

It's coming up on sunset, and it's finally time for Emma's wedding.

It's been a whirlwind afternoon. After dropping the bomb that Tyler was still on the island, Officer Anderson explained that he didn't make it onto the ferry after all and had been hiding out in his room since this morning. She was on her way to question him and, if her suspicions proved sufficient, to place him under arrest until her colleagues could get here.

In the meantime, with it looking like Tyler was behind everything that had happened so far, we got the green light to go ahead with the wedding.

Once that was established, I sprang into maid of honor mode.[69] That meant locating Shawna and Harper, advising the guests that we were going ahead, tracking down the photographer from *People*, and making sure Emma still wanted to go through with it.

She assured me she did, but then started to fret about the smaller details—like who's going to do her makeup (her, we decided) and my makeup (also her) and press out her dress (me) and get the flowers together (also me, plus Shawna and Harper) because her glam squad and florist were scheduled to arrive today, but that's out with everything that has happened.

---

[69] Which, to think about it, I haven't really been in till now. What's that about?

What else?

Oh. The storm is getting closer.

The sky has darkened, and the surreptitious peek I took at my cell phone confirms Hurricane Isabella has moved up the coast and is threatening San Diego as we speak.

As I write. Whatever.

The point is, in a couple of hours the wind that's already tossing the palm trees against the villa in a spooky rat-tat-tat and littering the paths with debris is going to increase to seventy-five miles an hour. And the clouds, which look so pretty with the sun reflected through them, are going to turn black and release inches of rain.

That's what's coming.

But before all that is a moment of, well, calm.

"I'm getting married today," Emma says, looking at me through the mirror she's seated in front of. Her hair is swept back off her face and tumbles to her shoulders in waves I can never get my hair to make, because she's good at hair, too, and I'm kind of hopeless with girly things.

Oh, well.

Can't be good at everything.

Not that I'm good at everything.

We just established that I'm not.

We're alone in the bedroom in her suite. It's filled with light from the French doors that lead out onto a back patio, and there are rose petals strewn on the bed.

We'll walk down to the Beach Club together in a few minutes, but for now, it's just us and a glass of Champagne each.

Okay, maybe two or three glasses, but who's counting?

"I'm happy for you."

She meets my eyes in the reflection. I've cleaned up pretty nice, too, with her help, and the eggplant-colored dress I'm wearing suits me, even if the taffeta in the skirt is itching a spot on my hip where the slip has a gap. It's a small price to pay for the happiness I see in front of me.

"Are you?" Emma asks.

"Yes, of course. If this is what you want."

"I do want him."

"Even with . . ."

She smiles at me. "It's okay. I know you've been keeping things from me."

"I . . ."

"Fred told me everything after that policewoman left . . ."

Officer Anderson had questioned Fred and Emma before Oliver and me. She'd also talked to Harper and Shawna, David and Allison, Simone, and even Inspector Tucci before she got to us.

I was trying not to take it personally that she'd left Oliver and me for last.

It probably was because she knew it couldn't be us.

Right?

I mean, I *could* have done it. I'm right here on the spot. I might not have a motive—that I've told you about—but that doesn't mean everything.

Maybe I'm a sociopath waiting for my moment to strike. Because the perfect murder is one where you *don't* have a motive.

Kidding!

I didn't do it, I promise. And the fact that we haven't found Fred's burner phone, even though I ripped my room apart and sent Oliver back to the crime scene to check, well, that is just a loose thread that I'm sure is going to be explained eventually.

It's a gap like the one in my slip. An irritant, and nothing more.[70]

"What did Fred say?"

"He told me about his second phone and the texts. It was some ex-girlfriend who wanted to get back with him. He gave her that number so he'd have an excuse not to answer her regularly."

"Why not just block her?"

---

[70] Sure, Eleanor. SURE.

"Because she's someone you can't do that to." Our eyes meet again, and I get what she's saying. She's one of *those* ex-girlfriends. The famous ones. The ones who can call up TMZ or *People* and plant a story from "close sources" that will ruin your career if you cross them.

"Did he meet with her?"

"A couple of times, to tell her things were over and they weren't going to get back together."

"Like never."

Emma laughs. We used to sing that song together a lot when we were in our early twenties because we were dating guys who were in their early twenties.

"People have trouble letting go sometimes," Emma says.

"Like Tyler."

"Yes."

"I can't believe you remembered his number all this time."

Emma blushes and looks down. "It's not what you think."

"No?"

"It was because he was calling me. I saw it flash on my screen so many times."

"Ah."

She reaches for a pair of earrings on the dresser in front of her and starts to insert the diamond studs into her ears.

"Why did Fred have that phone in the first place?"

"Because of Tyler. He didn't want me to know about the money."

"I see."

"And I'm deciding to trust him."

"It's just all been so fast."

"I know it has, El. But when you know, you know."

"Do you know?"

"Did you know about Oliver?"

I want to say no, but the answer is yes. "I did."

"See?"

"Okay, yes, I do. And I do see that you love him."

"And what I love about him?"

"Yes, of course. He's Fred Winter!"

"I'm marrying Fred Winter!"

I lean down and rest my cheek against hers. "So crazy."

"I'm really happy, El."

"That's the most important thing."

"I thought the most important thing was you being able to take credit for this match?"

"There is that."

She smiles at me again, then kisses my cheek. "I hope you can be this happy soon."

"I'm working on it."

Tears spring to my eyes, and I stand up.

"No tears at my wedding."

"Yes, ma'am. Are you okay with your parents not being here?"

Emma considers this for a second. "You know what? I'm fine with it. It would just be an added stress, and the Winters are *a lot*, as you've seen."

"They seem like a lot."

"Thankfully, they're moving to Florida soon because the taxes are too high in California. Anyway, the point is, they'll be gone, and the movie will be over, and Tyler is probably going to jail, and we can start our life fresh."

"It's all working out . . ."

According to plan, as the rest of the saying goes, and a chill runs down my spine.

Was *this* the plan all along?

To get rid of Tyler? To pay him back for Fred *not* repaying the money he owed?

Emma and Fred together could've planned all of this.

They *did* plan it—the wedding was *their* plan, despite the storm. What was it that Fred had said? It was all arranged already. They couldn't put it off. Is this what he meant?

But no, no. It can't be.

It would be a great plan, though—create an elaborate series of near misses to make it look like someone wanted to kill *them*.

Emma could've sent those notes to herself—if there were any notes. There was only one that was kept, she said, the one she showed me. And she has access to scripts just like David does. Just like anyone on set.

She could've been leaking to that Twitter poster and the gossip site.

And the schedule she approved that announced the murder.

And Fred could've given José his number.

It didn't have to be Tyler.

So maybe this *was* the plan all along. And José was collateral damage, so they could plant the murder on Tyler and get away with everything.

Even the threat on the dock. Fred could have goaded him into that to make him look *guilty*.

Shit.

But wait, wait, wait. There were texts on José's phone with *Tyler*. They were in touch. Tyler *was* the one behind it all.

So no. My best friend and her fiancé aren't behind all of this. Emma's not a killer.

Phew.

"El?"

"Yeah?"

"Were you just trying to decide if Fred and I are murderers?"

I clear my features. "What makes you think that?"

"You were talking out loud. You know, how you do."[71]

"What did I say?"

"'But what if it was Fred and Emma together?'"

---

[71] I do talk out loud sometimes. It's like an odd kind of sleep talking except I'm awake. Other writers I know suffer from it, too. Maybe it's because we live in our heads and we forget which is real. Not sure. But it's <u>not</u> a good trait for someone trying to act like a detective.

Oh dear.

"I'm sorry."

"It's okay. I know it's the way your brain works. I love you for it."

"You love me for considering you might be a murderer?"

"I love you for you."

"Ditto."

She cocks her head to the side. "So, did I do it?"

"I concluded that you had not. Didn't say that part out loud, huh?"

"Nope."

"Tyler was communicating with José. So unless you were in cahoots with him, too, you're in the clear."

"Glad to hear it." Emma reaches out and slips her engagement ring onto her finger.

"You swear you're not mad?"

"I'm not mad."

"So, what now?"

"I think you have to walk down the aisle in front of me."

"Let's do it."

The wedding is tasteful and subdued. A man died, after all, but maybe that's also just Emma and Fred. Despite all the glitz and glamour and outward flash—the exotic location, the photographer from *People*, the cameras set up recording the whole thing, Mrs. Winter crying loudly into her handkerchief while Mr. Winter rubs her hand to soothe her—it's still only a wedding. Something people do every day.

Two people facing each other and making those age-old promises.

To love.

To cherish.

Even to obey.

It's my personal belief that the only people who hate weddings are sociopaths. Because they're in a room full of people they have to pretend in front of. That they understand love. That they can live a simple life and do the things that everyone does. Couple up. Make promises. Be there for each other. That puts a strain on a person who can't feel anything for anyone but themselves.

You might disagree, but I'm not a sociopath.

I am, however, pretending, too.

That everything is okay with me and Oliver.

That I'm not jealous of Emma.

That I believe Tyler killed José.

I might not be a very good actress, but I *do* walk down the aisle with a smile on my face, holding a bouquet of exotic fresh-cut flowers that are stand-ins for the understated tulips Emma wanted. And when I reach Oliver in his seat, he holds his hand over his heart and mouths *I love you* and *You look beautiful* and I know all's forgiven, that we'll make it through this wedding intact after all.

I mouth it back and walk toward Fred. He's beaming like he's a little boy who's won a prize, and of course he has.

Emma.

She's a radiant bride. Under the glare of the lights and the flashes from the photographer, she walks without hesitation into Fred's arms, not saving the kiss until the end of the ceremony.

Everyone laughs, releasing the tension, and the ceremony proceeds without a hitch, with Inspector Tucci reading their vows from a printout he got off the internet.

I'm not guessing this; he told us so as part of his spiel.

It was, how do you say, said to get a laugh.

Like this.

Everyone is performing.

It's a room full of professional liars, after all—actors and those who orbit around them.

I should've kept that in mind.

Because—and you should know this from the page count—someone's sitting there without a genuine smile on their face.

Someone's plotting a murder.

Someone's already committed one.

But who?

Let's spin the wheel of suspects: Fred. Emma. Shawna. Connor. David. Allison. Simone. Mr. and Mrs. Winter. Harper. Oliver. Me.

Did I leave anyone out?

Oh, Inspector Tucci, though I doubt he did it.

He is, how do you say, not *that* stupid. Or he doesn't have a motive. Take your pick.

So step right up if you have a theory. We're in a circus, after all. Spin the wheel, pick a prize, solve a murder.

Have *you* figured it out yet?

"Have I told you that you're beautiful?" Oliver asks me as he spins me around the dance floor during the reception. He's dressed in a tux because it's a black-tie affair, and I've already told him that I'm going to insist that he wear one at least once a month from now on.

It's late—we've eaten dinner and dessert, and Emma and Fred cut the cake with a large knife and then Emma smooshed a piece of it onto Fred's face before kissing him. The storm has started outside, the rain pattering against the windows, streaking them with water like they're in a car wash. The lights have flickered several times, but have never fully gone out.

But those are outside problems. Inside, the party rages on. The band never made it, but there's a sound system pumping out wedding hits, and people are dancing and making liberal use of the open bar. Fred and Emma are glowing and happy, roaming among the tables, stopping to talk to each guest for a few minutes, kissing and hugging.

And I'm so happy for her.

I'm happy for me.

"You *have* told me I'm beautiful already today," I say to Oliver, "but you can say it as many times as you like."

"You're beautiful."

"Thank you."

I tuck my head against his shoulder and breathe him in.

"You think she's having a good time?" Oliver asks.

"Who?"

"Officer Anderson."

I pull my head back and scan the room. She's sitting off to the side, her back against the wall, observing. She's still in her uniform—I guess she didn't have anything else to wear—and I can't put my finger on why she'd come. But Tyler's locked up in a jail cell in Avalon, so I guess she had nothing to do.

"Is she hoping someone's going to confess?" Oliver asks.

"Unclear. You don't think Tyler did it?"

"Nope. And you don't either, I'm guessing."

I sigh. Oliver does know me well. "Who then?"

"I don't know."

"But you have a theory," I say because I know him, too.

He tips his head and looks down at me. "It's speculation."

"Tell me."

"How about we *not* talk about murder tonight?"

"You're right."

"It happens."

"Ha ha." I kiss him. "I'm happy."

"Good." He spins me away from him and back slowly. Someone gives out a wolf whistle, and the music rises and swirls into another song, a faster number that has a beat to it.

"I'm going to get us some drinks," Oliver says.

"Good idea. I'm going to find the ladies'."

"See you in a minute."

We kiss again briefly, and I wend my way through the crowd as the beat of the song thumps through me. I find myself bopping to the music as I go, my heart swelling, a smile creeping onto my lips.

But I should know better than to celebrate or let my guard down.

You should, too.

Because I've shown you this scene before.

Did you forget? I forgive you.

I get to the door I think leads to the bathroom[72] and turn the handle.

The room is dark. It's one of those annoying bathrooms where the lights are supposed to be movement-sensitive but aren't.

I wave my hand around, trying to provoke the light, but when nothing happens, I step inside and search for the light switch on the wall. I grope around for a minute until I find it, then snap it on as it hits me.

That *smell*.

Metallic, heavy metal.

Blood.

My eyes adjust, and a body comes into focus on the floor in front of me.

Dark blond hair. Tux.

Fred. Actually dead this time, I promise.

So, first of all: *Fuck.*

And second of all: It's one minute to midnight.

Which means this murder is right on time.

---

[72] I stopped counting the number of Champagnes I drank when it got to four.

SUNDAY

CHAPTER 22

Is It Wrong to Pretend This Never Happened?

Okay, Eleanor, you've been here before.

Literally and figuratively.

You need to breathe.

But when I breathe, all I can smell is *blood*. Fresh in the air like the abattoir I visited once for research.[73] But this isn't my next steak dinner.[74]

It's *Fred*.

I fall to my knees, the edge of my gown just missing the spreading pool on the floor. I want to look away from him, but I can't.

Emma, poor Emma. She's going to be devastated. How is she going to recover from this?

But also—now it definitely can't be Tyler who killed José.

Because Tyler's locked up in Avalon.

No. It's someone *here*, at this party.

Because of course it is.

We should've seen this coming.

You should've, too. In fact, why didn't you warn me?

---

[73] I was sick for days and vowed <u>never</u> to do any research again.

[74] Not my best work.

Sorry. I'm tired and a bit drunk, and also, there's a dead body a few feet from me.

This isn't your fault.

I lean my back against the wall. The smell of blood is mingling with the whiff of bleach that hangs in the air. There's a bucket and a mop next to me, and part of me wants to clean this mess up and hide the body and go back to the party like nothing happened because that way I won't have to tell Emma she's a widow before she ever had a chance to be a wife.

But I know that's not realistic.

Instead, and even though I know I shouldn't, and even though I was *just* warned not to do this very thing by Officer Anderson, I force myself to stand. I slip off my shoes, then walk around the body slowly, looking for clues.

Fred is face down in his tux with a knife sticking out of his back. His feet are toward the door, his arms extended toward the far wall like he was briefly in flight before he landed.

I bend over him to get a better look at the weapon. I don't know for sure, but the knife looks an awful lot like the one they used to cut the cake.

Is that a message? Or convenience?

Come on, El. Someone used the cake-cutting knife to knife the groom at his wedding.

It's a message.

Nothing else seems out of place. So how did he get in here? Who did he come to meet? Why are there no signs of a struggle? His back is to the door, so he could've been taken by surprise. But who would he let surprise him in here?

Did someone follow him? Did he come in here by mistake like me? Or was he here to meet someone, lured here like he was lured to the basement?

Fred's not the sharpest tool in the shed, but is he dumb enough to answer a summons to a secluded location *twice*?

No, so it can't be that. Whatever brought him here had to be something else.

Personal.

Comfortable.

Because you don't turn your back on someone you're afraid of.

A knife in the back. That's a crime of passion. The knife was driven in deep. It takes a lot of strength to do that unless you know what you're doing and your knife is very sharp.[75]

So it's probably a man, but it could be a woman full of rage.

Who hates Fred that much?

Who hates Fred so much, but that he wouldn't be afraid of?

Think, Eleanor. Think.

Who, besides Tyler, would be so mad with Fred that they'd want to kill him on his wedding day?

And it's then that I notice it. His left hand is ringless. Someone stole his ring? Or . . .

Oh, no.

Oh, *shit.*

This isn't Fred.

My heart starts to race and tears spring to my eyes. Because if it's not Fred, then there's only one person it could be. Someone else with the same haircut and build who even I mistook for Fred more than once.

My God. My God. Someone finally did it. They killed *Connor.*

And I'm not sure how to feel about it.

No, I'm lying.

I'm *sad.*

Goddamn it.

I need help.

I wipe my tears away and turn to the door, grabbing my shoes. It's

---

[75] I know this because of <u>research</u> I conducted on the <u>internet</u>. Not because I've tried to do it.

time to leave and go to Officer Anderson and get the wheels of justice in motion. But if I do, it'll be real. A world without any Connor in it. Something I've fantasized about more than once.

But now it's happened, and it's going to change everything.

Shit.

Did I say that already?

Connor's death has me so upset I'm *repeating* myself.

I open the door and step back into the hall, ready to raise the alarm, and smack right into something, my shoes tumbling out of my hand and falling to the floor.

Someone.

"They're not going to run out of alcohol, El. You can slow down."

"Connor?" I look up and it's *him*. His tux still immaculate, his thick hair in place.

My heart skips a beat.

Is this relief, or am I having a heart attack?

"El, have you hit your head?"

"You're alive!"

I hug him hard, breathing in his musky aftershave, and just as quickly let him go.

"What?"

I clench my hands and take in a slow breath. "Someone's dead in the broom closet." I point over my shoulder and pray that the tears I shed for him aren't visible.

"And you thought it was me?" His eyes dance, because even though I've just told him someone is dead, his focus is always on how that impacts him.

See, Harper? People don't change.

"Yes, I did think it was you for a moment. Clearly, I was wrong." I don't look him in the eye. He doesn't need to know. Nothing good can come of this.

"Who is it, then?"

"I thought at first it was Fred, but . . ." I turn and open the door again.

Connor stands beside me and looks at the body, sucking in his breath. "That's Ken."

"Ken?"

"The stand-in."

"Oh my God, you're right." My eyes trace over the body, and I can't believe I missed the little details. His less expensive shoes. His rougher hands.

Sherlock Holmes, I am not.

I'm not even Cecilia Crane.

"Why would anyone want to kill Ken?" Connor asks.

"I don't—"

"What are you two doing in there?" Simone says behind us. "My God. Is he *dead*?"

"I . . ."

"Fred is dead?"

I turn around. Simone is wearing a dress in a deep wine color, and her thick, dark hair has tumbled out of the updo it was in earlier. Her eyes are shining like she might be about to cry.

I take hold of her arms. "It's not Fred, it's Ken. And keep your voice down."

But it's too late. The word "dead" tends to carry in any environment.

"What is going on?" Mrs. Winter slurs behind me. "What are you saying about my Fred?"

I make a desperate gesture with my hand to Simone, and she reaches for the door and closes it. I turn around slowly. Mrs. Winter is wearing a silver turban with a brooch in the middle of it like she's Elizabeth Taylor in her turban era. Her eye makeup is similar, too, that elongated liquid eyeliner that extends beyond the creases of her eye like a thick black whisker.

"It's nothing, Mrs. Winter."

"It's not nothing. You're hiding something in there. What is it? And why did *she* use that word?" She points at Simone.

"What word."

"'Dead.' I heard someone say 'de—'" Her hand flies to her mouth. "Is my son in there? Is he *dead*? Did *you* kill him? Oh, you killed him, you killed him." Her voice rises above the din of the party.

"No, Mrs. Winter," I say. "He's not dead. He's not. It's someone else in there, not Fred."

"I told him to stay away from you," Mrs. Winter says to Simone as she strains against me. "I told him nothing good would come of it. But does he listen to me? No. No. My poor boy. My poor son. My love, my love, he's dead."

She flings her hand against her forehead and slumps against me.

Deadweight, I think, because I can't help myself.

But she's not dead. Not even fainted. Not really.

She's just overcome by her dramatic self.

I lower her to the floor as the music stops abruptly. I crouch down, fanning my hands in front of Mrs. Winter.

"A little help here?" I say to Simone and Connor.

"She just accused me of murder," Simone says.

"You seem to be handling this well on your own," Connor drawls. "I'll go find . . . Ah, here she is."

I follow his gaze, and here comes Officer Anderson with her jacket off and her gun out.

"Step back, everyone. Step back slowly."

I stand, leaving Mrs. Winter against the wall, and follow directions as a crowd gathers behind us.

Whatever I was hoping to do a few minutes ago—to tamp it down, or cover it up, or pretend it never happened—there's nothing I can do about that now.

CHAPTER 23

If You Gather All the Suspects in a Library, Will Someone Confess?

"How long is she going to make us wait in here?" Mrs. Winter asks an hour later, her voice rising to a level that could reach the farthest row in a dinner theater.

"I'm sure she'll be here soon, Mother. Just try to relax. Did you take your pills?" Fred looks to his father, who I don't think has said two words since Officer Anderson asked us to wait in here half an hour ago.

I told Officer Anderson what I found, but that's obvious since the dead body is kind of hard to miss. I explained about meaning to go to the bathroom as I slipped my shoes back on and said something about my feet killing me, which I don't think Officer Anderson bought and Connor definitely didn't.

A problem for later. Regardless, I left out the time I spent alone with the body or the fact that I thought Ken was Connor or Fred. The second isn't relevant, and the first could get me thrown in jail.

Officer Anderson phoned the body into her headquarters on the mainland, and then there was a debate about what to do about the party.

Could it continue while someone lay dead in a broom closet?

It could, apparently.

We wouldn't want to cause a panic.

But the central guests—I mean suspects—were told to come to this room, the—wait for it—*library* down the hall from the reception.

Me, Oliver, Harper, Shawna, Simone, Fred, Emma, Inspector Tucci, Connor, Allison, David, and Mr. and Mrs. Winter.

We're in here waiting for Officer Anderson among the old hardcovers and the new paperbacks and the dark oak furniture that might've been burnished with cigar smoke. We can hear the thumping of the music through the walls, and the rain slapping the windows. The lights have been flickering for the last ten minutes, dimming down but not quite out, as the windows are lit up by flashes of lightning out over the ocean.

Because of course they are.

We're sitting in a circle like we're at an AA meeting.[76] Only we're way too dressed up and there's no one reciting the Serenity Prayer. We've all been looking at one another with the same thought ringing through our heads.

Who killed *Ken*?

I assume that's what you're wondering, too.

Let's eliminate me right off the bat. I know I've said I'm out of it before, and you might be thinking that's a misdirection. I promise you it's not. This is not that kind of book.[77] I have no reason to kill Fred or Emma or José or Ken. Emma's my best friend. She doesn't owe me money. I'm not secretly in love with Fred. I've been paid already for this movie, and I'm not invested in its financial success, other than tangentially.[78] I'm not a sociopath. So it's not me.

---

[76] Not that I've ever been to an AA meeting. In case you were wondering.

[77] The next one might be, though. *This Weekend Doesn't End Well for Anyone* might be <u>exactly</u> that kind of book.

[78] I mean, sure, if the movie is a success, I'll probably sell some books. And there's a formula in my contract that means that if it makes a ton of money, I might see some more. Then again, maybe not. Studios are famous for their creative accounting.

Ditto for Harper and Oliver. They have even less of a motive than I do.

And Tyler must be out of it as well. If he hadn't been arrested, then I might be thinking this was an *And Then There Were None*[79] scenario and he's hiding somewhere on the island, but nope, he's in the Avalon jail. Unless he's working with someone else, which is always a possibility, but doesn't seem to fit the facts for reasons I can't quite put my finger on.

I know one thing, though. Fred is worth more to Tyler alive. And I doubt he's stupid enough to threaten to kill Fred in full public view if that was his plan all along.

"Where's a whiteboard when you need it?" Connor says, his tone light, almost jovial.

"Oh God, not that again," Allison says. "Once was enough."

"What do you mean?" David asks.

"We used one in Italy," I explain. "To try to solve the murder there."

"Ah, like outlining."

"Sure. If you outline."

He blinks at me slowly, and I can't help but wonder: Is *David* feeling desperate right now? Trying to figure out how to finish the task he screwed up?

Because killing Ken had to have been a screwup.

His only crime is looking too much like Fred.

"We *are* already here," Inspector Tucci says. "I do not see what the harm would be in trying to help Officer Anderson, given our expertise."

There's a flash of lightning outside and then a thunderclap almost immediately, its boom echoing through the room, rattling the window frames.

Emma jumps, and Fred puts his arm around her, making a shushing sound. Emma's always been, well, *deathly* afraid of thunder.

---

[79] Sorry if I spoiled that for you. But how have you not read that book yet or at least seen the movie?

"For the last time, you are *not* the authorities," Simone says. "And you have no expertise."

"We could try to figure it out just the same," Connor says.

"Why would we do that?" Simone asks.

He cocks a smile. "Aren't you curious?"

"About?"

"Who did it and why. I would've thought the fact that you're likely sitting in a room with a murderer would motivate you."

A frisson goes through the room, which was Connor's intention. He has a flair for the dramatic. It's, perversely, one of the things that makes him appealing.

"Why don't we wait for Officer Anderson?" I say.

"Come now, El. You can't honestly tell me that you're not intensely curious as to who killed Ken instead of Fred?"

"*Instead* of Fred?" Emma says, her voice quavering. She's still in her wedding dress, and I'm sure deeply regretting that she didn't change into a second dress. It had been a long debate, but she'd run out of time to find something that she liked.

I'm sure she's going to want to burn this dress after tonight.

I would, anyway.

"Well, certainly," Connor says. "Unless you think someone killed Ken deliberately?"

I'm sure he doesn't quite mean to speak in that tone, but it's there, just the same.

As in, is Ken even worthy of being killed?

News flash: Everyone is.

"That seems unlikely," Oliver says. He hasn't said anything about me and Connor finding the body together, maybe because he doesn't know that part yet.

He didn't see me fling myself into Connor's arms in relief either, thank God.

He doesn't need to know about that.

No one here does.

You'll keep my secret, right?

"So, we're agreed then," Connor says. "Fred was the intended victim. Which means you, you, you, and you are suspects." He points to Emma, Simone, Shawna, and David. "And I suppose you lot." He flicks his gaze to Mr. and Mrs. Winter.

Mrs. Winter pulls her sparkling shawl tight over her shoulders. There's one half of a fake eyelash loose against the side of her eye, a crack in her facade.

"I do not like your tone, young man."

"Excuse me?" David says. "What about *you*?"

Connor scoffs. "Why would *I* kill Fred?"

"Because Tyler hired you to."

"I am not a murderer for hire."

"He makes a good point, though, Connor," I say. "You *are* working for Tyler."

"Seriously, Eleanor? You think I'm capable of that?"

Is that *hurt* in his eyes?

"If you were desperate . . . If you needed the money . . ."

"I'm fine."

"In Italy, you were in dire straits. That was only three months ago."

He juts out his chin. "I just sold my novel in a three-book deal at auction."

"You . . . what? The rom-com?"[80]

"Yes."

"Who bought it?"

"Vicki."

My blood runs cold. "Vicki as in Vicki my editor?"

---

[80] I learned in Italy that Connor was writing a rom-com with a plot like one of those Hallmark Christmas movies. Small-town girl returns home to hometown boy, etc.

And Oliver's. Jesus.

"Yes."

"Holy shit."

"And last week I optioned the film rights for high six figures. So I am *fine* financially. I agreed to some detective work for Tyler, yes, because I like to keep my hand in, and the book deal payment hasn't gone through yet. He was willing to pay a handsome finder's fee if I recovered his money—"

"Connor loves a finder's fee," Harper says.

"I do. But murder? No. Absolutely not. And I certainly wouldn't confuse Fred and Ken. Please. Give me that credit, at least."

Another flash of lightning, and a loud clap of thunder that's even closer this time. It feels like it shakes the building to its roots.

Emma gives a little squeal.

"It's okay, Emma," I say.

"No, it's *not*."

Fred makes that shushing sound again. If Oliver did that to me, it might make me break up with him. But it seems to soothe Emma.

"It's true about the book deal, El," Harper says.

I look across the circle to her. "How do you know?"

"I've been, um, working with him on it."

Wait, *what?*

"Working on it, how?"

"You know, editing, working through the dialogue with him. Like I do for you."

"Oh," Oliver says. "*That's* what you were talking about on the phone."

"You've been listening to my phone calls?"

Oliver looks embarrassed. "Not on purpose. I just heard . . ."

Harper's eyes widen. "The read-through. Oh my God. You thought I was with Connor?"

"I didn't know what to think."

She looks at me. "And you, El? You thought that?"

"You were defending him! Telling me he'd changed. What was I supposed to think?"

"Ugh. No."

"No need to be quite so disgusted, surely?" Connor drawls.

"What are we even talking about?" Emma asks.

"I'm sorry, Em. Where were we?"

"We've just eliminated Connor as a suspect," David says. "Who next?"

"You?"

He tips back in his chair. "Me? Whyever?"

"Eleanor, please," Allison says. "Be serious."

"I *am* being serious. I don't trust him. And you shouldn't either."

"Why not?"

"Because he wrote you into the movie, and now you're dating him. Doesn't that raise a red flag?"

She looks uncertain. "I hadn't thought about that."

"And didn't Emma get you fired off a movie, David?"

Emma sits up. "That's true."

"You did?" David asks. "You expressly told me you hadn't."

"I only meant I knew that you thought I did."

"So convincing."

"So, you've been mad at Emma ever since?" I say.

"It was years ago. And yeah, I wasn't happy. But if I was going to kill her for getting me fired, I would've done it back then. Not now."

"But you thought about it?"

"No!"

"I don't think it was him, El," Emma says. "He might hate me, but why would he want to kill Fred?"

"Yes," David says. "Exactly. Why would I?"

Everyone turns to look at Fred. He holds his hands up. "Don't look at me. I *like* David."

"What if he did it for publicity?" Harper says. "For the movie?"

"That's a bit extreme, isn't it?" Oliver says.

"Not if *he* has money problems. David, I mean. And that's who gets blamed, right, if the movie doesn't succeed? Not the actors, unless they're women, but Emma's already well established. But the writer and director? Especially if they're people of color . . ."

"We don't need you to defend us," Simone says. "You can keep your white-savior act for someone else."

Two spots of color tinge Harper's cheeks. "That's not what I meant."

"What *did* you mean?" David asks.

"Only that you might be desperate to save your career. This is only your second credit, right?"

"I . . ."

"I was checking out your IMDb page," Harper says. "Lots of staff writer jobs, but this is only your second film. And you're, what? Forty-five? And the writers' strike . . . That took a lot out of people like you, didn't it? Months of no work . . ."

David turns his palms up. "So I killed two people?"

"Maybe the original plan was just to scare everyone. And then José didn't want to go along with it anymore, and you ended up killing him, maybe by accident. And then you had to cover up that crime. Maybe Ken saw you do something and was trying to blackmail you, so he had to go, too. As Connor says, who would confuse Ken and Fred? Certainly not from the front."

Harper sits back, a little out of breath. And I have to admit it.

I'm impressed.

So is Simone because she starts a slow clap. "Bravo."

"Don't be a bitch, Simone," I say. "Wasn't Mrs. Winter just accusing *you* of Fred's murder?"

"She doesn't know what she's talking about."

Mrs. Winter throws her a look. "I've *never* liked you."

So I guess those rumors of Fred and Simone dating all those years ago are true.

Huh.

"Me either, Mrs. Winter," I say, and immediately regret it.

In my defense—nope, it's not defensible.

"Nice, Eleanor, nice."

"I'm sorry, but Harper's theory is plausible."

"Please. Someone's committed two murders to guarantee a box office success? That's the stupidest plot I've ever heard. And what about the sequel he's already writing? Not going to happen if one of the leads dies."

"That's what the sequel could be about."

"And you think David is behind it?" She makes a dismissive wave of her hand. "No."

"Central casting again?"

"Yes. But also that theory could apply to any one of us here."

"That doesn't mean it's a bad one," I say. "Maybe that's what's brilliant about it. Get a bunch of people together with the same motive so no one sticks out and you confuse the police . . . It's been done before."

Simone arches an eyebrow. "So a brilliant person designed this plan? Does David strike you as being that smart?"

I consider her. "Why are you defending him?"

She puts her hands out in front of her. "I have no skin in this game."

"But you have the same motive as me," David says.

"No, I don't. I've already booked my next gig."

"What is it?" I ask.

Her composure slips for a moment. "A film I wrote."[81]

"What's it called?"

"*Untitled.*"[82]

"Congratulations."

The room falls silent, the only sound the close grumble of thunder

---

[81] Another <u>writer</u>? Seriously?

[82] Damn it, that's a good title.

and the clatter of the rain and the party that won't end, though I don't blame them.

I'd rather be out there doing bad dance moves to hits from three decades ago than in here with a bunch of people tossed together because they have the means, motive, and opportunity to kill someone.

"I think we're all forgetting something," Oliver says, scratching at his chin in the way he does when he's working on one of his uber-detailed book outlines.

"What's that?"

"Maybe Fred wasn't the intended victim."

"You think it was Ken?" I say.

"No, that theory seems wrong to me—sorry, Harper."

"Then who?"

But as he says it, I know.

There's one other person that could be mistaken for Fred.

"Connor."

There's another massive CRACK, and then the lights flicker again and go out. Emma squeals and Mrs. Winter starts to mewl like the cat she almost killed yesterday.

Oliver tells everyone to remain calm, but we're sitting in the dark with a murderer.

We all know how this is going to go.

The lights will come back on and one of us will be dead.

I hug myself, keeping my ears and eyes as alert as possible.

But it's total darkness. The wind is howling now, a primal shriek. The hairs on my arms are standing straight up as I hear the sound of a chair scraping back, then a door opening.

Oh, shit.

"Don't do it," I say. Though I don't know who I'm pleading to.

And then there's a whine and a flicker as the generator kicks in and the lights come back on. I search the circle as my eyes adjust to the light. Everyone's still here, alive.

But in that moment of darkness, something *has* changed.

There's a figure in the doorway, a silhouette.

A woman is standing there, wet to the bone, holding what looks like a club above her head as if she's about to strike.

It's . . . Crazy Cathy?

CHAPTER 24

How Many Stalkers Does It Take to Commit a Murder?

Crazy Cathy is framed in a flash of lightning and the flickering lights as the rain pelts the windows and the wind howls through the palm trees. The two together create a strobe light effect, where the room shifts between light and dark, and the people do, too.

FLASH!

Cathy raises her arm above her head. She's holding what looks like a piece of wood but might be a baseball bat.

FLASH!

Someone gets behind her—a dark figure looming with their face obscured by shadows.

FLASH!

Cathy's arm comes down and is stopped right above David's head.

FLASH!

Connor and Oliver have Cathy by the arms and are pulling her back.

FLASH!

Emma screams that piercing scream of hers as another *BOOM* hits the ground so near our structure that it shakes like there's been an earthquake.

FLASH!

Officer Anderson is standing in the doorway with her arms out straight, her gun leveled at the group. She's outlined by the light from the hallway.

"Freeze!" she yells, and everyone does.

But that's a mistake because Oliver and Connor loosen their grasp, and Cathy wrenches herself free and runs toward the far doorway that she must've come through.

FLASH!

Officer Anderson's arms swing around and follow Cathy as she yells "Stop!"

But Cathy doesn't stop, and the next flash we see is from the barrel of Officer Anderson's gun.

BAM!

A chunk of wood splinters next to Cathy's head but that doesn't stop her from wrenching open the French door. And then she's out into the night in a flash of yellow rain slicker.

Officer Anderson tears after her as the lights finally stop flickering, leaving us all in stunned silence.

Except for David.

He never seems to be at a loss for words.

"Who *was* that?"

"That was Crazy Cathy," I say. "My stalker."

"*Your* stalker."

"What? I can't have a stalker?"

"Why was she trying to hurt *me?*"

"I have no idea."

"What should we do?" Oliver says as he leans down and picks up the thick piece of wood Cathy was holding. It's not a bat, but some discarded scrap of construction lumber from God knows where. Oliver hefts it in his hand, then drops it back to the ground, startling us.

"Stay here, I think, until Officer Anderson comes back," Allison says calmly.

Emma slumps into her chair as Fred drags his chair even closer to her. "I can't believe Officer Anderson shot at her."

"She *was* trying to kill me," David says.

"Let's not exaggerate," I say.

"Come now, El," Allison says. "We all saw it. But where did she come from? Has she been here all along? She must've been."

"To what end?"

"She must be behind everything."

"Cathy?" I say. "I don't think she has it in her."

"You're the one who got a restraining order against her," Connor says.

"Yes, but that was *before* Italy. We've made up since then."

"You made friends with your stalker?" Simone says.

I ignore her. "I don't see how she can be behind any of this. She doesn't know Fred or Emma or Tyler. The wedding was a secret. And what about changing the word to 'murder' on the schedule? She couldn't have been behind that."

"What if it was a moment of opportunity?" Connor says. "Coming over here *was* on the shooting schedule. She didn't have to know it was a real wedding."

"And what? She decided to try to kill Emma and Fred because . . . ?"

"She's a stalker, El!" He spins a finger next to his head. "You said so yourself. Her logic isn't going to be something we understand."

This stops me because Connor, once again, as much as I hate to admit it, is right.

Cathy's obsessions and solutions have never made sense. She used to want to make me feel uncomfortable, even though she professes to love me, but now that we're "friends," maybe that's flipped. Maybe she felt the need to protect me against people she perceived as my enemies.

Like David.

But how could she know I don't like David?

And even this crazy logic doesn't apply to Emma and Fred.

I doubt she knows anything about Tyler or even who he is.

And how would she have convinced José to work with her? Last time I checked,[83] Cathy was collecting disability because of a back injury she suffered in a car accident ten years ago.

Not that it looked like she had any problems with her back when she was getting ready to brain David.

But a doctor told me once that they search for one medical issue to explain all of their patient's symptoms because the chance of them having two issues at once is very small. It's the same with murder mysteries. There can't be *two* plots at work at once.

You have to find a solution that explains *everything*.[84]

"Something doesn't make sense," I say.

"*None* of it makes sense," Fred says with his arm around Emma's shoulders. They make a striking pair, even now. Emma in her white sheath dress and Fred in his tux. "This is our *wedding*. It's supposed to be a time of celebration. Not a place to air out old hurts."

Fred's quoting from something again, I'm not sure what. But he might also be onto something.

"What do you mean, Fred?"

"As just established before the fracas, someone is trying to kill Connor, not *me*. *Your* stalker is here. You've been acting as if this is all about me, or me and Emma. But it's clearly about *you*."

Harper gasps, and the room turns to me as a sinking feeling fills my heart.

Is he right? Have we been looking in the wrong direction all along?

---

[83] I did a background check on Cathy when I got the restraining order against her.
[84] Does that apply to book series? Hmmm.

Am I the main character in this story after all?[85,86]

The lights flicker again and the French doors open, bringing in a swirl of rain and a very wet Officer Anderson hauling Cathy in front of her. Her hands are cuffed with a zip tie, her hair is matted down, and there's a streak of dirt on her cheek.

"Let me go!" she says as she struggles against Officer Anderson's grip.

"Stop moving or I'll tighten the restraints."

Cathy settles as Officer Anderson leads her to a chair in our circle and pushes her down into it. "Sit here. Do. Not. Move. I will be back in a moment." She looks at Oliver. "Please guard that door."

Oliver moves to the door, blocking the exit with his arms crossed over his chest.

Officer Anderson walks toward the other door, with her radio up to her ear, which is squawking with a disembodied voice.

I guess she's calling in yet another crime, but what can dispatch do about it?

Nothing until the storm clears.

Which I assume will last conveniently long enough for us to figure out what's going on.

Or until we're all killed.

"Cathy," Harper says, "what are you doing here?"

Cathy looks at her through her dripping bleached-blond hair. "El was in trouble."

"What?" I say.

Cathy looks around the room, her eyes unfocused until she gets to Mr. and Mrs. Winter.

---

[85] I mean, obviously, yes. But also, no, right? Like the medical symptoms, I can't be the target of *two* different people's plots to murder me. I'm not *that* bad of a person, am I?

[86] Like the chapter titles, this is a rhetorical question.

"I didn't know *you* were here," Cathy says. "I'm a big fan! I've seen every episode of *Trial by Night!*"[87]

"Thank you, dear," Mrs. Winter says. "Perhaps I could sign something for you later?"

"I'd love that. But I left my autograph book at home. But maybe—"

"Um, Cathy?" I say. "This is *not* the time."

She turns her eyes to me, and they soften, like eyes do when they look at something they love.

I shiver, but I don't look away. "Why did you come here?"

"I read the stories online. I heard someone died. I came to save you."

"You came here in the storm?"

"I took a boat."

"How? Did you steal one?"

She shakes her head, letting droplets of water fly. "It was the ferry."

"The ferry is running?"

"On Friday."

"You came here on *Friday*?"

She tries to cross her arms but is stopped by the restraints. "I was invited, wasn't I?"

"Invited? By who?"

"Them," she says as she points to Emma and Fred. "'Emma Wood and Fred Winter cordially invite you to their wedding on Catalina Island.'"

"Do you know about this, Emma?"

"We didn't send out wedding invitations," Emma says. "Remember?"

"Oh, right. You didn't. So how did she get one?"

"Someone brought her here," Harper says.

"Or she's lying," Connor adds.

"I'm not a liar!"

"Where have you been all this time, Cathy?" I ask.

---

[87] The name of Mrs. Winter's biggest nighttime soap, on before I was born.

"In my room. As instructed."

"As instructed? By who?"

Confusion clouds her features. She must've been quite attractive, once, but wet and crazy is not a good look for anyone. "I'm not sure. I assumed it was Harper."

"Harper?"

"Cathy texts me sometimes."

Um, *what*?

Harper's shaking her head. "About events and things. And El's news-letter."

"You texted me back."

"Harper?"

"Once. I did that once. *Before* the restraining order."

I give Harper a look, then turn back to Cathy. "Was it Harper who told you to stay in your room? Her number?"

"No, the number was blocked."

"Why did you think it was her, then?"

"Who else would it be?"

Thunder cracks again, making the ground shake and the lights flash.

I shudder. I have a terrible feeling of déjà vu. In Italy, someone invited Cathy on the book tour to divert suspicion and create chaos. And here she is *again*.

But why?

No matter how crazy Cathy is, and she's not *that* crazy,[88] no one would reasonably think that she had anything to do with a plot to murder Emma or Fred. But Connor, on the other hand . . .

Connor is another story.

If Connor *was* the intended victim, then bringing her here makes sense.

---

[88] At least, that's what I tell myself because you can't live your life looking over your shoulder all the time.

You'd want to have more than one person who had a motive to kill him on the scene.

Like me.

Like Oliver.

Like Harper.

Like Allison.

Like Cathy.

Like *Italy*.

Because I've seen this movie before.

I've lived it.

I search the faces sitting around me. Fred is consoling Emma, stroking her hair like she's a child. Mr. and Mrs. Winter are in a similar position, like a fast-forwarded version of Emma and Fred. Simone is standing over Cathy, with an expression that's daring Cathy to try something, anything. Oliver's by the door, watching me. Connor, Allison, Harper, and David are clutched together, waiting for something to happen.

Maybe for me to provide the solution.

And Inspector Tucci has his notebook out, but God knows what he's writing.

Doodles, probably.

But wait.

Someone's missing.

"Where's Shawna?" I ask.

Harper's head swivels, like she might be hiding in a corner. "She was just here."

"When's the last time you saw her?"

"I . . ."

"Anyone?"

"She was here before the lights went out," Oliver says.

"I haven't seen her since then," Allison says. "But she's so quiet, it's easy to overlook her."

"Simone?" I say. "Did you see her leave?"

"No, but that girl isn't reliable."

"She's been at your beck and call for *months*," Harper says with a flush to her face. "Making your movie happen, making this wedding happen. Doing everything."

Simone's eyes flash. "What do *you* know about it?"

"We've all seen how you treat her on set."

"What has that got to do with anything?"

"It doesn't. But you're a jerk. No one likes you."

If circumstances were different, I might throw out a "You go, girl" to Harper, proud that she's sticking up for someone, even if it's not her. But now is really not the time for a Norma Rae moment.[89]

Besides, Simone doesn't seem to care that she's being judged.

But also . . .

"Harper," I say, "what do you know about Shawna?"

"What do you mean?"

"Has she said anything to you?"

"Anything to me about what?"

"Me? Or Connor? Or Italy?"

"What are you talking about?"

"This all feels *way* too familiar. Everyone gathered here, and someone trying to kill Connor, and Cathy being here . . . you see?"

Her eyes dart back and forth quickly. But she's always been the smart one. It doesn't take her long to get there. "You think this has something to do with what happened in Italy?"

"Maybe, yeah. One of the Giuseppes is still on the loose, isn't she?"

"You think Shawna is Marta?"

"She could be."

"Come on, El. I *knew* Marta. I met her many times. So did you."

"I met her twice. Maybe three times. A year ago and in a completely different circumstance. I doubt I'd recognize her."

---

[89] Is this reference too dated for my age? It was one of my mom's favorite movies.

"Well, I would."

My brain is whirring. "What about the other sister? Rosa. There were three of them. Maybe that's who Shawna is?"

"That doesn't make any sense."

"I know, but where is she? And what is Cathy doing here? Someone is fucking with us. With *me*."

"Because everything's always about you?" Simone says. "Even this."

"Shut up, Simone."

"You can't talk to me that way."

"El," Oliver warns, and I clamp my jaw shut because he's right.

This isn't helpful.

But somehow, deep down, I know I'm right.

About all of it.

"We have to find Officer Anderson and tell her Shawna is missing."

"Shawna's missing?" Officer Anderson says, coming through the door with Mr. Prentice. "Since when?"

"We're not sure. She was here before the lights went off. But no one's seen her since then."

"She must've left during the chaos of Cathy's entrance," Oliver says.

"I was *told* to come here, I'll have you know."

"Wait, what?"

"I was telling you before," Cathy says to me. "That same person who was texting me, they told me to come help you."

"They told you to club David?"

"No, but I assumed that's what they meant."

"Why?"

"You've been complaining about him for months, haven't you? Saying how he was ruining *When in Rome*?"

"Where did you hear that?"

She hangs her head. "I can't say."

I cycle through all the times I've complained about David. On the beach with Oliver and Harper, in my brain, once on set, and many, many times at home.

In my home.

"Have you been . . . listening in on my conversations somehow?"

Cathy's eyes flash with defiance and pride. "It was for your own good."

"My own . . . what?"

"You were almost killed in Italy! And two of them are still out there. I was just keeping watch."

I feel sick to my stomach. Cathy *is* dangerous. And I'm an idiot. "How did you do this?"

She clamps her jaw tight. "I refuse to answer because it might incriminate me."

"Oh my God, you broke into our house?" Harper says. "What the *fuck*."

You know things are going badly when Harper sounds like me.

"Officer Anderson?" I say.

"Yes?"

"Are you going to arrest her?"

"For what?"

"She was trying to kill David."

"I was *not*."

"She's been spying on me. She crashed this wedding. You saw it, you shot at her."

"She was fleeing the scene," Officer Anderson says in a robotic voice, like she's trying to convince herself. She's probably never fired her service weapon before.

"She needs to be locked up."

"She's under restraint and will remain that way until my colleagues arrive."

"What about Tyler?" Emma says. "Is he going to be released?"

"I say," Fred says, "he could still be involved."

"Why would Tyler want to kill me?" Connor asks. "Or do you think *I* killed Ken by accident?"

"Of course not."

"This has nothing to do with me."

"Who, then?"

"You," Connor says with emphasis.

Fred takes a step toward him.

"Fred!" Mrs. Winter calls, a plaintive note in her voice.

"Not now, Mother."

"But Fred, I . . . I . . ."

"Are you quite all right, dear?" Mr. Winter says.

"I . . ." Mrs. Winter goes pale and then paler again, and before anyone can reach her, she faints dead away.

"Now, that's what I call making an exit."

"Shut *up*, Tucci!"

CHAPTER 25

If One of the Dash Girls Isn't Sleeping with a Criminal, Is It Even a Vacation Mystery?

"I can't believe this," Harper says an hour later over a stiff scotch one of the bartenders was kind enough to pour her. The party's finally been shut down and everyone shepherded back to their rooms.

We're supposed to be there, too, but Officer Anderson is occupied getting everyone locked in for the night with the help of Mr. Prentice and a couple of the staff.

I'm sure we'll get in some kind of trouble when she finds us, but what more trouble could we be in?[90]

Two people are dead, and we have no idea who did it.

Not Mrs. Winter. She was revived off the floor by a few words of kindness from her husband and a stiff drink of brandy brought by the hotel manager. Mr. Winter then led her to their room, and I think we all breathed a sigh of relief.

But it's what gave me the idea to bring Harper in here. She's been acting strangely since Shawna went missing, but I didn't want to question her about it in front of everyone.

"What's the matter?" I ask. "I mean, besides the obvious."

"I just can't believe Shawna had something to do with it."

---

[90] Yes, this is also a rhetorical question.

"Well, we don't know her, do we? So who knows what she's capable of."

Harper shoots me a look. "You're very dense sometimes."

"Rude."

"It's true." She starts gesturing to our images in the mirror behind the bar. "You thought I was sleeping with Connor."

"You'd done it before. And Oliver did hear a compromising conversation."

"Uh-huh. Two plus six equals seven."

"Harper, I know we've all had a shock, but what am I missing?"

She stares down into her drink. "It's Shawna."

"Who's the murderer? I mean, probably, but why?"

"No, dummy. *She's* the one I'm sleeping with."

"*Plot twist.*"

She glares at me. "We're fine with it."

"Of course we are. Sorry, I just . . . You took me by surprise."

I take a large gulp of my drink. I'm having a scotch, too—okay, it's a double, which I'm sure Oliver will disapprove of when I return to our room.[91] But I told him that the Dash sisters needed a moment, and the fact that I was talking about Harper and me in the third person convinced him to give us a beat.

Anyway, I am 100 percent okay with my sister sleeping with whoever she wants.

I'm just taking a minute to process.

"How did . . . how did you meet?"

"On set. We have a lot in common."

"You do?"

"Our jobs, for one."

"Working for unreasonable women, you mean?"

---

[91] Not because I have a drinking problem—I just tend to get drunk when there are murderers around, which is hazardous to my health.

"You said it, not me."

"Fine. So where is she?"

"I don't know."

"Maybe this is all some misunderstanding," I say, patting her on the hand.

"How can it be?" Harper's arms are slumped in front of her, her body hunched over in defeat. She didn't have to wear a bridesmaid dress, so she's in a slinky black number, which she told me with defiance when she showed it to me a couple of weeks ago was giving "sexy funeral vibes."

"I don't know, Harper."

"You don't have to be nice to me. I know I fucked up."

"This isn't your fault."

"Connor, Shawna . . . What's *wrong* with me."

"You see the good in people."

"I get taken advantage of."

I look into my glass. The half finger of Scotch I haven't downed yet is glowing under the bar lights. We're sitting at a mahogany bar on red stools reminiscent of the ones I met Connor on in Italy, and which were so accurately re-created in an early scene in the movie.

I'm not jet-lagged, but it feels like it.

I can only imagine what Harper's feeling.

"I should've seen it coming," she says.

"Why?"

"Because I'm the smart one, remember?"

I laugh, but it's true. "Even smart people make mistakes."

She tosses back part of her drink. "Maybe she *is* a Giuseppe. She was always apologizing. They grew up in Canada, right? That's where they shipped those girls after you and Connor exposed the dad. A fitting place for future criminals."

"Canada's not Australia."

"It might as well be in our lives."

"Okay, fair. But . . . apologies are not enough to equate to master criminal."

"Right. But wait, wait, wait . . . She speaks Italian. She does! I heard her tell Inspector Tucci to shut up in Italian. How does she know Italian?"

"Lots of people know Italian. You can't go around thinking everyone in your life is out to get you. It's okay to trust. It doesn't make you stupid."

"So *you* say. But why, though?"

"Why what?"

"Why seduce *me*?"

"I don't know. But she can't be a Giuseppe. It doesn't make sense. She must be involved somehow, but not because of that."

She rests her head on my shoulder. We sit there like that, under the muted lighting, breathing together as I count out the beats in my head.

After a moment, I feel calmer.

I doubt it makes a difference for her.

She's going to need time, but we don't have that much of it.

We need to solve this thing before the storm clears. Because I don't think I can just go back to my life with a murderer on the loose. Not again.

"What are you two doing out of your room?" Officer Anderson's voice sounds weary. One of her braids has started to come undone, and she looks exhausted. When I'm tired, I look old. But Officer Anderson looks like she's gone through one of those de-agers they use on *Star Wars* actors. She was in her mid-twenties when she started, but now she's just a kid.

"You'd be drinking if you were us, too," Harper mutters, then finishes her drink and motions to the bartender to bring her another.

Officer Anderson shakes her head but doesn't disagree. Instead, she pulls up a stool and sits on the other side of Harper.

I think about offering her a drink, but that would be bad form.

Police aren't supposed to drink on the job. Right?

Officer Anderson puts her elbows on the bar and sighs heavily.

"Tough day?" I say, and maybe I bury my sarcasm.

Maybe.

"This is my first assignment. I only started in the job last week. It's why I got stuck here when everyone else evac'd with the storm."

"Yikes."

"That's one way of putting it."

She eyes Harper's glass, but I'm not sure if it's because she wants what's in it or because she's worried about Harper.

"Any sign of Shawna?" I ask.

Officer Anderson frowns at herself in the mirror behind the bar. "No."

"What about her room?"

"She's not there."

Harper lifts her head. "I'm sure she's inside somewhere. It's dangerous out there."

"Rain is letting up a bit. Storm should be gone by morning."

There's a loud *CLAP* of thunder, as if the weather disagrees with her.

"That's what the weatherman's saying, anyway."[92]

"So, we're just supposed to wait till morning with a murderer on the loose?" Harper asks.

"It's not an ideal situation."

"You don't say."

"Did you find anything in her room?" I ask.

"She had several phones." She opens her satchel again and plunks three evidence bags down on the counter, each with a phone in it.

I recognize one of them. "That's Fred's burner phone." I point to the one in the middle. "The one that was missing after we found José's body."

"Interesting."

---

[92] Have you ever noticed that weatherman is the only job where you can be wrong every day and not get fired?

"That one's hers," Harper says, pointing to an iPhone in a black case with decals on the back. I look more closely. It's a sprig of lemons and a coastline that looks like the Amalfi Coast.

"How did she get this?" I say to Harper, pointing at it.

"What's the significance of the sticker?" Office Anderson asks.

"It's a promotional sticker for *Amalfi Made Me Do It.*"

"Your next book?"

"I gave it to her." Harper puts up a hand. "Don't say. Don't."

"I wasn't going to say anything."

"I can feel your thoughts. I had a box of them, and she asked for one, okay?" She picks up her drink and finishes it. "She said she was a fan."

"Maybe she is."

"No, she used me. For her sick plan."

There's nothing to say to that, so instead, I ask Officer Anderson if she found anything on the phone.

"It's locked. With a real password this time."

"I guess the techs will get into it."

"Hopefully."

"And what about this third one?" I point to the other phone, a larger Samsung device. "Have you seen that before, Harper?"

"No."

"Is it locked, too?"

"Yes." Officer Anderson picks it up as the screen flashes with an incoming text.

"What's it say?"

She tilts it toward me. It's a message from someone named Jim Post. *Tyler, why aren't you answering your*—and the rest of the message is cut off.

"That's a text to Tyler," I ask. "Why would Shawna be receiving texts to Tyler?"

"It must be his phone," Harper says, slurring her words a bit.

"No," Detective Anderson says. "His phone was confiscated when he was arrested."

"Cloned phone?" Harper says.

"Shawna cloned Tyler's phone?" I say. "That would explain the texts to José."

Officer Anderson flips the phone over slowly in her hand. "That's pretty sophisticated."

"Not really. I learned how to do it when I was doing research for one of El's books. Remember, El? It was child's play. Like, people believed *Connor* could do it, so . . ."

I stifle a snort. The alcohol's getting to me, too.

"So, Shawna cloned Tyler's phone and has Fred's burner . . . Looking pretty bad for her," I say.

"I agree," Officer Anderson says. "Plus, there's this." She pulls another evidence bag out of her satchel and places it on the bar. It's a copy of the *When in Rome* script with a white cover.

"It's normal that she'd have a copy of the script, isn't it?"

"Sure, but this one's got a bunch of words cut out."

"She cut the words for her note to Emma from the script of *When in Rome*? Jesus. That's not subtle."

"Murder rarely is."

"Are you quoting from something?"

She scrunches her face. "I'm not sure."

"Hmmm." I pull the evidence bag toward me. Something is off about this script.

Oh, the color!

This one is white. The cover of my script is green.[93]

I start to open the bag.

"What are you doing?" Officer Anderson grabs it away from me.

"I need to check something."

---

[93] Scripts have different cover colors during filming depending on the revision, starting with white (the color you start with on day one of shooting) and then blue, pink, yellow, green, all the way to cherry (ninth revision).

"You can't. It's evidence."

"It might be a clue, though."

"It *is* a clue."

"No, I mean to what's really going on. That's an older version of the script."

"So?"

"I'm not sure, it just feels significant."

Harper sighs and picks up her drink, but all that's left is ice. She rattles her glass at the bartender, but I shake my head *no*. She'll thank me in the morning.

"Shawna has the script," Harper says. "She has the burner phone. She's *missing*. It seems like case closed to me."

And then the thunder *CLAPS* again, the weather punctuation and underlining all at once.

WHEN IN ROME

ACT 3, SCENE 12

__INT. HOTEL HALLWAY - NIGHT__

Cecilia and Connor trip down the hallway, drunk and happy, their arms around each other.

They stop in front of his door. Connor pushes her up against the door and kisses her passionately.

> CONNOR
>
> You're amazing.

> CECILIA
>
> You're amazing.

> CONNOR
>
> We make a fantastic team.

> CECILIA
>
> I can't believe the capo had his son killed. Gianni didn't deserve that.

> CONNOR
>
> He was going to tell on him, I think. And don't let Italian charm fool you. Gianni was not someone to be trusted.

> CECILIA
>
> Yes, but still. Murder. It's so . . . final.

> CONNOR
>
> Loyalty is important. Especially to the Mafia.

> CECILIA
>
> Yes.

Connor kisses her again.

                    CONNOR
But now the case is over and we are free. We
should go to Monaco next. You're my lucky charm.

                    CECILIA
Don't spend that finder's fee all at once.

                    CONNOR
What's life without a little risk? Come with me?

                    CECILIA
I can't.

                    CONNOR
Why not?

                    CECILIA
I have to go back to real life.

Connor smirks at her seductively.

                    CONNOR
Living the high life in LA?

                    CECILIA
Something like that.

                    CONNOR
I'll persuade you.

He kisses her again, then reaches for the key in his
pocket and opens their door, pushing her inside.

INT. HOTEL ROOM - NIGHT

Cecilia and Connor are in bed. She wakes with a start
and sits up. <u>Something</u> is bothering her.

She gets up. Looks at Connor sleeping peacefully. She
slips on her robe and leaves the room.

INT. LIVING ROOM - NIGHT

Cecilia is going through the papers strewn all over the table—maps of the city with markers of where the robberies occurred. She stands over it, looking at it, searching for a pattern.

And then a phone that's resting on the table FLASHES with an incoming message.

She picks it up. It says ALLISON.

She glances back into the room where Connor is sleeping. He's still out. She enters his password.

There's a message in Signal—an encrypted app. She opens it and reads:

I'm expecting my cut of the finder's fee—wire it to the usual coordinates. Don't bring the girl to Monaco. Get rid of her.

Cecilia almost drops the phone. She's <u>horrified</u>. But there's more. There are other messages in the app. Messages from someone named GIANNI.

Her hands are shaking as she scrolls through to the older messages.

> *—GIANNI: We almost got caught last night. Pick a better location next time.*
> *—GIANNI: That bank is too close to the polizia.*
> *—GIANNI: I am not making enough for the risks I am taking.*
> *—GIANNI: I want 50% of the next job.*
> *—GIANNI: If you don't give me your share I'm telling my father that this was all YOUR idea.*
> *—GIANNI: This is your last warning. I'll tell my father tomorrow.*

She checks the date of the message—three days ago.

> CECILIA
> *(muttering)*
> Oh my God. Oh my God. Connor was behind it all.
> He and Allison were behind everything.

Cecilia puts down the phone. She has to get out of here.
She heads for the door of the suite, grabbing her clothes
from the floor as she goes.

> CONNOR
> And where do you think you're going?

CHAPTER 26

How Can You Sleep When the World Is Burning?

I put Harper to bed, muttering and drunk in a way I'm not sure I've ever seen her.[94] I leave water, a garbage can, and some Tylenol by her bedside. She'll be embarrassed and in pain in the morning, and if I could use some device to erase her memories, I would.

And yeah, I know there are consequences to doing that.

That's what the movies tell us, anyway. But I'm not so sure. If we could find a way to eliminate memories of our worst mistakes, wouldn't we all be better off?

But for now, Harper *is* forgetting. Because that's what sleep is. A way to shut out the day and live in another world. I'll let her do that for as long as she likes.

I close her door as quietly as I can and let out a long sigh.

"Is she okay?" Oliver asks.

He moves behind me and starts massaging my shoulders. I lean against his chest, and a large part of me wants to turn around and put

---

[94] Okay, maybe once when she was a teenager, but a drunk driver killed our parents. That puts a cap on alcohol consumption. Not that I don't indulge—you know this about me—but I never drive if I've had a glass of wine. And I'm always checking to make sure my consumption is reasonable overall. Please note all you've ever seen is me on <u>vacation</u>.

my mouth on his and end up in the bedroom, where we can't talk and can't remember either.

"She'll live," I say. "But she won't ever be the same."

"It's hard to believe . . . Shawna, of all people." I can feel Oliver's breath against my neck.

I turn around. Oliver's taken apart his bow tie, the ties loose around his neck, and undone the top buttons on his shirt. He looks tired and comfortable at the same time, like a rumpled bed you want to crawl into.

But I shake that impulse away because I can't let my guard down.

Not with Shawna on the loose.

"Did you lock the front door?"

"Yes. And I put the chain on and a chair under it for good measure. I'll keep watch."

"I'll do it with you."

I move away from him, walking to the window. It's rain-streaked. The ocean looks black. Or maybe all I'm looking at is the night, dark and menacing.

It occurs to me how very isolated we are here.

Because of course we are.

But even if we weren't, that doesn't matter.

One person with a determined plan can cause so much chaos whether it's dark out or not.

I know that better than most.

I pull the curtains closed.

"What did Officer Anderson tell you?" Oliver asks.

I catch him up on the details. What she found in Shawna's room. How Shawna's still missing. What it must mean for what's been happening. How there are still so many things that don't make sense.

"What's this about the script colors?" Oliver asks.

"The final script before you start shooting has a white cover. And then, every shooting day, we get sides—that's the pages that are being shot that day—with the call sheet. If there are any revisions, they give you those pages in the revision color so you can swap them out in your script. And then a new cover for the script with the new version number on it."

"Why do they do this?"

"No idea. But here, you can see my script."

I locate it in my bag and pull it out. It's got a green cover and the words "REVISION #5" written on it with a date from near the end of filming. I'm a bit anal about certain things, so I'd collated the new pages along with the old, which means my script is multicolored.

The cover page says that the script is co-written by David Liu and Simone Banerjee. I hadn't noticed it at the time, and Simone's name isn't on the script that was found in Shawna's room. This means Simone had to have changed at least 50 percent of the script since filming began. Which, now that I think about it, David mentioned before.

Is that relevant to this, though? It's not a crime to make changes to a script.

Only a book.

Ha.

"Remember what Harper said earlier about David?" Oliver asks. "About how he had hardly any credits?"

"You think it's relevant?"

"I'm not sure." Oliver rubs at his stubble. "This is all too familiar."

"I was thinking the same thing. You think he's involved in what's been happening?"

"Maybe, maybe not. But I don't think Shawna was working alone. She also doesn't have a motive. And she's too junior to have enough sway over what happened..."

"You think she was working for David?"

"She could be."

"Why?"

"Call it a hunch."

"Do you know something you're not telling me?"

"No," Oliver says. "But it feels like we're missing something. *Someone.*

You know how when you're working out the plot and you can't quite close the loop on the mystery?"

"Of course."[95]

"That's what this is like."

"You think there needs to be a third-act twist."

"Doesn't there?"

"I wish there wasn't. Maybe we should talk to David and find out."

"I'm sure Officer Anderson wants us to keep out of it."

"She does for sure." In fact, she'd said that very thing to me when I was getting Harper out of the bar. *Don't go investigating this yourself . . .*[96] "But I feel like we can get things out of people that she can't."

"Magical thinking."

"Is it? She doesn't know us. She doesn't know the personalities at work."

"Lucky her."

"And we *did* figure it out in Italy."

"Not before you almost died."

"True, but that was the drinking. I'm sharper than that now."

Oliver gives me a look because I've been drinking tonight, too.

"I'm not proposing going up on any tall buildings, just talking to David and Allison."

He puts a hand on my waist. "I worry about you."

"I'm glad." I pull in a deep breath.

"So we talk to David and Allison."

"Agreed. Should we go over there? Invite them here?"

"They're one room over," Oliver says. He points to a door in the wall. "Through there."

---

[95] I feel like that all the time. One of the downsides of being a pantser. But it <u>always</u> comes together in the end.

[96] That Officer Anderson would assume I'd follow her directions to stay out of it is either very naive or very trusting, neither of which are great qualities for a cop. Or a mystery writer.

"We have an adjoining room with a potential murderer?"

"I'd expect nothing less."

After a private moment where we pluck up our courage,[97] we knock on the door and Allison answers it after I tell her it's me.

She's dressed down in comfortable-looking sweats and a hoodie. David's in a pair of flannel pajamas. They look domestic and innocent and like we might've interrupted *them* in an intimate moment. I brush away my embarrassment as it occurs to me that we haven't examined Allison as a suspect.

If it's *Connor* who was the intended victim, that puts her in the hot seat. Maybe she got a taste of Connor almost dying in Italy and liked it. And the fact that he's still here, still in her life, was suddenly too much?

Of course that logic could apply to me, too.

Nothing's *really* changed since Italy, has it?

No, something *has* changed.

Things are better between us. We're bantering. We're working together without friction.

And it's ruining my life.

Okay, "ruining" is a big word. But it's definitely affecting me and Oliver. So it needs to stop. I need to put Connor in my rearview.

But not by killing him.

Besides, as you may have noticed, I'm not a long-term planner.

But Allison?

Allison *is*. She could've set all this up—I'm not sure how, exactly, but she has the *means* to do it. Means, motive, opportunity. She has the motive, too. Oh! Even more of one now that Connor just signed a huge book deal (!) because if he dies, the balance of her divorce settlement is due.[98] Before, it wasn't clear if he had enough money left to cover it, but now . . .

---

[97] No, we didn't have sex. That would have taken <u>too long</u>.

[98] I found this out in Italy.

high six figures just for the film rights. That's a lot of money. More than I can believe he got for his book. But never mind about that.

She has a motive.

And as for opportunity—she's been here the whole time. She was on set, too. She could've left the notes. She'd know about all of the ins and outs of production from David.

Wait, wait, wait . . . I've been thinking *David* was the one who seduced Allison, but what if it was the other way around? What if she saw that he was weak, and he was her way into the *When in Rome* production?

I mean, who auditions to play *themselves* in a movie?[99]

"What do you want, Eleanor?" Allison asks. "It's been a long day."

"Don't you want to know who did it?"

"It's Shawna, isn't it?"

"Is it?"

"What's that supposed to mean?" David says. "I don't like your tone."

"We don't think Shawna was behind it. Not exclusively."

Allison frowns. "Why do you think that?"

"Have you met Shawna?"

"She was acting, obviously."

"No one's that good of an actress."

Allison lifts her chin. "You don't know anything about it."

"Oh? Please tell me."

"What are you implying?"

"That maybe there's more than one good actress on this trip."

Allison stares at me for a moment, and then she throws her head back and laughs. "Oh my God, Eleanor. You know you're bad at this, don't you?"

"No, I'm not."

---

[99] Okay, John Malkovich in *Being John Malkovich*, but that movie was <u>cool</u>. And yeah, fine, Keanu Reeves did it, too. Whatever, you get my point.

"You are, though. You think *I'm* behind all of this? How could that possibly be true?"

"I haven't worked it out yet, but you have a motive, you have the means, and you had the opportunity."

"A motive to kill Emma and Fred?"

"No, Connor."

"I see. And I was in cahoots with Tyler to do this? I only met him a few weeks ago. And why would Tyler want to kill Connor?"

"Tyler was a red herring. Shawna had a cloned phone for him. He wasn't the one texting with José. *She* was."

"I don't even know what that is."

"Easy to say."

"Please. Is that all you have?"

I'm starting to get that desperate feeling when I know I'm right, but I can't explain why. "You're the one who did it in the script."

"Excuse me?"

"Like I said yesterday at the ropes course . . . The big twist. It was all a long con between Connor and Allison. They identified Cecilia as an heiress and targeted her to get her money. And they get away with it. Cecilia doesn't even find a way to get back at them."

I know, right? It's stupid. And it's not what happened in *When in Rome*, the book. But that's the movie we've been filming. At least I think it is. There have been so many changes along the way it's hard to keep track.

I may have . . . lost the plot.

And yes, I *have* been saving that one in my drafts folder for a while.

You know me that well by now, right?

"That's not how the movie ends."

"What?"

"You were there, Eleanor. Remember Shutters? Connor and Cecilia and their happy ending?"

My brain starts to whir. Allison's right. That's the scene we shot.

Cecilia and Connor clinking Champagne glasses, being all loved up at Shutters.

Am I losing my mind?

No.

I mean, yes, obviously, but not about this.

"Okay," I say, "but if that's true, how come you were there on Thursday? You were on the call sheet."

"That's for the alternative ending," David says.

"The *what*?"

"You know, sometimes they shoot two endings to a movie and see which one tests better."

"What's that got to do with anything?" Allison asks.

"Something, I think," Oliver says in a measured tone, but his voice is harder than it usually is, and this gets Allison's attention in a way my spinning theories hasn't.

"You think this is about the movie?"

"Not the way you mean, but . . . David, you wrote the script a long time ago, yes?"

David nods slowly. "Tyler hired me to write it when it was first optioned."

"And you'd worked with him before?"

"That's right. One credited script and a bunch of backroom rewrites."

"And then what happened?"

David gnaws at his bottom lip. "Hollywood."

"Fred?"

"That's right."

"Tell us."

"It's an old story, isn't it? Write a script, everyone gets excited, an actor comes in and tells you how much he loves it and how much he's going to make it happen, and then . . . poof, the project is dead."

"Was that Fred's fault?" I say.

David takes a beat. "He took another film. In fact, I believe he used the interest in him for this movie to parlay a better deal for himself on that film."

"Doesn't that sort of thing happen all the time?" Oliver says.

"Not to *friends.*"

I try to keep my face impassive. I doubt very highly that Fred was a friend. He's not the type to have friends in the lower classes of Hollywood.

"You got paid, though, didn't you?" I ask.

"Um, no." David laughs bitterly. "Have you never heard of development?"

"I know it can take a long time."

"Right, and if it's the beginning of your career or even the middle, it's often free."

"You wrote a whole script for free?"

"I did."

"Why?"

He makes a dismissive gesture. I should know this, he's saying. "Because Tyler was where my work was coming from. And Fred was involved. It was green-lit. It was happening. I'd get paid on the first day of principal photography."

"Which only happened a couple of months ago."

"Yes."

"You resent Tyler," I say.

"Wouldn't you?"

"And Fred?"

"Fred is a lightweight."

"And you don't like Emma," I say. "Because she got you turfed from the only other movie you've ever done."

"And you came back to this project," Oliver says. "Why?"

"I wanted to get paid."

"Where are you going with all of this?" Allison asks. "Why are you excavating David's career?"

"Because David has a motive," I say.

"For what?"

"To kill Fred and Emma and pin it on Tyler," Oliver says with a solid certainty.

Oh, how I love this man. I really don't want to lose him.

"I thought Connor was the intended victim?" Allison says.

"No, I don't think so."

"David didn't do it, Eleanor," Allison says.

"Why are you so sure?"

"Why would he? At this juncture? Right when he's finally getting the success he deserves? And sorry, darling, but planning isn't his strong suit."

"I don't think that's fair," David says.

"Are you trying to convince us that you *could* have planned this murder?"

"Well, no, of course not—"

"The point is," Allison says, "it would be counter to his interests to kill anyone right now, especially on the production. Assuming that killing someone is a reasonable or even possible response to Hollywood being Hollywood."

"She has a point," Oliver says.

I sigh. "I know."

"So what now?"

"It's obvious, isn't it?" David says.

"What's obvious?"

"Who's behind it all."

"Oh, really? Tell us then."

"It's Fred."

CHAPTER 27

If Someone Dies on Your Doorstep, Are They Giving You a Clue?

"Wait, *what?*" I say, my brain spinning like a top that might fall over at any minute.

"It's Fred," David repeats. "It must be."

"Why do you think that?" Oliver asks.

"Stands to reason. Means, motive, opportunity . . ."

My heart starts to race. "You're stealing my lines now?"

David is unfazed. "I thought you complained when I *didn't* use your words."

"Stop it, you two. Just explain, David," Allison says.

"I'm sorry, my dear. But Fred is definitely the prime suspect. He's the one who needs money. And he's marrying a rich woman who he stole from Tyler."

"That's not right," I say. "He didn't *steal* Emma. She's not a painting. And things were never serious between her and Tyler. Plus, it was over long before filming started."

Allison gives me a look. "Is that what she said?"

"What do you know?"

"Just what I've heard."

"Which is?"

"That it *was* serious. They were on and off for years. And then Fred came along . . ."

My stomach twists. Would Emma lie to me about her and Tyler? Then again, she didn't tell me about it in the first place. Not until she had to. But there are lots of things I haven't told Emma. That doesn't mean anything nefarious. It doesn't mean anything at all.

Besides, there's one important thing David hasn't thought of.

"Tyler isn't dead," I say. "So none of that matters."

David makes a dismissive gesture with his hand. "But he *is* in jail."

"What does Fred get out of that?"

"If Tyler is blamed for José's and Ken's deaths, he's not going to be focused on collecting on his debts, is he? And Fred rides off into the sunset with Emma. Who would think Fred *Winter* would kill anyone? It's kind of brilliant, really."

"Don't write the sequel *just* yet."

"You must admit it makes a certain amount of sense," Allison says.

I think it over. It does on the surface, but it doesn't explain another crucial detail.

Two.

"Why bring in Crazy Cathy?"

"To add to the suspect list. Emma knew about her, yes? She could have told Fred about her."

"Okay, but . . . what about Shawna? How does she fit in?"

David doesn't look concerned. "They planned it together."

"Fred and Shawna?"

"Yes."

"Why? How?"

"Maybe *she's* a red herring," Oliver says. "The thing that seems like it fits but doesn't."

"No. She's involved. So why would Fred bring her into this?"

"She's unobtrusive. No one notices her and she has access to every-thing."

"And *Fred* came up with this plan?" My voice can only be described as incredulous. "Does he strike you as a criminal mastermind?"

"No, but—"

"We should talk to Fred," Oliver says.

"Now you *want* to investigate?"

"Hey, now, I'm not the enemy."

"I'm sorry. But you were so against it earlier."

"We're here, aren't we? In for a penny . . ."[100,101]

We stare at each other, and I can't read his expression. But there's a sense of urgency emanating from him, and I feel it, too.

The solution is just out of reach.

We need to grab on to it while we still can.

"All right, let's go see them." I check outside. The rain finally seems to be letting up, but the wind is still howling. "We need to be careful. David, Allison, you should come with us. The more people we are, the less likely someone will try to harm us."

"Aren't we supposed to stay in our rooms?" David says.

"I don't personally have any desire to sit here and wait until a mur-derer comes knocking, you?"

"Why would the murderer knock?"

Lord preserve me from pedantic writers.

✻   ✻   ✻

---

[100] In for a penny, in for a pound. But why, though? You could just put the penny in, couldn't you?

[101] Oh, I see. It's about people without money. So if you owe a penny you might as well owe a pound. And apparently a synonym is "hanged for a sheep." Um, *what?*

I convince them to follow me to Emma and Fred's room, which is not far away as the crow flies.[102] It's still wet and very windy outside, but the worst of the storm seems to have passed us by. Some of the lights are out, so it's very dark, and we pick our way along the path quietly, our phone flashlights lighting our way.

"Where are you going?" a stern voice says when we're a couple of hundred yards away, startling us.

"Connor. Jesus. What are you doing out here?"

He steps out of the shadows. He's wearing a long black rain jacket, the kind of thing Dexter might've worn if he was committing a murder in a rainstorm. "I could ask you the same thing."

"You *did*," Allison points out.

"We're going to Fred and Emma's room, if you must know," Oliver says. "You?"

"Same."

"Why?" I ask.

"Because Fred did it."

"See," David says. "I told you."

"We're not taking *his* word for it," I say.

"Could you be making any more noise?"

"Harper?" She's standing there in a red rain jacket with a light illuminating her face like she's the villain in a horror movie. "I thought you were asleep."

"I *was*. And then you guys were banging around the room asking about candles and flashlights."

"Sorry."

"I'm used to it."

---

[102] I'm going to stop pointing out the origins of these kinds of expressions, but the English language truly is fascinating.

"Should we get a move on?" Connor says. "I, for one, do not want to get caught out here by Officer Anderson."

"He never did like authority," Allison says.

"Can you blame me?"

"*Yes.*"

"Enough of this," Oliver says. "Let's go."

We follow along behind him, tripping over branches and slipping on the wet path, but we make it to Fred and Emma's door without getting accosted. All the lights are on in their villa, so we don't need to worry about waking them up, even though it's almost midnight.

I get it.

It's not the kind of day when you tuck yourself in early.

And they got married today.

Shit. Somehow I lost track of that even though I just changed out of my bridesmaid dress.

Is Emma married to a murderer? That can't be right, can it?

Is her judgment that bad?

I mean, she did get involved with Tyler.

But we're all entitled to one mistake.

Or two. Whatever. Bygones.

Oliver knocks on the door and there's a long pause, and then Fred's voice. "Who is it?"

"Oliver and Eleanor . . . and just open up, Fred."

"Why?"

"We want to talk to you."

"What about?"

"It will be easier to explain inside," I say, coming up next to Oliver. I try to look through the peephole, but it just gives me a telescoped view of Fred's face. "Emma? You in there?"

"I'm here."

"Tell Fred to let us in."

"Fred, let them in, for God's sake. Oliver and El are not here to murder us."

"All right, hold on."

A chair scrapes back and then the bolts are turned and the chain rattles. The door opens slowly. Fred's still in his tux pants and shirt, but he's lost the jacket. "What's all this about? And . . . what are you all doing here?"

Oliver pushes open the door and walks inside, everyone following him. Emma's out of her wedding dress and is in the bathrobe she was wearing when we were doing her makeup earlier today. Her hair is down and her face is free of makeup.

"We wanted to talk to Fred," I say.

"Why?" Emma asks, but then she looks at our faces and she knows. "No, no, no. El. Fred didn't do it."

"Do what?" Fred says.

Is he the world's best actor or simply an innocent?

Why are those the only two possibilities?

"Kill Ken and José," Connor says.

"What? No. I didn't."

"You had the means and the opportunity," David says.

"What did I ever do to you?" Fred asks.

David shrugs his shoulders. "It's not about me."

"El?" Emma's eyes are pleading with me.

"He's in a lot of debt."

"But José?"

"His accomplice."

"And Ken?"

"A diversion." I think it over. "To make him look like the victim."

"I would *never* do that."

"Me thinks the lord doth protest too much," Connor says.

"It's 'The lady doth protest too much, methinks,' you dolt," Fred says. "*Hamlet.*"

"Does that mean you can't be a murderer? Just because you've memorized some Shakespeare?"

"You're the one working for Tyler. And I thought we'd decided Shawna was trying to kill *you*. You and *El*."

"I don't think so, Fred," I say.

Fred looks around desperately. "Emma, please. You're not buying this, are you?"

"I . . ."

"I love you," Fred says to Emma. "I do."

"I know."

"Oh!" Harper says.

"What?"

"I just thought of something . . . those texts. The texts on Fred's burner phone. The ones about meeting up at all those dates and times. Those could've been with *Shawna*."

Why didn't I think of that?

I take out my phone and pull up the photographs I made of the texts. "What's Shawna's number?"

She recites it from memory. It's the same number.

"I'm sorry, Harper."

Her eyes fill with tears.

"What are you talking about?" Fred says. "I never texted Shawna. *Never*."

"I have photographs of the texts, Fred. It's the same number."

Fred's shaking his head slowly from side to side, but the performance isn't convincing.

"Just tell us, Fred," Emma says, taking his hands.

"I didn't do it."

"You told me the texts were from an ex-girlfriend. Did you mean Shawna?"

"No, I told you who it was."

"But it's not her number."

"I don't know how to explain that. Someone must've tampered with the phone. I wasn't involved with Shawna. I'd never. I've barely even spoken to her."

"Then who, Fred? Who did you think you were texting?"

He meets Emma's eyes, and maybe he's going to say something, offer up some excuse, but before he can, there's a hard *KNOCK* against the door.

"What the hell?" Allison says. "Does *everyone* want to talk to Fred tonight?"

She reaches for the door and swings it open.

Shawna's standing there. Pale as a ghost and wet to the bone.

She takes a step into the room, then falls to the floor.

"Shawna!" Harper rushes to her, turning her over. There's a bloodstain blooming on her chest and she's gasping for breath. "Someone call for help!"

"There isn't anyone," Allison reminds her.

"Shawna, what happened? Who did this to you?"

"I . . ." Shawna gasps out. "I'm sorry."

"It's okay. It's okay. Just tell us."

Shawna's eyes pool with tears. "I . . . was . . ."

"Yes?"

"Doing . . . what . . . I . . . was . . . told . . ." Her head slumps to the side and the light goes out in her eyes, and there's no escaping it.

Shawna is dead.[103]

---

[103] Yes, a murder victim <u>did</u> just give a clue with her last words. Deal with it. I told you the chapter titles were rhetorical questions.

CHAPTER 28

Are You Near the End When the Third Murder Happens?

Harper is curled around Shawna's body, and it's in this moment that it occurs to me that there are so many secrets surrounding us that I don't know how I'll ever make it out of them.

I had no idea of the extent of Harper's relationship with Shawna, which is evident to everyone as pain streaks her face like tears.

But everyone here is hiding something.

Like Fred.

Like David, and how he really feels about Tyler and Fred and Emma.

Like Emma, and the true nature of her relationship with Tyler.

They're all woven together, but I can't figure out the pattern. There are other tensions, too, other threads I haven't figured out yet. Some connective tissue that brings all these disparate events and people together.

It's not just the movie—which seems to me to be the *occasion* of the crime rather than the purpose—but something deeper, something more sinister. Something that might make it seem okay to dispose of people like tissue paper.

"What did she say?" David asks. "After she said she was sorry?"

"Something about doing what she was told," Oliver says. He's standing behind Harper, looking ready to step in if necessary, just like he always is, but there's nothing anyone can do for Shawna anymore other than close her eyes and cover her with a sheet.

"Is she a Nazi?" Allison says.

"What?" I say.

"Doing what she was told? Isn't that what *they* said they were doing?"

"What is wrong with you?"

Allison shrugs in that way she has—like nothing serious will ever impact her that deeply. Like she can brush off life like it's dandruff on her shoulder.

"She's just a lost kid."

Harper looks up at me. Now the tears have come, shining on her face that is so like mine, but so different, too. "It was because of you and Connor. That's why this happened."

Her words hit me like a slap, but I understand where they're coming from.

After all, I was just blaming myself for this very thing.

"No, Harper," Oliver says, as always coming to my rescue. "No."

I've never seen Harper like this. She almost looks dangerous.

She wheels on me. "And *you* protected him . . . The two of you together. *You* did this."

I glance at Connor. For once, he doesn't look like he has anything to say. And I'm at a loss for words, too. Because she's right. Shawna wouldn't be here if it weren't for Connor and me.

None of us would.

"Harper, please . . ."

Harper's breathing hitches, and she lets out a wail of grief. It's a horrible sound, one that sends a chill through the room, freezing everyone to the spot.

We are terrible with grief, with wounds.

No one ever knows the right thing to say.

But I have to say something. I have to *do* something.

I inch toward Harper, then bend down and wrap my arms around her, pulling her up and away from the body. The front of her shirt is stained with blood, and the air is filling with that horrible metallic smell.

I turn her so she's facing me. "I know you're upset. But this isn't my fault or Connor's. Shawna *chose* to be here, to be involved in whatever's going on. That was *her* decision."

Harper won't look at me.

"Look at me, Harper. Listen to me." She turns her face. Her eyes are red and puffy, the tears falling in large wet beads. "Someone else did this to her. And we're going to find out who it was."

"I should've seen through her."

"No. This isn't your fault. And you can blame me if you want, if that's easier, but it isn't anyone's fault but hers. Shawna and whoever she was working with. They're the ones to blame. *Them.*"

"It hurts."

"I know."

Her body's shaking now, the shock setting in. "Why does this keep happening?"

"I don't know."

"I'm scared."

"Me too. But we're safe here. We're safe, and we're going to get Officer Anderson to come, and we're going to figure out what's going on before anyone else gets hurt."

"You can't promise that."

"I *am* promising that. This has to stop. It's going to stop."

I'm not sure who I'm speaking to, but it feels like someone.

Instinct drives me to focus on Fred. He's standing next to Emma with his hands by his side. Not comforting her, I notice. She has her arms wrapped around her waist, and part of me hates Fred because even if he's not behind all of this, he should be thinking of her in this moment.

Helping her.

"This has to stop," I say.

Fred puts his hands out in front of him, but he doesn't say anything.

My suspicion builds in me like a head of steam.

Was he working with Shawna?

He had to be because of the texts.

The texts with all those dates and times and instructions to meet.

No, orders.

Is that what Shawna meant? That Fred was the one she was taking orders from?

Is that why she came to *this* room?

His room.

But why? To warn him they were about to be discovered? To ask for his help to extricate herself? To complete the plan?

Or was she hiding on the property, hoping to escape, and then ... someone got to her first and this was the first room she could get to?

Did Fred get to her first?

But that can't be because Fred was here. Fred was here when someone was killing Shawna. So if he's involved, he can't be the only one.

The room is eerily silent, only the questions loud in my head.[104] But maybe everyone else is thinking this way, too?

I search the room until I find Oliver. A moment of eye contact un-sticks him from his place.

He crosses to the room's phone and picks up the receiver.

"What are you doing?" I ask.

"Calling Mr. Prentice so he can locate Officer Anderson."

"Good idea."

As he makes his call, I walk Harper away from the body and sit her down on the couch. I can feel Fred's eyes on me as I do it, but I don't get any sense of danger from him.

Still, I have to ask.

---

[104] Did you know that some people don't have an internal monologue? Like they don't hear thoughts in their heads at all? It must be so quiet. I'm all internal monologue.

"Was he here all night?" I ask Emma. "Fred?"

"What? Yes."

"Are you sure? You didn't fall asleep?"

"No. We came back here when Officer Anderson told us to, and we were talking until you showed up."

"What about when you took off your dress?"

"I did that alone. And took a quick shower . . . But it was only a few minutes."

"I didn't kill Shawna," Fred says. "How would I have even known where she was?" He's speaking in that half-British accent he puts on when he's being theatrical. It's a bad tell.

"But you're involved in this. You have to be."

"Why?" Allison asks.

"Because of the texts on his phone. The phone no one knew he had."

Fred clamps his jaw again and I realize my mistake. Others *did* know he had that phone. Tyler. José. Shawna.

Who else?

Just because there weren't texts with anyone else doesn't mean he didn't send them.

Texts can be erased.[105]

Oliver hangs up, and it's only a moment before Officer Anderson is at the door.

She's not alone.

She's followed by Simone and Inspector Tucci. They've both changed out of their wedding clothes, Simone into one of her sets of coveralls and Tucci into what looks like flannel pajamas with a British hunting jacket over them.

---

[105] It's actually very hard to erase texts. That's what a law enforcement official told me when I talked to him for research purposes. Also, he was cute. Whatever. So not the point right now. All I'm saying is when you think you've hidden what you've done, you're probably wrong. Everything leaves a trace.

Officer Anderson takes in the scene, then drops to the floor to check the body, but it's obvious to all of us that Shawna is dead. She slips on a pair of gloves and pulls Shawna's coat back. She's still wearing the suit she wore to the wedding, but the white shirt is red now, caked thick, and it's hard to see where the origin of the blood is.

But if I had to guess, I'd say it's coming from her heart.

"Was she stabbed?" I ask because it doesn't look like a gunshot wound.

And also: I want to know if someone on this island has a gun.

Besides Officer Anderson, that is.

"I think so. But the lab techs will have to determine that. When they can get here."

I shudder. *Two* stabbings and a broken neck. This killer gets up close to their victim and then strikes. These aren't stranger murders. They're committed by someone who instills trust and confidence.

"Any idea how long ago it was done?" Oliver asks.

"It looks like she's lost a lot of blood. Theoretically, it could've been hours ago."

Oliver goes into the bedroom and returns with a sheet. He unfolds it and drapes it over Shawna as we watch him.

Officer Anderson's words ring in my head. Shawna could have been stabbed *hours ago*. And who knows where Shawna has been since she escaped during the blackout.

We were last all together at one in the morning. It's now three a.m. That leaves two hours unaccounted for.

I know where I was—with Harper and then with Oliver.

Oliver was alone for part of the time, but if there's someone here I know isn't involved, it's him.[106]

David and Allison were in their room when we got there. But that leaves at least an hour unaccounted for. I assume they were together, but

---

[106] This is <u>not</u> my way of telling you it's him.

I don't know that. Then again, Allison made a mistake last time, in Italy. She kept a crucial piece of information to herself, and I almost died for it.

"Allison, where were you and David?"

"In our room, where you found us."

"You sure? Neither of you left?"

"Yes, I'm sure."

"Unless you're working together," Oliver says.

"That could go for all of us," Allison points out. "We all have alibis in twos and threes."

"A conspiracy of murder," David says.

"That sounds like one of those book titles generated by AI."

"What I want to know," Oliver says, "is why Shawna was coming here. To this room."

"I had the same question," I say. "And what are you doing here, Simone? And you, Tucci? Where have *you* been?"

"I was with Officer Anderson," Simone says.

"Why?"

She gives me a contemptuous glare. "She was questioning me."

"And you, Tucci?"

Inspector Tucci runs his hand over his head, spraying out water as he goes. "I was investigating."

"Give me a break," Simone says.

"As I have been telling you since the beginning, I am a trained detective. I can help solve this murder. And the others, too." I try to cut him off, but he puts up his hand. "As you were saying, Shawna came to see Fred and Emma before she died. She must've done that for a reason. Did she say anything? The victim usually says something before they die. Or perhaps she had something clutched in her hand?"

I take in a slow breath. Tucci's like a child bashing around on a piano. Every once in a while, he hits on something that sounds like a tune.

"There wasn't anything in her hand," I say, even though I didn't check. But she was waving her hands around when she came in and they were empty. "She did speak, though only to say she was sorry. And that she was doing what she was told."

"I can't believe *you're* going along with him, of all people," Simone says.

Inspector Tucci ignores her. "Ah, well, now, that is *very* interesting indeed." He looks at Emma. "She was coming to see you, wasn't she?"

"What? No."

"It makes sense, of course."

"How?" Emma says.

"The least likely suspect."

"Seriously?" I say. "Simone's right, you're a nut."

He gazes at me. "Isn't that what you write in your books? You go through all of the suspects starting with the most obvious to the least likely, and that's the one that it is."

This is *exactly* what I do.

Not like I'm the only one. It's a common technique.

But being called out by Inspector Tucci about it?

Do not recommend.

"What has that got to do with anything?" Harper asks. "Are you getting to some point? Because Shawna is dead right there on the floor, if you didn't notice?"

Inspector Tucci is not deterred. "This is a play." He puts his hand out in front of him in a sweeping gesture. "All a performance."

"Tucci, I swear to God," Simone growls.

"No, let him talk," Oliver says. "What's your theory?"

"We have been behind the killer the entire time. A new clue, a new misdirection, a new victim seem to happen right when we think we are figuring it out . . . But what ties them all together? What is the connective tissue?" He looks around us as if it should be obvious. "It's Emma."

"What?" Emma says. "Me?"

"Yes, you. Where did this all begin?"

"With the movie," Connor says. "*When in Rome.*"

"No, it was before. Long before." He sweeps his hands in front of him, then forms a square like he's directing the scene. "A love affair gone wrong."

"What are you talking about? Fred and I only got together on set."

"You and Tyler. I have watched you all this time, young lady. I have observed and noted, and it is clear you are not being truthful about that relationship."

Emma rolls her eyes. "Give me a break."

"It is true. You claim now that it was not serious, yes? That your heart was never involved. But I saw the way you looked at him. How your eyes followed him around the room and would not let him go."

Emma starts to laugh. "So I'm in love with Tyler, but I married Fred? Why would I do that?"

"To make him jealous."

"What?"

"That was your original intention. Perhaps you took it too far. Perhaps you fell in love with Fred and changed your mind about the whole thing. I cannot fathom your actions."

"That doesn't make sense, Tucci," I say.

"Which part?"

"You're saying Emma was in love with Tyler, so she took up with Fred to make him jealous and then, when that didn't work, she decided to try to kill him at her wedding?"

"Precisely."

"You've lost me."

"Me too," Allison says.

"Me three," Oliver adds.

"Spell it out," Officer Anderson says. "From the beginning."

"I don't have all the details, I grant you. But when Tyler rebuffed her attempts to reunite, she decided to use Fred to get back at him. Make him jealous. Win back his heart. And when that didn't work, she decided to get revenge. To lure everyone here under the guise of a wedding and to kill Tyler."

"And instead, I killed José and Ken and Shawna?" Emma says.

"They were your accomplices. Your decoys. No one would suspect the bride. It was the perfect plan."

"Is anyone buying this?" Emma says. "Because this is the worst script I've ever heard of."

My head is spinning trying to follow Tucci's logic, but that word stops me: "script."

The *script*.

Tucci is right about one thing.

This *was* all scripted.

It still is.

"You're not making sense, Tucci," Connor says. "You haven't explained half of what you've said, only made vague assertions without any evidence. You're as incompetent as the original."

Inspector Tucci puffs out his chest. "I'll have you know that—"

"I agree," Officer Anderson says. "Your theory leaves too many unanswered questions. Shawna, for example. We haven't uncovered any connection between her and Emma except for a superficial one."

"She was working for her, as I said. Like *Shawna* said. She was just doing what she was told."

Oh, *shit*.

Tucci's right. Again.

He's right.

Not about Emma. That part is stupid, and as Emma herself just said, the worst script ever.

But Shawna *was* doing what she was told. The whole time. The whole movie.

She was taking orders from one person.

Simone.

CHAPTER 29

Have We Gotten to the Least Likely Suspect Yet?

"That's it," I say.

Emma turns on me with hurt in her eyes and a layer of disbelief. "You think *I* did it?"

"No, that's ridiculous. You're not capable of murder."

"Gee, thanks."

"I didn't mean it that way. It was a compliment."

"What are you talking about, Eleanor?" Simone asks, her contempt for me as evident as always.

And I should've seen it. I should've known. The least likely suspect, standing in front of me the whole time. Almost begging me to call her out.

And maybe that's what her antipathy is about?

A shield from my eventual accusations?

But no. *No.* She's too arrogant for that. She never thought I'd catch her. She had to be sure of that. Because that's what murder really is.

Arrogance.

I have to find a way to stop her.

But I can't just accuse her like Tucci's done with Emma. I have to have evidence. I need to make sure.

"What's your problem with me, Simone?"

She flicks her hand up. "Let me count the ways."

"No, tell me. Tell me what it was that I did to you that made you hate me so much."

Her eyes narrow. "You truly don't remember? This isn't some act?"

"I'm not an actor."

"Unbelievable."

"What did I do?"

She pauses, maybe for dramatic effect, and maybe because she can't quite believe that she has to tell me. "Aiden."

Aiden. *Aiden.*

Oh my God, Aiden.

This is *actually* about a boy?

I was eighteen and it was the end of high school. It was a few months after my parents died. I was taking care of fifteen-year-old Harper and, if I'm being honest, already resenting it.

It felt like all my dreams had been ripped away. I was supposed to be going to New York in the fall with Emma. We'd both gotten into the acting program at Tisch. But that was all on hold. I was stuck in Venice Beach, temping at my father's advertising agency, a grown-up before my time.

I needed to do something. Anything that felt like the old, irresponsible me.

So I went to a party in the Valley with Emma.

A night for myself, I'd said.

One night where I could make stupid mistakes and be a teenager before Emma left and I settled into being an adult for real.

Aiden was the cool guy in our class in high school, the one everyone wanted. Six feet. Blond. Baseball team. You can imagine him, can't you? Every high school has one.

I'd always crushed on him from afar—we didn't run in the same circles. I knew he and Simone had been a thing at some point, but were they still together that night? They weren't acting like it. I mean, *he* wasn't. I don't remember if she was there.

I just remember tossing back a drink and walking toward him while a slow smile played on his lips because he'd been watching me all night. Tracking me.

All I knew was I'd been chosen and I wasn't going to say no.

We hooked up. You can imagine it.

The next morning, I collected my things from the floor of his room and snuck out of his house before anyone else was awake.

I wasn't ashamed. I was *proud* of myself. But I knew it didn't mean anything. Not to him or to me. In fact, we never spoke again.

"Eleanor?" Emma asks. "What's going on?"

"I slept with Simone's boyfriend."

"Recently?" Her eyes track to Oliver.

"Right after high school. You remember that party in the Valley?"

"There were many."

"Maybe for you," I say. "But I only went to one."

I can almost see her reach back into her memory and fix on it.

"That's right," she says. "You did."

I turn to Simone. Her face is flushed with rage. "That can't be it," I say.

"That can't be what?"

"One mistake when I was eighteen with some guy I didn't even know you were with. That can't be the reason all of this is happening."

"You always think everything is about you," Simone said.

"I mean, we're in the movie about my book, so . . ."

"You don't know *anything.*"

"I've been slow, I grant you . . . but I'm putting it together now."

"What are you talking about, Eleanor?" Connor asks.

"It's Simone. The one Shawna's been taking orders from. That's what Shawna meant. *She's* the one in charge. The one behind it all. *Directing* it all."

"Do you have any evidence of this?" Officer Anderson asks.

"It's been right in front of us the whole time."

"What has?" Emma asks.

"The original ending of the movie—it was that Allison was in on it with Connor. It was all a scam to defraud Cecilia of her inheritance. That's why Connor seduced her and involved her in his investigation. But that wasn't the ending that was shot. Instead, it was Connor and Cecilia all loved up because of the rewrites by Simone, right, David?"

He nods in response.

"What's all this about?" Harper asks.

"The script for *When in Rome*. The one *Simone* rewrote enough to get partial credit for. It's what must've given her the idea. But then she needed to cover her tracks. That's why she made the changes. Not to make it better but to hide what the plan was." I turn to David. "When did Simone start rewriting the script?"

"In pre-production. She pitched me the new ending; I didn't really have a say."

"So that's what this is about." I look at Officer Anderson. "It's the oldest motive in the book: money."

"Isn't that what *I* said?" Inspector Tucci says.

"Whose money?" Harper asks.

"Emma's."

"But then, that would mean . . ."

"Yes."

"Mean what?" Emma asks.

I meet her eyes and try to convey something that I can't. Because I'm not an actor.

He is.

"I'm sorry, Em."

"Sorry for what?"

"It *was* Fred. Fred and Simone."

"*What?*"

There's a cacophony of voices. I'm not even sure who's speaking.

But it's clear in my mind. Finally.

I turn to Simone, who's standing stock-still. "You were bailing him out, weren't you? It wasn't your idea, it was *Fred's*. This is all his fault. *He* owed money to Tyler and didn't have a way out. He had to make the movie to pay back his debt. And then he brought you on as the director as, what? An apology?"

Simone's chin lifts. "I deserved the job."

"Of course you did. But you've been in the wilderness for years, just like David. This was your shot. He probably didn't even tell you about his plan to seduce Emma and marry her for her money at first."

"He did *not*."

"Of course he didn't. He thinks he's smarter than he is. But nothing he does ever fixes anything. It only makes it worse." I pause, waiting for her to say something more.

I don't even search for Fred in the room, but I can feel him backing away from us.

Only there's nowhere to go.

"And then what happened?" I say, working it out aloud. "He went and fell for Emma for real, didn't he? He left you for her. He was going to get his cake and eat it, too, and leave you out of it. After everything you did for him."

"Fred?" Emma says. "What's she talking about? Is this . . . Is this true?"

And now we all turn to look at him. He seems smaller than he did a few minutes ago, like the key light he's usually standing under has been dimmed.

"Of course not, darling, I promise. I love you." His voice sounds hollow. "That's the only thing she's said that's true. I fell in love with you, I did."

"And her?" Emma's hand rises and points toward Simone.

"She's nothing to me."

Simone winces.

"But you were with her ... You told me it was casual, but you lied. And your mother. Your mother hates Simone. She wouldn't hate just some random girl you'd been with. She wouldn't accuse her of murder." Emma's head shakes slowly from side to side. "Is *she* the ex? The ex who was texting you? The one you couldn't let anyone know about?"

"No."

"I don't believe you." Emma slides down to the floor, her knees catching her in a deep bend. "Oh my God. Oh my God. You were going to kill me, weren't you?"

Bile rises in my throat because it's sickening, that thought. But also, it must be true.

"I would never do that."

"But you'd have to. We signed a prenup. If we got divorced, you wouldn't get anything. But if I die ... if I die, then you get *everything*."

"Oldest motive in the book."

"Shut up, Tucci!"

"You were going to kill me." Emma's swaying on her heels now, still crouched. Maybe she feels safer, closer to the ground.

She needs help.

Fred isn't helping her.

That motherfucker.

"You were going to kill me," Emma says again, popping up, her voice stronger, but her face so pale I think she might faint.

"I ... no ..."

"Perhaps we should go somewhere private to talk," Officer Anderson says to Fred.

"You don't have any evidence," Fred says, just like an *innocent* person. Ha ha.

This isn't a laughing matter, but his response is laughable.

And now I *can* help Emma.

Because Fred is wrong.

"There is," I say. "I can prove you were communicating with Simone. That she's the one you were meeting with." I pull my phone out and dial the number I can visualize from the texts I've read over too many times.

There's a pause, and then a phone starts to ring. It's coming from Simone.

"What does that prove?" Fred says as Simone reaches into her pocket and silences it.

"That's the number on your burner phone. The one you were arranging all those meetings with. Not Shawna. *Simone.*"

"But Shawna had the phone with that number," Harper says. "That's the number I called for Shawna."

"Simone cloned Shawna's phone," I say. "Just like Tyler's. She probably needed Shawna to be able to communicate with Fred if necessary. And if Emma found Fred's phone, then it wouldn't trace back to her."

I press dial again. Again it rings.

"Will you stop that," Simone says.

"Take out your phone."

"No."

"It doesn't matter. We all know it's you."

"Do we?"

"You're the only one who could've pulled it off. You were in charge of everything. And you were the one scaring Emma with those notes. You wanted them to call off the wedding."

Simone pauses, her eyes narrowing. Then, "Why would I do that if this is about getting Emma's money?"

"It was all about money for *him.* But you? Look how hard you love. You're still mad about some stupid boy I slept with in high school. And that must've made it all the sweeter, right? The fact that it was *my* movie. Duping *my* best friend."

"I already told you. This isn't about *you.*"

"No, it's about José and Ken and Shawna. Why did you kill José? Was he going to tell on you? Tell everyone Fred had him set up that potential electrocution at the pools?" I stop, remembering. "Fred told Emma to go there. Remember, Emma? He said you should go and have a soak."

Emma blinks rapidly. "He did."

"He called and told you Emma was going there, right, Simone? When he was going to the ferry to meet his parents. That's why you came to the pools? To, what, supervise?"

"This is ridiculous," Simone says.

"Was it you or Fred who killed José? Breaking a grown man's neck . . . It must have been Fred. He must've asked José to meet him at the ropes course. He killed him and rigged the course so it would seem like an accident. That's why I fell through it.

"And then he sent himself that text to meet José in the basement from José's phone. He erased the other texts between them. And then he dropped the phone by accident and couldn't find it because he didn't have his phone. And then you must've hit him on the head in the basement to make it look realistic." I shake my head at myself. "It was an *alibi*. To make us think José was still alive long after he was dead."

"And Ken?" Oliver says. "Why Ken?"

"Because he looks so much like Fred. If Fred was the victim, then he couldn't also be the murderer. Easy enough for him to slip away for a minute and do it. His prints were already on the knife from cutting the cake. And Ken trusted him. He'd go anywhere with him."

"And Shawna?"

"That was Simone, it must've been. She was coming here to tell Emma everything." I turn back to Simone. "So you stabbed her before she could get here. But you must've gotten a bit sloppy because she didn't die. She made it here anyway." I wait. "Nothing to say, Simone?"

"I'm not some villain in a bad movie. You have zero evidence of any of this, and when we get back to the mainland, I'll be speaking exclusively to my lawyer."

"In the meantime, the phone will be enough to hold you. You and Fred, right, Officer Anderson?"

"I have *nothing* to do with this," Fred says. "I would never be with *her*."

"Fuck you, Fred," Simone says in a whisper, and her breaking heart is plain for all to see. "I am *not* taking the fall for you."

They stare at each other, and it's impossible to know what's passing unsaid between them. But then Simone shakes her head slightly from side to side, her eyes narrowing, some plot forming.

I see it. Fred sees it.

And now *Fred* is scared. "I'll confess, Officer Anderson. She *did* want me to marry Emma for the money. But not to kill her. If we were married, I'd have access to it, prenup or not. Resources. Credit. *She's* the one who killed José. And Shawna. And Ken. She never told me half of what she was doing—"

"Stop it. Stop, stop, *stop*. You . . . This was my one shot. My one chance to prove myself, and you just threw it away. Because you're Fred Winter! You always land on your feet. Even when you were stupid enough to lose all that money. Tyler was never going to do anything to you. That's what you never understood." She clamps her jaw shut.

"As I was saying—"

"Shut up, Tucci!" half of us say together.

Not Emma. Not Harper. Not Fred. Not Simone.

The victims and the perpetrators.

They're silent, locked in this tragedy together, everything changed forever.

I know the feeling, but I'm apart from it.

The hurt doesn't touch me the way it touches them.

And I can't even feel the satisfaction of solving it because I didn't want to know this.

I wish it weren't true.

Officer Anderson takes out a set of zip ties and walks toward Fred. It feels like it's happening in slow motion, this big dramatic rise to one more moment before the curtain falls.

CRASH!

The door slams open and the wind howls as Mr. and Mrs. Winter burst in through the door. Mrs. Winter stops as her eyes sweep the room, her cheeks two high spots of color. "What is happening? Where are you taking my son?"

"Mrs. Winter, please calm down," Emma says.

"No, I will *not* calm down! That Mr. Prentice told me that there was a body found in your room and I thought . . . I thought . . ." She glances at Shawna's body on the floor, covered by a sheet. "What is happening, Fred? Tell me at once."

"Just leave it, Mother."

"I will not." Mrs. Winter looks around the room desperately as her eyes come to light on Simone. "Is this because of *you*? It is, isn't it? I told him and told him to stay away from you. That you were nothing but trouble. But did he listen to me? No, no, he never has."

Simone just stares at her. "Your son did this on his own."

"I doubt that very highly."

"Why, Mother? Because I'm not smart enough? That's what you think, isn't it? Fred's the handsome one, not the smart one. Fred takes after his father. Fred isn't meant for academics. Fred only got that Oscar because it was a weak field."

"I never said any of those things."

"Yes, you *did*."

"So it's my fault? All of this?" She points dramatically at poor Shawna on the ground, covered by a sheet, the blood easing out of it and staining the floor.

"Just be quiet, Mother. For once in your life."

Mrs. Winter's hand goes to her heart and she falls back dramatically onto Mr. Winter, and I have a moment where I think that maybe she's had a heart attack, but no.

Mr. Winter catches her with a practiced hand and rights her as Officer Anderson puts the zip ties around Fred's wrists and pulls them tight.

There's a minute of silence while the storm gathers outside for one last fight, slamming against the windows like a lung that inhales and exhales.

The building shakes, then settles.

No one knows what to say.

Well, not *no one*.

"So, this had nothing to do with me?" Connor says.

Some people never change.

CHAPTER 30

Is Anyone Going to Get a Hollywood Ending?

There was no sleep after that.

—Three people dead.

—A broken marriage.

—A broken heart. No, three.

But even though Emma does love Fred, I think she'll find in time it wasn't a lasting love. Not one that could've sustained them past the bubble of the movie.

She'll never know. He might've had real feelings, or he might've been acting. She'll wonder about that, too. She'll blame herself and say that she should've seen it. Seen through his veneer and her old crush and found the very heart of him.

I understand how she's going to feel because I feel guilty, too.

I always thought one of the good things about being a writer is that you have insight into people. A kind of antennae for motivations and wants. Because you have to put yourself in everyone's shoes. You have to feel the darkness and imagine what could bring someone there. Even if you're not writing about yourself—and I never really was, only a shadow on the wall with better hair and better decisions—you have to make it feel like you are. You have to make your readers believe that you feel what your character feels.

Writing *is* acting.

But I wasn't thinking about that when I was spending hours on set with headphones around my neck, sitting in a chair marked WRITER.

I was thinking—this is cool.

I was pissed at the changes in the story.

I was wrapped up in myself, so I never saw this coming.

Murder times three.

"Do you think they'll confess?" Oliver asks me. We're standing on the balcony of our villa, looking out at the ocean. It's early, the sun just rising, and the storm has finally passed.

The literal storm, not the theoretical one.

Is there a difference at this point?

"Does it matter?" I say, then lean my head against his shoulder. He feels warm, and I'm cold inside.

Something in me feels dead.

Maybe it's my optimism.

That things will work out. That there's a solution just around the corner.

But don't worry. I've already told you I don't feel things for nearly as long as I should.

"I would've thought you'd want to know how it all came together," Oliver says.

"Right?"

"So, why don't you?"

"I'm tired. Three people are dead. Harper's heart is broken. Take your pick."

"And Emma's?"

"Hers, too."

He squeezes me to him and we stare at the surf. It's high, the waves crashing into the bay. Gulls are squealing and circling above the water, diving in, looking for something. Food, I guess. You can't fish during a hurricane. They must be hungry.

"You know," I say, "I'm starting to have met an awful lot of murderers."

"All the way back to high school."

"She was so popular in high school. How did she get from that to murder?"

"A lot of attention is never good for anyone."

I smile. "I've always thought there were two kinds of people. Those who want to go back to high school and those who don't."

"And which are you?"

"High school was a nightmare."[107]

"So, no high school then?"

"Oh, no, I'd go back."

He bursts out laughing. "Why?"

"Look at what I've accomplished. Those bitches would be jealous."

"What bitches?"

"All the bitches who told me I wasn't pretty enough or thin enough or smart enough."

He frowns. "They said that?"

"It was implied."

"Hmmm." He plants a soft kiss on my forehead. "This mess is quite the story."

"How would you write it?"

His mouth twists. "Your next book?"

"I do owe them a manuscript." I touch his hand. "Tell me."

"I think Simone was one of those girls to Fred—the ones who are there when you need them but that you can never admit you're with in public."

"A hidden girl," I say.

"Yeah."

"You never did that, right?"

---

[107] I like "So High School," though. Taylor and Travis 4Ever.

"No."

"Good." I run my hand on his cheek. It's scratchy with stubble. "Go on."

"So they have this on-again, off-again thing. Enough for her to know his parents and for them to disapprove. She has real feelings. He doesn't. They break up, and then he goes on and becomes a huge star. But he keeps her around. Because she's normal to him. He knows she wants to be with him because of him, not who he is."

"Men think like that?"

"They do."

"Noted."

"Years go by. Fred makes some stupid decisions, loses his money, gets in a fight with Tyler, and is feeling pretty desperate. And then Italy happened," Oliver says. "It was all over the news. And the book was back on the bestseller list."

"And Tyler owned the rights."

"Tyler *and* Fred."

"Who suggested they make the movie to make them square?" I ask.

"Fred. He saw it as the solution to all of his problems. He also suggested they hire Emma, aware of her long-standing crush, and then he moved in. It was all laid out for him in the script."

"And Simone?"

"They wanted to make the movie quickly. She was available . . ."

"When did she discover his plan?"

"Maybe she always knew."

"I don't think so. I don't like her, but Simone wouldn't see murder as a solution. In an emergency, yes. But not more than that."

"You know her better than I do."

"I guess." I hug myself. "There's still something missing. I can't put my finger on it." I think it over. "Who was tweeting? And what about the murder on the schedule . . . If the plan was to kill Emma, why signal it? Why put her on her guard?"

"To divert suspicion away from Fred?"

"Maybe? Anything else?"

"I can't figure out how the cat plays into all of this," Oliver says.

"Maybe Fred put something in his mother's food to make it taste bad?"

"Why, though?"

"Was he . . . trying to kill his mother? Who inherits when she dies? God, I didn't even think of that." I bite my lip. "Or it could have just been to create generalized suspicion? To feed the narrative that there was a killer out there to divert suspicion away from Fred?"

"Is that what the electrocution was?"

"It must've been . . . because that was *before* the wedding . . . If Emma died then, Fred wouldn't inherit anything, right? Wait, no. That's not right. Emma said they had already changed their wills . . . when they went to sign the prenup. So it didn't matter when Emma died. Only that she did. Ugh."

Oliver frowns. "You really want to write this?"

"What if we write it together?"

"Is this a pity invite?"

"It's a love invite. I want to be tied to you forever."

"Like Connor?"

I wince, but I deserve that. I take a step toward him and wind my arms around his neck. "No, not like that. Not like that at all."

"Vicki isn't expecting a book from two of us."

"She'll get over it. Besides, she'll be busy editing *Connor*."

"I did *not* see that coming."

"Right?" I kiss him. "So, what do we call it?"

"How about *I Went to Hollywood and All I Got Was This Lousy Murder*?"

"Um, we'll work on that. But we make a good team."

He pulls me closer. "We do."

"So you'll do it?"

"What's the worst that could happen?"

"I thought we promised we'd never say that to each other again?"

He smiles. "I'm feeling reckless."

"I'll say."

"I will promise you one thing."

"Oh, yeah?"

He brushes his lips against mine. "The ending will surprise you."

I kiss him back. "Good."

And if this were some other kind of book, I'd cue the rising music—maybe "Sweet Nothing" because there's a perfect Taylor song for every moment—and we'd end it here, me and Oliver in a clinch.

But it's *this* kind of book.

Oh, wait. Did you think this was the end?

Ha ha.

No.

Anyway, Oliver does kiss me again, but then I notice something out of the side of my eye.

Someone.

"Who is that?"

Oliver squints. "Is that Tyler?"

He's right. Tyler's picking his way up the path toward our villa. He's dressed in the clothes I saw him in on the dock, casual businessman, but he looks like someone who hasn't slept well in a couple of days because he spent the night in jail. Hair a mess, stubble, a hunch to his gait.

"They let him out of jail, I guess?" I say.

"Makes sense."

"Is he coming to talk to us?"

"Not sure."

I watch him as he looks up at our balcony, then turns away. "He's going to Emma's."

"Why?"

My heart skips a beat. "My God, that man doesn't give up."

"You think he's trying to get back with Emma on the day she discovers her husband is a murderer?"

"I wouldn't put it past him." I take Oliver's hand. "Let's go."

"You don't think we should leave them alone?"

"No."

I tug him through the villa and out the front door to the path. By the time we get there, Tyler has disappeared.

"Come on, hurry up."

"Are you worried?"

"Call it an instinct."

We reach the front door to Emma's villa. Earlier, after Officer Anderson took Fred and Simone away, she'd said she was taking a sedative and was going to go to sleep. We'd offered to stay with her, but she said she needed to be alone. I thought it was a bad idea at the time, and that feeling is increasing, my stomach in knots, my hands shaking as I try the door.

It's not locked, and I can hear voices inside. Tyler's and Emma's.

I put a finger to my lips and ease the door open.

"—I can help you," Tyler says.

"I don't need your help, Tyler."

"Clearly you do."

I look back at Oliver. His face is creased with concentration.

"I'm handling everything fine."

"You call this handling things? And what happens if I tell Officer Anderson that you knew? Are you going to kill me, too?"

Wait, *what?*

"Don't be ridiculous. You're not telling Officer Anderson anything." Emma's voice drips with contempt. "What did you think, coming here? That I was going to want you *now?*"

"I want answers."

"About?"

"Why you tried to frame me for murder."

I lose my grip on the door handle and the door swings open with a loud *CREAK*. Shit.

"You might as well come in, El," Emma says, her voice oddly calm.

I step through the door with Oliver right behind me. My throat is tight, my mind whirring.

What. The. Fuck. Is. Happening?

We walk into the living room. Emma's wearing a pair of white joggers that I know say BRIDE on the butt because we ordered them together one night over a bottle of wine. Her hair is up in a high ponytail, her face free of makeup. She looks calm and composed, the complete opposite of how I left her a couple of hours ago.

"How did you know I was there?" I ask, trying to make my voice sound normal but failing.

"Tyler told me you spotted him. I knew it was only a matter of time before you stuck your nose in."

"What's going on?"

"Nothing. Tyler was just leaving."

"No, Em, I'm not."

"Tyler?" I say. "What are you doing here?"

He takes in and releases a slow breath, deciding something. "She knew."

"Knew what?"

"About Simone and Fred."

My eyes fly to Emma. She doesn't react, just stands there, patient.

"How?"

"I told her."

"When?"

"Right after they got engaged."

Oh my God. My God.

"Em?"

She looks at me, and it's like I'm looking at her for the first time. Like

I'm finally seeing her and she's not someone I recognize. She's a stranger on a screen.

"So?"

"You've been lying to me. To everyone."

She's been *acting*. Acting like she didn't know about Fred and Simone. That she didn't know about his debts. That she didn't know about any of it, which means . . . which means . . .

"It's more than that," Tyler says.

"*You* killed them?" Oliver says. "José and Ken and Shawna?"

Emma blinks slowly and now I do recognize her. It's what she does when she needs a minute to process. When she's taking a beat.

"You think I overpowered a two-hundred-pound man and put him in a climbing harness after he was dead? And why would I kill Ken? Or Shawna?"

I hold my face in my hands, my brain whirring, whirring, whirring.

"It was *Fred* you wanted to kill," I say. "If Tyler told you about the cheating after you got engaged. No way you'd just let that go. 'Trust but verify,' right?"[108]

I work it through, the pieces of the puzzle clicking into place like they always do eventually. The solution is there in the things you've already experienced. You just have to know where to look.

"After Tyler told you that, you went looking and found his burner phone, didn't you?"

She says nothing, and this is how I know I'm right.

I think I'm going to be sick.

But I can't stop now.

"What would you do once you found that? It had those texts on it, with Tyler, so you asked him about the money, right? And he told you?"

---

[108] I told you this was her motto a while back. And also that she's totally the kind of girlfriend who'd read her boyfriend's texts.

"Yes," Tyler says. "I told her about all of it. That he was either broke or hiding assets."

"And that he'd suggested Emma to play Cecilia?"

"Yes."

"And then there were the meeting times on the phone. With someone else. You'd want to be sure about that, too. So, you followed him and you saw him with Simone. And it wasn't innocent. Not someone telling off an ex who he could've talked to at any time on set without raising suspicion. And you knew you'd been betrayed. But it was more than that. Something pushed you over the edge. You figured something else out . . . Something clicked into place for you. What was it?"

I stop to figure it out. It's so quiet in here you could hear a pin drop, and I hate that I have to break this silence. That I have to fill in the gaps and come to this conclusion but there's nothing to be done about that.

CLINK.

"The Twitter feed. You found that on his phone, too, right? On his regular phone. He was tweeting gossip about you, making it seem like someone was out to get you. So why would Fred be taking up with you, marrying you, but still be with Simone? Why would he be tweeting about you? Making it look like someone hated you? A man with money problems. A gambler. And the script changes. The script moving away from it all being a scam to get Cecilia's money to them having a happy ending, you saw what that meant. You figured out that they were planning on killing you."

Again Emma says nothing.

"Why not just pull out of the film?" Oliver asks. "Break things off and leave?"

"She couldn't. Not without damaging her career in a way that might be fatal. You can't show that kind of weakness—especially not if you're a woman. And it wouldn't just be the shoot but also the press tour and having to do endless interviews about your love story gone wrong. And then, maybe a sequel . . ."

"Sounds unpleasant, but—"

"It's more than that," I say to Oliver. "I know Emma. It was the betrayal. Emma's had a crush on Fred since she was a kid. He used that. He used *her*. He wanted to kill *her*. No. It was too much. He deserved it."

"You think that?" Oliver says.

"Emma thinks that."

Our eyes connect, and that silent communication that's always been possible between us works as usual. I know this is what she was thinking. I know what she's done.

"She didn't kill José. That must've been Fred. And he *did* try to electrocute her in the hot tubs. But she knew he was going to do that. She was on her guard." I pause, rethinking the scene. "She was going to put Harper's phone in the water to ensure Fred hadn't done anything to it."

And if Harper's phone hadn't been there, she'd have found something else to put in it first.

Maybe Harper. Maybe me.

Fuck.

"Fred is an idiot," Emma says, finally breaking her silence.

"Yes."

"But Ken . . ." I keep my eye on Emma. "She killed Ken. It could've been done by a woman full of rage, and it opened up so many possibilities. Everyone would assume it was a mistake for Fred. But it could also have been Connor. Which is why Cathy is here. *She* invited her. Emma knows all about Cathy. So why not add her into the mix? Make it seem like it might be about me and Connor. The more suspects, the better."

A lump forms in my throat. If she killed Ken because he looked like Fred, was she going to kill me because I looked like her?

Despite everything, I shy away from that possibility, but I shouldn't.

Because once you see murder as the answer to your problems, then all bets are off.

"And Shawna?" Oliver asks.

"That was her, too. She and Fred were alone for enough time. She told me she took off her dress and had a quick shower. There's a back door in her room. I saw it when we were getting ready for the wedding. Is that what happened, Em? Shawna came to see you? She was coming to warn you. She knew Fred and Simone were planning to kill you. And you couldn't have that. Not after everything you'd gone through to keep it silent. So you stabbed her and shoved her out into the rain and you thought she was dead. That you could blame it on Simone. So she'd go to jail, and Fred would die before the weekend was out. She had *something* in mind. I'm not sure what . . . Oh! That's why she had the knife she used on Shawna. She was going to kill Fred in his sleep. It must be here, somewhere. Hidden."

"Or she got rid of it after Officer Anderson left. That's why she wanted to be alone," Oliver says. "To get rid of any remaining evidence."

"That makes sense."

"What about me?" Tyler asks. "If I was locked up, I couldn't be responsible."

"No," I say. "It was *Fred's* plan to blame you for Emma's murder. But then he had to kill José, so he shifted to pinning that murder on you. He must've decided to wait to kill Emma in some other way. Or to live off her money like he said earlier. Either way his problems were solved. Or so he thought."

"But what about what I knew about Emma? I could've told on her."

"I think Emma was pretty sure you wouldn't. You came here to confront her instead of telling Officer Anderson, didn't you? You do want to get back with her. If she had to, she'd string you along until she'd convinced you she didn't do anything."

Tyler's head hangs with the truth of what I'm saying, and I can't even look at Emma now.

"Did we forget anything?" I ask. "The murder being announced— Emma approved the schedule. She told me so herself. And she didn't invite her parents to the wedding. She wouldn't want them around for this. She showed me the note Fred left for her so I could testify that she was the intended victim. Wait. *That's* what she was going to do—she was going to kill Fred and say he attacked her. Then she'd uncover his plot to kill her and say she had to defend herself and the police would believe it because it was true."

I think it through again. This is what we were missing all along—two interwoven plots, one spurred by the other. There *were* two things to diagnose. Because what do doctors know about solving murders?

"Aren't you going to defend yourself, Emma?" Tyler asks.

"What's the point? You think I did it, that's why you came here, isn't it?"

"I realized in jail . . . I put it together. You could've come to me. I would've helped you."

"You don't get it, do you?"

"What?"

"I was never going to be with you."

Tyler goes to say something and Emma puts up her hand. "Just stop. You too, El. I'm not going to confess. I am not stupid and weak like Simone or Fred. You don't have any proof. And I'm not giving you any."

"They'll find it," I say. "And everything you tried to hide, it'll come out anyway."

"So be it." She lifts her chin and turns to the window, and she looks so alone in this moment, so far from me, even though she's just across the room.

My best friend. My oldest friend.

I failed her.

I could've stopped this and it's all my fault.

I remember saying to Harper once that nothing good ever happened to me in Italy.

But that's not true.

It's *When in Rome* that's brought me tragedy, over and over again. It doesn't matter what the format is.

Someone dies in every iteration.

Someone dies every time I go on vacation.

But no one's supposed to die at a wedding.[109]

"I happened to be walking by, and . . . can I be of assistance?"

"Shut up, Tucci!"

---

[109] Am I writing <u>song</u> lyrics at a time like this? Looks like it.

EPILOGUE

Are All Epilogues Three Months Later?

"How long is it to the resort?" I ask Harper as we wait in line for the shuttle bus to our hotel. I was nearly certain she'd told me they were sending a private car, but even though I searched for a sign with my name on it being held by one of the many uniformed men awaiting our flight, the name Dash didn't appear on any of them.

Hence the shuttle bus.

"Not far."

"Like actually not far, or Dad not far?"

Harper shrugs. She buried her head in a book[110] the entire flight here, and now she's wearing a scarf over her hair and large sunglasses, like a '50s movie star who doesn't want to be recognized.

She probably doesn't.

I can't blame her.

She's been struggling ever since we left Catalina. Shawna's betrayal has hit her hard, and Emma's, too. She was like a sister and finding out that we didn't know her at all is a blow it's going to take both of us a long time to recover from. Maybe you never can. Stay tuned to find out, I guess.

---

[110] *Jackpot Summer* by Elyssa Friedland. So fun. Read immediately after you finish this.

In case you haven't picked up on that by now, being flip is how I deal with pain.

Because sometimes all you can do is laugh to escape the pain of life.

That's my excuse, anyway.

How do you cope?

Anyway, she's why we're going to this weekend-in-the-sun, learn-how-to-write-a-murder-mystery thing in the Bahamas. I thought it would be a good place for her to relax and forget about life for a while.

It *wasn't* because I needed her to organize my life, even on vacation.

I swear.

"About twenty minutes," Oliver says.

"Great." I fan my hand in front of my face. It's hot out and it's going to get hotter. I'm already regretting agreeing to this trip, even though we could all use a change of scene.

It's been a hard three months for me, too.

Not that anyone's asked.

I'm just telling you in case you were interested.

After we failed to get Emma to confess that Sunday morning, we went and found Officer Anderson and told her what we'd discovered. Then we went back to our villa and sat on the balcony until we saw the police boats arriving, two sixteen-footers that chopped through the waves and dispensed what looked like a small army of lab techs and officers and one older, grizzled detective who looked like he wanted to be anywhere but on an island where he had to arrest two major movie stars for trying to kill each other.

The media wasn't far behind. By the time Fred, Simone, and Emma were led to one of the boats in handcuffs, there was a flotilla of them in Avalon Bay, long lenses at the ready. There might've been a few media frenzies like this one before, but it's hard to remember them.

It was the 9/11 of celebrity stories, consuming everything.

It consumed me, too.

All I could do was spin and spin and spin, turning over every little detail, trying to convince myself I couldn't have figured it out earlier.

That I couldn't have stopped Emma from her course of action once she'd decided on it.

It's taken me thirty-five years to realize you can still feel guilty about something you have no control over.

After a couple of days, Harper and I decamped to Oliver's house in North Hollywood because too many people knew where I lived. But we couldn't go anywhere. I'd never really been recognized in public before, and guess what? It's not that fun! Especially not if it happens because your best friend killed two people.

Deep breaths, Eleanor.

Maybe one day that phrase won't be a punch to the gut.

But not today.

Allison and David kept in touch with us by text—they were at some undisclosed retreat in Arizona where they make you hike ten hours a day for your sins. David was hard at work on *When in Rome You Go to Catalina*, because, yes, that's exactly what Hollywood is doing with this.

Tyler's at the forefront, bemoaning the indignity of his arrest and pressing a lawsuit against the Los Angeles Sheriff's Department. But he's also going to be a star witness in Emma's trial, which is something else I don't want to think about right now.

Crazy Cathy became a minor celebrity when she did the rounds on TMZ and the other online tabloids. She and Inspector Tucci were the only ones who'd talk to them, but once they started spinning conspiracy theories, the more reputable news organizations stopped booking them.

I hear Inspector Tucci's in talks to get his own Nancy Grace–type show on Fox News, though.

Enough said.

Oliver and I mostly spent the time together writing our book. No surprise that Vicki was happy to take the manuscript, which is a dramatization of what happened on Catalina.

We wrote it as a dual narrative—me writing Emma's part and him writing Fred's. Only we called them Emily and Ted.

Yes, yes.

Did you *not* get the part about us cashing in on a tragedy I was involved in?

It's what I do, after all.

It's not my fault you want to read all about it.

Let's see, have I forgotten anyone?

Mr. and Mrs. Winter moved into one of those retirement homes for once-famous actors. It turns out Fred had gambled away their money, too. I'm not sure what the worst blow was for Mrs. Winter. Discovering that her precious baby boy was a murderer, or that she wasn't going to be able to continue to live the lifestyle she'd become accustomed to.

Thank God for her SAG pension and her residual checks from the 1980s, which started multiplying once her old shows were added to every streaming platform after Fred was arrested.

Seems like everyone's cashing in on this tragedy.

I'd expect nothing less.

Which brings us to Connor.

I almost forgot about him.

His book came out early, and we were invited to his lavish book launch at Zibby Books in Santa Monica. It's a small store, but the choice of location was intentional. There was a line two miles long to get in there for Connor to sign a copy.

Not that I went to his event. I just saw the pictures on Instagram.

I think he was pissed we didn't go.

But I didn't want to be in that maelstrom.

I read it, though. And it pains me to admit this, but it was *good*?

ANYWAY.

"Bus arriving," Oliver says as a dark blue minibus with the Footprints logo on it pulls up. Ten other people have gathered around us while I've been summarizing, at least one of whom I recognize: Elizabeth Ben, the grande dame of detective fiction. She's in her eighties, thinning out and frail, and walks with a cane. But her dark brown eyes still shine with intelligence.

She's written fifty bestselling murder mysteries, and I've never figured out the ending of any of them.

It can't be a coincidence that she's here.

You should know me well enough by now to know it isn't.

Something is afoot.

Because of course it is.

You didn't think I was going to be able to go on vacation somewhere without someone dying, did you?

LOL.

But even though *I* should know better by now, I've found that moments of chaos are often preceded by moments of calm. Like the ride to the hotel down a palm-lined street while the Caribbean glimmers beneath a cloudless sky.

Like the glass of Champagne we're greeted with before we're even shown to our white stuccoed villa.

But there's no forgetting when the porter opens our door for us and stops short with a piece of our luggage in each hand, then drops them with a thud to the ground.

"What now?" Harper says with an impatience that's uncharacteristic for her.

But as she pushes ahead and her hand flies up to her mouth to stifle a scream, I almost don't have to look to know what she's seeing.

There's a body lying on its back in the middle of the room with a bullet in its temple.

Shit.

This probably won't come as a surprise for you, but: *This Weekend Isn't Going to End Well for Anyone.*[III]

[III] Coming soon!

ACKNOWLEDGMENTS

Another book done! Why does that always feel like a small miracle? Eleanor says she writes in a fever dream which is one of the many ways that we're different. But something we share is our passion to keep doing it, come what may.

And I'm so glad I did. In the summer of 2022, when I first conceived of this series, I felt like I might be onto something, but it's turned out even better than I could have written. Ha! Okay, I did have a list of things I wanted to happen and most of them did![112]

And that's because of you, dear reader! You fell in love with Eleanor and her many, many footnotes (or you skipped them, whatevs). You shouted *Every Time I Go on Vacation, Someone Dies* from the rooftops and told all your friends to read it (or you're about to do that, right?). And now you've read book 2! I am so grateful.

I also have to thank my amazing team at Minotaur and Raincoast— Catherine Richards, Kelley Ragland, Kelly Stone, Kayla Janas, Allison Zeigler, Sarah Melnyck, Jamie Broadbent, Christina Morden, and so many others who championed this book from the beginning and got it

---

[112] IndieNext. A review in *The New York Times*. A starred review in *Library Journal*. An Editors' pick by Amazon. A *USA Today* bestseller. A #1 Canadian bestseller.

into so many people's hands. A special shoutout to the audio team, too, and Elizabeth Evans, the brilliant narrator of this series.

This book literally wouldn't exist if my agent, Stephanie Kip Rostan, hadn't given me an enthusiastic *yes!* when I texted her the title for the first book. Thank you so much for always finding a way to make my crazy ideas come to fruition. And to the entire Levine Greenberg Rostan team—it's so great to have you in my corner.

To my management team at Gotham—Rich Green and Brooke Linley. Thanks for continuing to help me make my dreams come true.

To my book besties, Liz Fenton and Elyssa Friedland, for crying with me when I got my *New York Times* review and encouraging me to go cry on the internet. And Shawn Klomparens for fifteen years of friendship and encouragement. I hope you are resting in peace.

To Rachel Stuhler, my screenwriting partner, and Vince Marcello, for taking on our script and making it better. Let's make a movie!

To my tennis besties, Darina, Vivian, Rebecca, and especially Sandra, because they keep me sane, and if I didn't give her a special shoutout, she'd be mad.

To my lifelong friends Tasha, Sara, Christie, Candice, and Tanya for always being there when I need them. If I have to call one person from jail, I have lots to choose from.

To my family for helping when I ask.

And to David. It's been thirty years, babe. I guess you're stuck with me now.

ABOUT THE AUTHOR

Fany Ducharme

Catherine Mack (she/her) is the pseudonym for the *USA Today* and *Globe and Mail* bestselling author Catherine McKenzie. Her books are approaching two million copies sold worldwide and have been translated into multiple languages. Television rights to *Every Time I Go on Vacation, Someone Dies* and its sequels sold in a major auction to Fox TV for development into a series. A dual Canadian and US citizen, she splits her time between Canada and various warmer locations in the United States.

Harper, have you checked the latest forecast? There's not an ACTUAL hurricane coming to Catalina, is there? That's, like, fake weather news—right?